THE BLESSED GIFT OF DESPERATION

To Diana
God Bless you
Emma

Emma Sauer

ISBN 978-1-64670-858-1 (Paperback)
ISBN 978-1-64670-859-8 (Digital)

First Edition

Covenant Books, Inc.
11661 Hwy 707
Murrells Inlet, SC 29576
www.covenantbooks.com

1
CHAPTER

The Southwest Limited roared through the night across the deserts and plains, heralding its arrival in all the small towns between Los Angeles and Kansas City.

It was the era of the cold war, the end of the age of innocence, so-called, before the revolution of women, the sexual revolution, and all the other revolutions which would accomplish much and nothing.

In those days riding the train was a nice experience, before prepackaging and microwaves. You could get an elegant meal in the dining car and socialize with a drink in the club car. Nevertheless, twenty-four hours out of Los Angeles and the ride became a bit wearing. People who had boarded the train with excitement and expectancy were now reading or sleeping to pass the time away or looking anxiously ahead as if they could will the miles away.

Mary Lou was going home, home to the ranch, home to Daddy—the last place on earth she wanted to go. Unfortunately, all her other options had run out. There was nowhere else to go. It was one thing to look forward to a new beginning, to have hope that in a new place, in different surroundings, things would somehow be different. It was quite another to know that you were approaching a dead end; hope gone, the future stretching before you like a never-ending black hole.

Huddled in the train seat, she stared into the velvety darkness. She could have passed for a teenager in the dim light of the train car with her small thin body and long dark hair falling over the side of her face, her feet tucked up in the seat. In a better light, however, you could see a few fine threads of gray in the dark hair and the lines about her mouth and dark eyes. She had been pretty once—very pretty in fact—but now at thirty five, without makeup, she looked haggard and careworn, older than her years.

Up ahead, she could see the lights of her destination. Anticipating her arrival, a feeling of panic washed over her, making it hard to breathe. She wrapped her arms tightly about her stomach, trying to suppress the pain. The thought crossed her mind that she could use a drink.

"No use thinking about it," she told herself, "it would take more than one anyway."

She tried to still her mind by concentrating on the rhythm of the train, the rising and falling of the wheels, metal clashing against metal. She'd always loved riding the train. It was so anonymous, so safe, like a baby in the womb looking out on a world in which one is not required to take part, sleeping and being fed while the rest of the world scurries about in its race to nowhere.

How wonderful it would be, she thought, not to have to arrive at all, ever, just to speed right on through, keep right on going. But to where? This was the last stop, and unlike the returning prodigal son, there would be no welcome. It had been worn out years ago.

She had not called home or written in nearly two years. There was no telephone at the ranch. She had called the store and left word for her father to call her. Since the store was at least twenty miles away on the highway between the ranch and the nearest town, she could only hope that he might go there for some reason or stop on his way to town. She could have written, but since telephoning was only for extreme emergencies, he would be more apt to call her and then she could convince him of the urgency of her situation.

Fortunately, she heard from him sooner than she had expected. She remembered the apprehension in his voice as he spoke her name.

"Mary Lou," he paused, "what's wrong?"

He was torn with relief at finally hearing from her and a feeling of uneasiness, afraid to ask why she was calling. He knew from past experience she was not calling just to say hello.

"Mary Lou, what's wrong?" his voice rose, the hand holding the phone shook involuntarily.

Aaron Gerhardt was ordinarily a calm person, a man with a purpose, sure of his place in this world and the one to come. The Bible was his guidebook for living, along with the traditional values handed down through his stalwart German ancestry. Only one person had the power to shake his immutability: his rebellious daughter. Just the sound of her voice was enough to send a sinking feeling into the pit of his stomach.

Before he'd called her, he'd tried to prepare himself to be strong, to say no, to mean it, to set down conditions and not let himself be sucked into anything he'd regret. He waited.

"Daddy," she began plaintively, "I want to come home for a while."

He didn't answer for a minute, trying to compose his thoughts, hoping he hadn't heard right.

"What about your job?" he asked for want of something better to say. No answer. "What about your man?"

She smiled wryly. In the years he hadn't heard from her, he'd probably consoled himself with the vision of her busy with her *job* and a *man* to take care of her, hoping she'd married this man she'd written about so glowingly.

"Daddy, I'm sick, I can't work. Larry and I are separated. I had to leave him, Daddy. I just couldn't take the drinking anymore." This was the first he'd heard of Larry's drinking problem. She added quickly, "I don't drink anymore, Daddy, I just need some help till I can get myself together and get on my feet." She hesitated. "Dad, I know I've taken advantage of you in the past. I know I've never followed through on anything."

Still he was silent.

"Please, Daddy!" Her voice took on an urgency. "I wouldn't ask you if I weren't desperate. I have very little money, my rent will soon be up, and I won't be able to pay it! You have to help me…I have nowhere else to turn. Please, Daddy."

In the end, he'd relented, agreeing that she could come.

She promised he would not be sorry and that she would leave as soon as she was able to work again. She was glad he hadn't asked what was wrong with her health. She wasn't sure herself. The doctor she had gone to months before said something about nerves or maybe an ulcer. She had never called back to find out about the tests. Most of the time she was too depressed to get out of bed, too tired to fix anything to eat, wanting to sleep, afraid to sleep because of the night terrors. Sometimes she hyperventilated so badly she thought she would die. She broke out in rashes, the panic attacks kept her stomach in a constant state of pain. Most of the time she couldn't think straight. She thought about suicide all the time, but she couldn't think straight long enough to devise a plan.

The conductor interrupted her thoughts. "You the one getting off here?" he asked.

She nodded.

"Well, you better get your things together. We'll only be here a minute, long enough to let you off. You'll have to make it quick. I'll meet you at the back."

It figures, she thought as she rose unsteadily, even the damn train doesn't want to stop here anymore. As she lurched up the aisle, the train came to an abrupt stop, almost hurtling her into the lap of another passenger. Swearing under her breath she grabbed the two bags that held her worldly possessions; jumping down on the stool the conductor held, she twisted her ankle. She gave a sharp little cry, which he ignored, barely having time to jump back aboard before the train started to pick up speed again.

She stood for a moment, watching the receding train, a feeling of deep sadness overwhelming her. There was no returning. She had not acknowledged that completely until now. Her twisted ankle began to throb.

"Damn you!" she yelled at the receding train for no particular reason. The whistle blew derisively, the sound filling the night.

Even though it was past nine o'clock in the evening, the air was still warm. A slight wind was blowing and a tumble weed bounced along beside her, racing her down the track, passing her. Oh, to have the energy to race after it as she had when she was a child, racing the wind, chasing tumbleweeds!

The train had let her off so far down the track she had quite a walk before she reached the main street, which, except for the taverns, was dark and deserted. She hurried on, the soft strain of some cowboy song wafting through the air beckoning her. She had grown up on church music, but western music was her soul music. She rarely listened to it anymore; it recalled too many depressing memories of people gone, people dead, regrets, broken dreams.

Worst of all, it reminded her of Larry. She thought about the pain in his eyes when she told him she was leaving—this time for good. She had left and threatened to leave so many times before. Funny how he knew the difference between this time and all the others. He made no attempt to sweet-talk her out of it, promising to sober up, get a divorce, marry her, take care of her. He just bit his lip and nodded. He had surrendered to one truth at least. He would not, could not, do these things. She could stay and watch him drink himself to death or she could leave. Those were the choices.

He had been sober for a few months after he had left the hospital on his last drying-out spell. Sober was no good either, not for her anyway. The Larry she loved was the vulnerable Larry, the child-like Larry, the one who needed her. Sober, he was aloof, shutting her out. She wanted him to stop drinking, he had to, in order to live. But she didn't want him to change. She hated the Alcoholics Anonymous meetings, the new friends who talked about drinking but didn't drink.

For years she hadn't felt comfortable around people who didn't drink. Everyone she knew drank including herself. These people spoke a new language, twelve steps, Higher Power (God), a word she had dropped from her vocabulary years ago. She worried about the women who kissed him, telephoned him, and told him they loved him. She didn't believe for a minute that this was "spiritual." It was all so foreign.

In the end it didn't matter anyway. Larry went back to his first love, the bottle. This time it was different. He drank with a vengeance. He no longer cared whether she drank with him or not. Gone were the parties, the laughter, the fun. He sat alone and drank, went to bed and drank, no longer waiting until noon to have the "first one." The brakes were off. Eventually, he became abusive, threatening, unpredictable. She began to fear him.

In other times, they had spent days and hours in bed, making love, drinking, discussing their future. His desire for her seemed insatiable. No more, he seemed oblivious to her. There was no future. He was an *alcoholic*. He could either stop drinking or go insane or die. Life without booze was not an option. Not for Larry.

It had been a month since she had seen him, and not a minute passed that she didn't think about him.

At times the longing for him seemed almost more than she could stand—why had she left, if only she had stayed, let him kill her, what difference did it make? "Please, God," she prayed to a God she didn't believe in, "please, let me stop remembering."

She pulled herself together, took a deep breath, and resolutely moved on. She planned to find a cheap hotel room, spend the night, and her dad would pick her up early the next morning. There were two hotels in town. One, the larger one, had a restaurant and bar, frequented mostly by cattle men, traveling salesmen and conventioneers. The other was a small rundown place that catered mostly to permanent guests or people like her who couldn't afford much.

It was hard lugging two suitcases; the pain in her ankle throbbing with each step she took. She sat down on the curb to catch her breath and nurse her ankle, which was starting to swell. She longed for a cigarette. She was trying to quit since she would not be able to smoke in or around her dad's house. If only she could smoke, it would help to make life bearable.

Nothing ever changes here, she thought, as she looked up and down the dark street. It looked the same as it had when her father was a boy. So different from Los Angeles. You could never get attached to anything there; if you did, they might tear it down and build a freeway over it. Everything was so temporary. There was a time when coming to live in this town was as exciting as going to live in Hollywood had been later on.

Memories of another time came crowding in. Suddenly she was fourteen again, newly graduated from the small country school she had attended since first grade. Ready for high school, she remembered the excitement she felt, packing her new clothes into the cardboard boxes for the trip to Aunt Norma's house. Aunt Norma owned a large rooming house on this very street, only two blocks from where she was sitting.

She remembered sitting quietly beside her father on the long ride to town, barely able to contain her excitement and yet not wanting to appear too happy, because after all, her father had not wanted her to leave the ranch. If it had not been for her aunt, she probably would have been sent away to some religious school or she would have to stay home waiting for some rancher or farmer to notice her and marry her and secure her future.

Aaron knew she had to be educated. Her brother had left after the eighth grade to attend a Christian school in another state. But there was no doubt about his future; he would come home to be a rancher like his father and grandfather before him. It was different with Mary Lou. Aaron knew that this day would probably be the last day that Mary Lou would be a part of the land and the life he knew and loved. He sensed a restlessness in her, and it made him uneasy. She always found some way of upsetting life, nothing big, just little things. It was as if she could never accept things as they were. She craved excitement

He felt so impotent in the face of her moods. He wanted so much to please her and yet it was never enough, she was so easily bored. He knew that he would never be able to control her; the best he could do was provide an environment where temptation would be least likely to rear its ugly head, but that would not be for long.

It was a new adventure for a country girl—so different, so many things to do. Everyone at school had seemed so sophisticated. She never learned to fit in. She had lived in the country since the day she was born, forty miles from the nearest town. They never went to town except to buy what they needed and get home as soon as possible. She had never seen a movie, never learned to ride a bicycle, swim, roller skate, or dance.

She could ride the meanest horses, and she was a sure shot with a rifle, but that didn't count. Town people didn't care about those things. She was small, dark, and pretty, but she was socially awkward, gauche. Even though her aunt tried to help her in her choice of dress, genuinely wanting her to fit in and be happy, she herself was very old-fashioned, very religious, and hopelessly out of touch with the fashion of the day. As a result, Mary Lou sometimes looked like a younger edition of her maiden aunt.

The one thing she did have was a beautiful singing voice. People remarked about her beautiful voice, how she had the voice of an angel. She sang in the choir at church and at school. She began to dream of a singing career. Her voice would be her ticket to glamour and fame. She consoled herself with thoughts of the future. She chaffed at the restrictions of her life, bound by family, religion, and tradition. She daydreamed over the movie magazines she bought and hid from her aunt.

In her senior year she met Leonard. Lenny was a dancer and an artist. He too dreamed of fame and fortune and a life unconstrained by *convention* and small-town *provincialism*. That was the way he put it anyway. She learned so much from Lenny. He taught her how to dress, told her what books to read, how to dance, what music to listen to. He was very much influenced by his mother who hailed from a wealthy eastern family and prided herself on being a very cultured person in the midst of a *cultural wasteland*. After Mary Lou met Lenny, she suddenly had status as the girlfriend of a boy who came from a wealthy mainline family—Lenny's father's family being one of the first founders of the town.

The following summer after graduation, Lenny asked her to marry him and together they would go to Hollywood to seek stardom. It never occurred to her to ask herself whether or not she loved Lenny. Never having had any experience in male-female relationships, her father being divorced, her aunt a spinster, and her grandparents too old to ever consider them in this light, she had no idea at all about marriage.

Lenny too was a needy person, the type she would always be attracted to, and so she said yes. They had a nice wedding in her family church, although no one seemed too happy about it, Lenny's family not even attending. They had argued long and hard against it, hoping that he would change his mind and attend the prestigious college where he had been accepted. There was no arguing with Mary

Lou, and so her father, with a grim look on his face, marched his only daughter down the aisle.

One month later, they were packed and ready to take Hollywood by storm. Money was not a problem, Lenny having a regular income from an inheritance and Mary Lou a substantial wedding gift from her father. She had expected more. However it would be enough to keep her going for a while, since it wouldn't take long for Hollywood to discover her and Lenny and their incomparable talent.

A shadow of sadness fell over Mary Lou's countenance as she remembered her dad standing beside the station when her train pulled out for California. From her seat she could see him, and she could see him still, the cowboy with his boots, Stetson and denims, looking suddenly old. That was the only time she had seen her dad cry; the tears were coursing down his cheeks as he looked down studying the toe of his boot. She'd felt a momentary sadness—more sadness now in retrospect. At the time she had been filled with excitement. The dream was about to become a reality.

Mary Lou stood up, sighed, and took up her bags again. A lot had happened since then. Lenny had discovered his homosexuality, or was it bisexuality? He had taken up with an older lover who could and did promote his career. He became a successful dancer In Las Vegas. The last she'd heard he was happily married to a woman. Oh well, there had been rumors back in school about his sexuality. Such things had been beyond the realm of her experience at the time, and she had ignored the whispers and innuendos. Even so, most of her relationships after that were a step downward. In fact, Lenny was one of the few men in her life that she remembered with any affection at all.

After he left, she nearly starved to death, supporting herself by ushering in a movie theater at night and working in an Insurance Company by day as a receptionist, supplemented by periodic checks from her father. She soon found out that Hollywood was inundated by beautiful and talented young girls like herself waiting for that big break. She was young and not easily discouraged, however. Life was still just beginning. Later, she'd found a job singing in a cocktail lounge. She was sure that this was the break she'd been waiting for, after all, the man who owned the club had starred, well, not exactly starred, but had had a part in two B movies.

The letters to her family were full of glowing reports about how beautiful California was—the stars she had seen, the premiers she had attended (as an usherette). She wrote about her singing career in the supper club, not mentioning that the only supper served was booze. Meantime, she had learned to appreciate the elixir of the gods. Drinking cast a rosy glow over all the ugliness, coupled with the pills she took to keep awake. It gave her a feeling of well-being and confidence. She loved the people who drank. They lived in a world of their own. Relationships began and ended, world affairs were decided, all the important issues of the day settled without ever leaving the barstool. All cultural and societal differences melted away in the camaraderie of a shared bottle. Never had she had such close friends, known such acceptance. There was something almost "spiritual" about sharing your deepest thoughts, dreams, and hopes with someone as you drank in a closed bar until the sun came up. A few drinks and she became the person she had always imagined she could be—beautiful, sophisticated, intelligent, and of course, the life of the party.

When had all that turned to ashes, she wondered. Maybe her grandmother had been right, the things the devil tempts you with always seem good to begin with, otherwise, no one would ever fall into temptation. Thinking of Gran and her old adages and warnings about the devil and his traps almost brought a smile to her face. What a bunch of nonsense.

She pushed open the heavy door of the hotel trying to prop it with one suitcase while she reached for the other. The hotel clerk rose from his chair where he had been napping intermittently. He came around the desk to help her.

"You just got off the train?" he asked, trying to size her up.

Respectable women were rarely out alone after nine o'clock without a good reason. Not that there was any danger in being out alone, it just wasn't the thing to do. Respectable women did not go alone to motels and rent rooms in small towns like this one, unless they had a nefarious reason for doing so. Her father had tried to talk her into going to her aunt's house, but she refused, and he knew it was useless to argue with her.

"Yes," she replied in answer to his question, "I need a room just for tonight."

"Waal," he drawled, "you're just in time, I was about ready to close up here and go up to bed." Evidently the register wasn't used too much as he seemed to have trouble finding it and then he had to search even longer for a pencil.

"Name?" he asked, peering at her over his glasses.

"Mary Lou Gerhardt."

"Spell that?"

She spelled it out carefully, enunciating each letter, beginning to fidget impatiently. *Patience, Mary Lou,* she told herself. *This is not Los Angeles. People here move at their own pace, and God help you if you try to hurry them. You have to get in the rhythm of things, or you'll go nuts.*

"You from around here?"

"I used to be...just put Route 2." She could see that he was gearing up to ask a lot of questions.

"How much is that?" she asked brusquely. "And could I have my key, please...I'm exhausted."

"Waal now, let me see what's available." He peered at the row of four or five keys. "Do you have a preference, upstairs or down?"

"No," she snapped. "Please, anything, I am so tired."

"Okay, second floor, end of the hall." He handed her the key. "I'll help you with your suitcases."

"Thanks," she said and hurried on ahead of him in order to avoid any conversation. She reached her door, turned the key in the lock, and reached out to take her bags, shoving them in the room.

"Good night, and thank you," she said as she hurriedly closed the door in his face.

"Checkout time is twelve tomorrow," he called through the closed door.

The room was like the hotel, old and shabby, but it looked reasonably clean. Not that Mary Lou really cared too much at this point. She threw off her clothes, dragged an old tee shirt out of her suitcase, and got into bed.

"I should brush my teeth," she thought tiredly. "Oh, what the hell, tomorrow. I have got to sleep, I just have to, I can't go another night without sleep." She closed her eyes, soon she felt herself drifting off.

Suddenly, she was wide awake. She heard footsteps; they were approaching the bed. She opened her mouth to scream. She felt she did scream, but the footsteps kept approaching, closer, closer. Suddenly it was upon her. *It* was sucking the life out of her. She felt the life, the essence of herself leaving her body, rising above her in the room. Then she felt herself sinking. There was a terrible roaring in her ears. With all her strength she tried to struggle and fight back, but her body was leaden, and so she fought with her will, even though the temptation to let go seemed overpowering. It seemed that if she let go, that would be the end. And suddenly, as quickly as it had left, she felt the *life* reenter her body with what seemed like a *swoosh.*

She was awake, now she knew she was awake, drained. She moaned, moving her body. *It was a dream,* she told herself. *It had to be a dream.*

Yet it seemed so real! She had experienced these dreams over the past five years. They were occurring with greater frequency now, more frightening in their intensity. She was sure this was a struggle with death, and the next time she might not win, might not even want to win.

She turned on the light and looked at her watch. It was two in the morning. So she had been asleep. It was a dream after all. Still, she feared to fall asleep again, her heart was pounding, and that was no dream!

Could I die of fear? she wondered.

However, sometime before daylight she slept again, peacefully this time.

She woke to a gentle knock on her door. "Mary Lou, it's Dad," Aaron called through the door.

"Daddy," she cried, "wait till I get up, I'm still in bed! I'll just be a second." She threw on her shirt and jeans that she had already worn for three days, put on her tennis shoes, twisted a rubber band around her hair, not bothering to comb it, grabbed her sweater, and rushed to open the door.

"Hi, Daddy." She longed to rush into the safety of his arms as she had when she was a child, but something held her back. They were not normally an openly affectionate family anyway, and Mary Lou's wild willful ways had put a strain on their relationship, created an abyss that neither was willing to cross yet.

"Hi, Mary Lou." Aaron tried not to let the shock register on his face at her appearance. She looked so old! Worse than that, she didn't look well—her color was bad, her complexion blotchy and blemished, her teeth looked neglected, and her hair was lackluster, like straw. Her eyes were the worst, bloodshot and vacant-looking. A small fear began to creep into his mind. What was wrong with her?

She was aware that he was shocked at her appearance. "Daddy, I'm tired. I haven't slept for days, I can't sleep on the train, and I didn't sleep much last night. You look good." She surveyed him affectionately, noticing that although his normally dark hair was now very gray, he still had the strong and healthy look of the outdoorsman he was.

He smiled. "Feel pretty good for someone who just turned sixty."

He picked up her bags and she silently followed him to his pickup truck. Even though it was early morning, the midsummer heat was already bearing down, promising to be a scorcher. Even so, Mary Lou felt a chill and pulled her sweater tighter.

"I thought maybe since we're up here, we might stop by and see your grandma and Aunt Norma if it's all right with you?" He eyed her questionably.

A look of dismay spread over her face; the thought of seeing either of them was almost more than she could bear. "Dad, please take me home! I mean, unless you really want to, of course...Dad, I need some time."

"All right, we'll go on." Actually, he was relieved. He wanted to get home before the sun climbed much higher. The idea of sitting around all day with his mother and sister didn't appeal to him either. He wanted time to prepare them for Mary Lou's arrival. He was sure they would be full of questions and he wasn't sure they'd be all that happy to see her after what happened the last time she came home.

He wished he could be happy to see her. He just wished he could think of something to talk to her about during the long ride to the ranch. He didn't dare ask her what she'd been doing since he'd seen her last. He was sure he didn't want to know. Furthermore, he was sure she was not interested in the happenings in his narrow world either.

He did not dare bring up the past—it was too painful—and so they rode in an uncomfortable silence, each lost in their own thoughts. Even though Aaron would never admit it, even to himself, there was still a feeling of irritation, even anger toward Mary Lou. She had never listened to one shred of advice he'd ever given her, and yet she seemed to think nothing of throwing herself on his mercy each time she'd gotten herself in a jam.

Their thoughts wandered and came together always at the same place. She had returned home after leaving her latest relationship, destitute as usual. She had written to ask for money, but this time, Aaron had put his foot down. He would not send any more money. She had had her chance to make good in California, and it hadn't worked out. She was welcome to come home if she wanted to. He would support her until she could get on her feet.

She had returned home full of anger, bravado, and arrogance. Fortunately, she was able to find a job as a switchboard operator and receptionist in a hotel in town. It didn't pay much, but she was furnished a room in the hotel as part of her salary. At night, she hung around the hotel lounge, sometimes singing for tips and drinks. She was very popular with her dark good looks and great singing voice. She dated a lot of different men and drank a lot. It became harder and harder to keep up with her job. Even though it didn't amount to much, one still had to show up in order to do it. She probably would have been fired except that business in the lounge had picked up, noticeably.

This was about the time she met Charles L Pearson Jr. At first, she'd tried to avoid him, she really had. She knew he was trouble. He was the fourth son of a wealthy rancher (none of them worth shooting) according to all who knew them. But he was so good-looking! He drove a big car, wore a big hat, expensive boots, and seemed to have a never-ending supply of money to spend. He was a great dancer and a great lover. They waltzed and two-stepped in all the dance halls and saloons in the country and made love in all the hotels and back roads or wherever the mood struck. They were never without a bottle to share. She took him to meet her family and introduced him as the man she was going to marry, ignoring the lukewarm reception of this great news.

Unfortunately, he was already married, and worse, his young wife was pregnant with their first child. They rapidly became the talk of the town in a place where people live and breathe on other people's failings. People passed to the other side of the street when they saw her coming; she lost her job and was asked to move.

There was only one solution: they would run off together, nothing could stand in the way of their love.

It was just too hot to cool off. They drove to the ranch to pick up the rest of Mary Lou's clothes, drinking, laughing, clutching at one another passionately.

They roared up in front of the house, and her father came out to meet them. She could tell by the look on his face that the news had finally reached the hinterlands.

"Don't bother gettin' outa the car," he said quietly, trying to contain the rage that boiled in him.

"Dad, I came to get my things, we're leaving town," she said defiantly.

He shook his head. "No! Whatever you have here, I'll send to you wherever you are. I don't want you in my house, either one of you! Mary Lou, you're a whore, a Jezebel, I'm ashamed to call you my daughter!"

The man, who all her life had never scolded or raised his voice to her, who had always been a paragon of patience where she was concerned, had called her a whore! There was no argument in the face of his righteous anger. They left. At the time it seemed worth the loss of her reputation as well as her family to be with the only man, at that time, that she had ever really loved. Three months later, he abandoned her in Denver, returning to his pregnant wife. Daddy, his daddy, had cut off the pipeline to expensive cars, clothes, and worst of all, booze.

She had to swallow her pride and write home for money. She would return to California. This time she would make it. She had contacts, she could have a singing career, she would concentrate on that to the exclusion of all else. She had made some terrible mistakes in her choice of men. She was no longer interested in men or marriage. All that mattered was her career.

Aaron sent the money. Once again, he told himself, she deserved another chance. She was his baby girl. At night he got on his knees and asked his God to redeem her, reminding God that she was also his child and that if he loved her, he was sure that God loved her even more. Even though he had a fine son, who was the image of his father and who was married to a lovely, devout woman with three children who were the light of his life, he longed for this lost sheep to become part of the fold.

Mary Lou looked over at her father, intent on the road. How she longed to reach across the gulf that divided them, touch him, tell him how sorry she was that she had hurt him. But for him, that would never be enough. His feelings and his good name were secondary. In his eyes, she had sinned against God. That would require something more—more than she was capable of.

For twenty miles or more they drove on a two-lane highway traversed mostly by trucks, passing a few farms and ranches that could be seen from the road, and then they turned onto an unpaved gravel road crossing over a cattle guard. No telephone poles or roadside signs cluttered the view from this road. There was very little farmland to be seen except for a few small fields used to grow feed or corn for the livestock. All was prairie land, covered with the same buffalo grass that had been growing there since the beginning or since, as Mary Lou once believed, *the flood.*

About five miles down the road, they crossed over a creek which at this point had very little water in it, cottonwood trees lining the bank, their leaves shimmering in the sun as a barely imperceptible breeze blew through their branches. This creek started its journey in the hills west of their ranch, meandered past their house into the hills east of them, crossed the highway, and finally made its way to the river. There was never any water in it where it passed their house except after a rain, and then sometimes a wall of water would come falling and rushing past their house and they would sit on the front porch and thrill to the sight. Perhaps it had not even rained where they were, which made it all that more exciting.

They made a big splash as they sped through the water over the cement slab, put there to facilitate crossing. Many times, in the past they had not been able to cross at all if the water was high. There was nothing to do, except turn around and go home and wait for the water to subside or park on the bank and wait for hours. It didn't matter how important it was to get across, you were stuck.

They followed the road, passing only one ranch house belonging to a widow woman who lived in the house and leased her land to Aaron and his son. There were other ranches to the south and east of them, but from where they were now, everything, as far as the eye could see, belonged to the Gerhardts, or if it didn't belong to them, no one knew for sure who it belonged to. Their cattle roamed at will over all of it.

To the west, the flat prairie land gradually rose into hills and rocks and craggy cedar trees. As a child, Mary Lou had loved to explore the hills on horseback. Sometimes she would get lost, trusting her horse to find the way home, tying the bridle to his neck, lying down across his broad back. She always preferred to ride bareback, seldom using a saddle. From the highest mesa you could see all over the valley. She vaguely remembered the feeling of peace that would come over her, the feeling of being at one with the universe as she looked out over the flat prairie land, unchanging as far as the eye could see.

How could it be, she wondered, that she had loved it so much then—the vast, majestic loneliness of the land? Now she saw only hot, dusty ugliness—the loneliness, pressing in on her, stifling in its intensity.

As they pulled up over a small hill, she could see the house where she was born. It was a two-story house, part rock and part sod. They had built the second story when the grandparents came to live with them after her mother left. Her brother John lived on the original homestead where her grandparents had settled when they came from Oklahoma in a covered wagon. Now Grandpa was dead, and Grandma lived in town with Aunt Norma. The only people still living there were her father and the hired hand, Jake Callahan, who had been with them since she was a child.

There was a large front porch facing the road and a screened-in back porch facing the barn and the corrals. There was a row of tamarisks to the north, forming a windbreak, and the house was shaded by tall elms and cottonwoods, making it a comfortable house, cool in summer and warm in winter, except on a day like today when nothing could shut out the unrelenting heat.

A windmill gave half-hearted turns and then gave up altogether. It furnished water for the house and the horse tanks where the cattle and horses stood lazily swatting flies with their cockle burr laden tails.

To Mary Lou, it seemed as if time had stood still here in this spot. The only changes in the past forty years was the butane gas tank, which furnished refrigeration and gas cooking. The water had been piped into the house and you could take a bath provided the wind blew enough to provide enough water for both you and the cows, otherwise, the cows came first.

There was no electricity and no telephone. You could listen to the radio (they had never heard of television), again, depending on the wind whether or not it blew enough for the wind charger to keep the batteries charged.

As they drew near the house it was apparent they had company. Her brother and his wife and kids were standing on the front porch along with old Jake.

Damn, Mary Lou thought, *I really can't face seeing them, why did they have to come over right now?*

Aaron too was surprised. He had forgotten that he had mentioned that Mary Lou was due to arrive today. He could tell that Mary Lou was not happy seeing them. He himself was relieved. At least, there'd be others to fill in the awkwardness of the situation.

As she jumped down out of the pickup, Andrea, her niece, ran and grabbed her around the waist, squealing, "Aunt Mary Lou…oh, Aunt Mary Lou!" She was fifteen now—the picture of her mother, only thinner.

Rosalie, her sister-in-law, had gotten a little chubby in spots, but she still had the glowing complexion of a young girl. Dark red hair framed a face that was always serene. It was as if she'd read a sign, "Hear no evil, speak no evil," and had taken it as a motto for life. She was smiling as she reached out and hugged her daughter and Mary Lou together. "Oh, Mary Lou, we have missed you so much!"

Mary Lou was always amazed at the seeming sincerity of her sister-in-law. It was as if she'd never heard the stories of Mary Lou's disgraceful past. If it was true that she was really happy to see her, she was probably the only one in the entire country who was. Certainly, no one else looked particularly overjoyed, she thought as she surveyed her family. Rosalie and Andrea stood with their arms entwined, both in lookalike homemade dresses.

The two boys stood on each side of their father, hats in hand, like their daddy, looking shyly at her. With a sinking feeling, Mary Lou realized that she couldn't remember their names. They had been pretty small when she left, and even though their mother had faithfully sent their school pictures with their names and ages, to Mary Lou wrapped up in her problems, they had been just a shock of blond hair, freckles, and big teeth, or no teeth. *Where were all those pictures now?* she wondered. Lost in one of the many storage places, never to be redeemed, like everything else she had ever owned.

Her brother made no move to hug her or shake her hand. He just nodded. "How're yuh, Mary Lou?"

"Okay, and you?"

He gave a slight nod of his head.

Mary Lou turned toward Jake. "Hi," she said.

He nodded. "Hello, Mary Lou."

Mary Lou was twelve when Jake came to work for her dad and grandfather. When you came to work for the Gerhardt's, it was understood that you would go to church. It was not a requirement, but somehow when they told you "Church tomorrow," you went.

Jake always went obediently and sat in the back like an observer of the goings-on.

However, he was good help, he could do most anything, and he practically ran both ranches single-handed when her grandfather suffered through a long illness and finally died.

One Sunday, to the amazement of everyone, Jake suddenly stood up in church and walked forward to the front of the church and confessed that he had been a drinker, a woman chaser, and a jail-bird, and that he'd "seen the light" and wanted to be baptized! Mary Lou could never forget it, the look on her dad's and grandparent's faces, as if truly the angels in heaven were rejoicing over this repentant sinner.

To Mary Lou, who had never been that fond of Jake, he was a smart man who knew which side his bread was buttered on, because it went without saying, he now had a place to live and a job for life.

They all took a seat on the porch, the coolest place around, although, to Mary Lou, accustomed to the weather in California, it was an oven inhabited by horseflies.

"Well," Rosalie smiled, "Mary Louise bring us up to date…we haven't seen you for so long."

Rosalie was from the south, deep south, and she said, "Mary Louise," drawing out the name which Mary Lou hated.

John had met Rosalie when he had gone away to Bible College, the only time in his life that he'd ever left home. Rosalie was of another denomination, a denomination that spoke *in the Spirit* and *prophesied* among other things. There were times when she became filled with the Spirit and she would jump up in church and *prophesy*, which didn't go over too well with the conservative little congregation.

People were willing to overlook this strange behavior in Rosalie however, because she was filled with love for everyone. Having trained as a nurse, she was the first one there if anyone was sick and the first one there with food and comfort for any other occasion, sad or otherwise.

To Mary Lou, she was simply an enigma. She knew that Rosalie really did want to get close to her. After all, she was John's sister and there were very few women her age in this lonely expanse of prairie land, something she wasn't used to, having come from a large, close-knit family.

Mary Lou was aloof and uncomfortable around her. She avoided her as much as she possibly could.

Even though Rosalie had never in the slightest way passed judgment on her, just being around Rosalie was judgment in itself.

All eyes were on Mary Lou, and after staring at her expectantly—always before she had had a lot to say about her exciting life in California—Rosalie broke the silence. "Mary Lou, I'll bet you're tired. I brought some food, and maybe after you eat a bit, you'd like to go lie down. John, bring the food to the kitchen. Andrea, come and help."

"I'm sorry, Rosalie," said Mary Lou abruptly, "I just can't eat anything right now."

"Um… Dad, could I just go and lie down, please?" she entreated.

There was no time for niceties. If she didn't escape now, she would fall apart right there in front of everyone.

"Sure, Mary Lou." Aaron looked puzzled. He knew she hadn't had any breakfast, and it wasn't as if she had spent the night riding the train. He picked up her bags and motioned with his head for her to follow.

He led her to the room where she had grown up. It had never been used by anyone else. In fact, it looked the same as it had when she was a little girl.

"Thank you, Dad." She reached to close the door, indicating her need to be alone.

She surveyed the room—same wallpaper, same iron bedstead. Nothing had changed. It was not dirty, but not clean either. It just looked as if it hadn't been touched in quite a while. She sat down on the bed facing the dresser and mirror. The dresser scarf was gray from accumulated dust; her keepsakes and pictures were all there as if waiting for her.

The face of her mother, her beautiful dark-eyed, dark-haired mother, stared at her. Mary Lou stared back. Oh, how she had cherished that picture, all that she had left of her mommy. How many nights had she slept with it, talked to it, cried to it? She tried to push the memories down, but they came flooding back in a way they hadn't in a long while.

The wind was blowing, hard, whistling across the prairie. She could see the car, a big sedan, a man standing beside it—Carl, tall and lanky, his blond hair falling over one eye, smoking a cigarette, waiting.

She clung to her mother with the strength of a drowning seven-year-old, as indeed she was. Her screams tore the air, mingling with the sound of the wind. Her mother, trying to disentangle her, promised, "I will come back for ya, baby, We gotta get a job and a place to live. Soon as we do, I'll be here. We gonna live in the city, baby. Go to movies, eat ice cream every day. Won't you like that, honey? I love ya, darlin'. Just stay here with daddy 'til I get on my feet."

Mary Lou sensed her impatience, Carl was waiting. "Please, hon, ya gonna make me cry! Ya wanna make Mommy cry? Ya don't wanna do that, do ya, baby? Ya don't wanna see your Mommy cry, do ya?"

She beseeched her husband over Mary Lou's head. "Please, Aaron, please take her!"

Her father had loosened her clutching fingers and grabbed her thrashing body, holding her tight. But there was no comfort there. She continued to wail as if somehow she could convince her mother not to go or to take her with them.

She vaguely remembered Johnny, who was nine, standing beside their dad, his hands in the pockets of his overalls. Her mother had knelt and put her arms around him, hugging him close.

"Johnny, ya take care of your sister, ya hear me? I'll be back when I can."

John, so like his dad, looked off into the distance, his face impassive. "Goodbye, Mother," he said with a note of finality in his voice.

She stood, looked toward the car and then back at her children almost as if she might change her mind, but then she turned and ran to the car and they took off in a cloud of dust.

Aaron had married her mother against his parents' wishes. Her mother's family was dirt poor, eking out a living on land that was not much good for farming or ranching either. According to Mary Lou's grandmother, her mother's father was lazy and his wife and daughters did all the work. It was even rumored that he made bootleg whiskey and sold it. Among other things, it was rumored that he was a braggart and that he was mean to his wife, who was a quiet, overworked self-effacing wisp of a woman.

One thing he did have was three of the best-looking daughters in the county. They had all inherited the dark good looks of their father and the small thin shape of their mother. It was hard to say which was the prettiest. Martha, the oldest and Mary Lou's mother, was seventeen when she married Aaron. Her sisters were sixteen and fourteen. It was said that when they went to dances, the fellows stood in line to dance with them, and they did love to dance!

Aaron didn't go to dances. He met Martha at a box supper at the school. He was twenty-three years old and had never dated. Besides being a quiet, shy man who found it hard to talk to women, he hadn't had much opportunity since the country didn't exactly abound with young women his age.

The girls and women brought their suppers in a box, and the men bid on them in order to raise money for the school. They were not supposed to know which box belonged to who, although the women usually told their husbands or boyfriends so they would know which box to bid on. Aaron bid on Martha's box supper and got it.

He was tongue-tied when he sat down to eat with the beautiful and captivating Martha. He fell in love with her laughing eyes, her teasing ways, and her pure sensuality. He never questioned whether or not she loved him. He just wanted to be with her.

As far as Martha was concerned, marrying Aaron was an escape from a life of hard work. Even though there was work to do on the Gerhardt ranch, it was nothing like the work at home—milking cows, hoeing weeds in the garden, in the fields, feeding hogs, chickens. It was never ending. Besides, her father was pleased that she had found someone with money, someone that could take her off his hands.

However, it wasn't long before Martha was tired of life on the ranch, going to church twice a week. She began to long for the dances, the music, and the excitement. At first, Aaron went with her.

He didn't want to lose her. But the lifestyle, dancing and the drinking in the cars and other things that went on, began to clash with his deeply ingrained religious beliefs. He couldn't go and he couldn't keep his wife at home, and inevitably she found someone else, who, outside of the fact that he was a great dancer and fairly handsome, was *not worth shooting and never would be.*

Three months after she left, Martha wrote Aaron a letter asking him to send money for her to come home. It seems that Carl had taken up with another woman and asked her to leave, and she had nowhere to go and no money.

She missed her babies and wanted to be with them. She asked Aaron to forgive her if he could. She wanted to come home and be a wife to him, but if he could not forget what she had done, she would be willing to live in the house and take care of the kids. The letter rambled on about what a bad person she had been, how she had fallen into a trap set by the devil, interspersed with reminders about what the Bible said about forgiveness.

After much soul searching, Aaron sent her the money to come home.

Mary Lou would never forget the day they stood at the train station, the first snow of the season falling gently. It would soon be Christmas. Mommy would be home for Christmas! She could hardly contain her excitement. Her body trembled, her eyes sparkled, she could hardly breathe, she was so excited. The man and the boy stood, hands in pockets, impassive as ever.

There weren't any passengers arriving that day so long ago. She remembered watching the receding train, disbelief mirrored on her small face, her dad's "Come on, let's get outa here, we gotta get home ahead of the blizzard."

She and her dad and John never mentioned her mother again. Somehow, she knew it was useless to speculate about what had happened to her. Every day, for a long time, she had watched the mail, so sure they would get a letter explaining what had happened. When Christmas came and went with no word, she stopped waiting and watching.

If Mary Lou could point to a time when her rebellion against her father's God began, that was probably it. Mommy just wanted to have fun and enjoy life. God was against dancing and laughing. He had driven her away! In spite of her constant prayers, he had not brought her back. She had never actually formulated this in her mind, it just seemed too easy to drift away from God and finally to claim no belief at all. When she was old enough to think about it, it seemed that man could be in control of his own destiny. She could have the kind of life she dreamed of, money, popularity. God would not get in her way.

Mary Lou took the picture of her mother, opened a drawer, and threw it in. She slammed the drawer shut, lay down in a fetal position, closing her eyes tight, trying to blot out the memories, which in spite of everything, still had the power to hurt.

After a moment, she rose, opened her bag, and took out a large bottle of pills. Contemplating the bottle and the pills, she felt a moment of sheer panic. Should she take them all now? Or should she wait? Just take enough to get her through this one day? How many would it take? She would not be able to get anymore. Wouldn't it be better to swallow all of them now and get it over with, what was she waiting for? What if there weren't enough there to do the job? Maybe it would be better to take a few to calm her enough to sleep. She knew her father kept guns and she did know how to use them. She could take the pills and use the guns for the final solution.

Knowing that there was a way out when she was ready, helped to calm her anxiety. She took four of the pills and closed her eyes, but sleep did not come. She took four more pills and a drink out of a small bottle of whiskey she had in her bag. Then she took some cloves and chewed them slowly to kill the smell in case someone came upstairs. If only she didn't have such a high tolerance for all those pills. Soon she drifted into a heavy dreamless sleep.

In the meantime, Rosalie tried to straighten Aaron's kitchen so that she could put out the food she had brought. She loved to cook. She had brought fried chicken; her own friers were just right, potato salad, all sorts of things from her garden. She had even made ice cream, keeping it packed in gunny sacks and old quilts to keep it frozen.

This was really a special occasion! It would be so much fun to have Mary Lou back. Unlike her father and brother, she was always filled with laughter and fun. Andrea, especially, loved Mary Lou. When she had been there before, she was always entertaining the children, thinking up new games, putting on plays, splashing in the horse tank with them like another child. They had been crushed when she left without even saying goodbye.

Oh well, the first thing to do was get the swatter and kill all the flies and then sweep the floor. She picked up a rag which was used to wash dishes. Smelling it, she wrinkled her nose, rummaging around trying to find a clean one. She could not enjoy her food in this kitchen until it was clean. As soon as she finished washing the dishes and scrubbing everything else in sight, ever mindful of the scarcity of water in this dry country where droughts sometimes lasted for years, she dipped the water from the sink to use on the floor.

Dad can use Mary Lou's help around here, she thought. *Men cannot keep up a house.* Everything was left just where it was dropped, including saddles and horse blankets as well as parts for the vehicles and whatever else they happened to be using at the time.

An hour or so later, when Rosalie was ready to spread out the feast she had brought, Aaron went to call Mary Lou. First, he knocked several times, and when there was no answer, he opened the door and peered in. "Mary Lou," he called gently, "we're ready to eat." Still no response. He went to the bed and shook her lightly. She moaned and buried deeper into the bed.

"Are you sick, Mary Lou? Maybe you'll feel better if you eat?"

"Can't eat," she mumbled, "just wanna sleep."

Aaron stood for a moment, puzzled. *Had she been drinking? She sounded drugged.* He shook his head and walked out, closing the door.

"Maybe she'll want something later," he said to Rosalie. "I couldn't seem to rouse her."

"Well, I'm sure she will," Rosalie said. "She's probably just tired, it's such a long ol' way from California."

They all sat down at the large round table to indulge in the feast Rosalie had cooked. For Jake and Aaron especially, it was a grand feast since neither of them was a great cook. Although Jake could bake great biscuits and a fair gravy. They ate basically the same thing every day—a lot of greasy fried eggs, bacon, and steaks with very little vegetables or fruit.

Aaron asked God to bless the food, and for the next hour they gorged themselves on fried chicken, potato salad, fresh sliced tomatoes, corn on the cob, green beans, fluffy hot rolls with fresh churned butter, and to top it off, angel food cake and homemade ice cream. For the most part, they ate in silence, delighting in each morsel of food brought to the table at the height of its flavor and cooked to perfection.

At times, they would pause in their eating and listen for sounds of life from Mary Lou's room, each in their own way wondered who this quiet desperate-looking person was, so different from the old Mary Lou who ordinarily would be talking a mile a minute, regaling them with stories of celebrities she had met, her career, and much to her father's discomfort, her latest romance.

2
CHAPTER

Over a week had gone by since Mary Lou's homecoming. Aaron was repairing a fence to the southeast of the ranch. It was nearing noon and the searing rays of the sun were beginning to heat up the metal of the barbed wire. Aaron paused for a minute, removing his gloves and wiping sweat from his brow with his shirtsleeve. He stood for a moment, lost in thought, his brow furrowed, his eyes narrowed. As was his habit, he began to talk aloud to his friend.

"Lord, what am I gonna do about my girl?" He waited as if for an answer. "Something's terribly wrong. She doesn't eat hardly anything, just stays in the room, or gets up in the night and wanders around in the pitch-dark. I'm afraid she'll get hurt." He paused for a minute, groping for words. "It's like she's lost her will to live."

Saying that aloud was a revelation. Several times when he had tried to talk to her, she had seemed doped and once he thought he'd smelled liquor, but he'd been afraid to ask her about it. He didn't want to make waves as if he knew she was hanging by a thin thread.

Suddenly he stooped, picked up his tools, threw them in the back of the pickup truck, and headed for the house. It was as if he'd suddenly realized the urgency of the situation. He pulled up in front of the house, nearly running in his haste to get inside.

He rushed up the stairs to Mary Lou's bedroom, opened the door carefully, his heart in his throat.

"Mary Lou," he said softly. She stirred and he let out an audible sigh of relief.

"What is it?" she asked.

"Oh, I'm goin' to town." He tried to sound calm. "I just wondered if you wanted to go or if you needed anything."

"No," she said with finality.

He closed the door and went back downstairs into the living room. Why was he so afraid? It had come upon him suddenly, this fear. He was almost afraid to put it into words. Was it possible that she might take her life? There, he had put it into words in his own mind. He tried to brush the thought aside, but it continued to haunt him. Why was she in so much pain?

He knew she had just left her husband, but somehow, he failed to appreciate the tragedy in what was a long string of failed relationships. However, he knew he couldn't judge the depths of her feelings for this Larry.

He knew what it was like to lose the person you loved. He had gone through hell when Martha left with another man. Through it all, though, he had felt a strangely comforting presence. Before that time, his religion had consisted of obedience to a principal. Through the pain, he had come to know the Living God, the everlasting presence, the comforter, became a reality. Oh, that Mary Lou could somehow find that comforting Spirit.

He opened a closet in the living room and, taking out the guns one by one, he emptied them and then he took the bullets and another box of ammunition and headed toward the barn. In one way, he felt foolish, but maybe this was the Lord's leading and no matter how foolish it seemed, he knew that if you ask for advice you better be prepared to follow it.

He hollered for Jake to tell him he was going to town and asked if he would stay around in case Mary Lou needed him. Jake looked a little puzzled. He had never seen Aaron take off for town in the middle of the day. Maybe it had to do with his daughter. She was a strange one, he thought, always had been. Her doings had always been a worry to her dad. He was sorry to see her come back. He shook his head and went back to his chores.

Aaron was on his way to see his mother. He needed help to deal with this situation. He needed a woman's advice. He needed his mother with her no-nonsense, straightforward approach to life. He had missed her ever since she had gone to town to live with his sister. She had not really wanted to go, but she was over eighty and needed to be close to her doctor and her daughter. But right now, he wasn't thinking of that. He was thinking that she would instinctively know what to do about Mary Lou. He found he had to keep slowing down which was unusual for him. He seldom ever got in a hurry about anything.

His mother and sister were just sitting down on the screened-in porch to have a light lunch when he arrived. His sister Norma was a tall plain woman, her dark hair braided and coiled on top of her head. Like her mother, she had never been what one would call pretty, being tall and angular, but her features were not altogether displeasing and she had a beautiful smile, which softened her face and made her eyes sparkle.

She was an independent and liberated woman for her time. She had left the ranch to go to teacher's college and then came home to teach country school for a while. Perhaps due to a lack of eligible bachelors or the fact that she was so well-educated that she seemed unapproachable to the farmers and ranchers of her acquaintance, Norma never married.

When she was thirty she spoke to her father about moving to town to teach. Although she was thirty years old, her parents were apprehensive about her leaving home to live on her own, but they felt her loneliness and in trying to find her a suitable place to live, they decided to buy the large rooming house for their daughter. She had insisted on repaying them as soon as she was able, and over time she had.

There were three bedrooms downstairs plus a dining room and a large parlor with a veranda facing the main street. Stairs from the front led to the six single rooms and small bathroom upstairs. Norma had a view of the stairs from the parlor so that she could watch the comings and goings of her tenants, if need be. Since she mostly rented to young single girls who had to leave the farm to go school, she felt it was her duty to keep an eye on them. She was a strict, honest, no-nonsense person, perfectly capable of holding down a teaching job and running a boarding house alone.

Sometimes, she hired someone to help with the heavy work, but she was able to fix broken pipes, replace broken windows, and trim trees if need be. Like her parents and brother, she was very devoted to her church and her religion.

Aaron wanted to get right to the matter of what was troubling him, but it would have to wait until after lunch. His sister went to the kitchen to bring another plate and a glass for the lemonade.

"Mary Lou's come home," he announced between bites.

There was silence while they went on chewing their food. Finally, his mother asked, "When'd she get here?"

"Last Sunday night."

Nothing more was said until the food was eaten and Norma took the plates into the house.

"Surprised you didn't bring her by when you picked her up," his mother said.

"Well, I wanted to, but she was sick," he half-lied.

"Oh, what was wrong with her?" she asked, eyebrows raised.

Aaron sat studying awhile before he answered. "Ma, I don't know what's wrong with her! She don't eat nothin', she stares into space, she wanders around at night, she don't take no interest in nothin'. I tried to get her to go ridin', to church…course, I didn't really expect her to go." He sighed. "But she spends her time mostly in bed."

He steeled himself to say what he was going to say next. "I don't know why, but I have this feelin' she might do away with herself."

He watched her closely for her reaction. Her face was impassive. She said nothing of what she was thinking.

"Ma," he began again, "I was wonderin' if you could come and talk to her, you raised her. Or at least after you talk to her, you could let me know what you think."

What she was thinking was that Mary Lou was finally paying for all the heartache she'd caused everyone else and that the devil always received his due. Remembering the past, she too was not very happy about her granddaughter's return.

Alice Gerhardt was an older edition of her daughter, plain with gray hair pulled back severely. She was a tall woman too, in fact, she had been taller than her husband. Although, in her old age she had shrunk a little. However, she still held herself erect. Her blue eyes still snapped with fire when she was angry. Unlike most old people, she never discussed her health, and if one inquired about her well-being she always said, "'I'm very well, thank you."

She had no patience with "nerves" or other such weaknesses. She had buried her husband and two infant children on the prairie. Suffering and grief was a part of life. There would always be burdens to be borne and pain to be endured. It was just something you *got through* the best you could without bothering anyone.

"I reckon there's not much I can say to her, Aaron," she said. "She ain't never listened to anybody. Besides," she added peevishly, "she's been gone all this time and I ain't never so much as got a post-card from her."

Aaron lowered his head resignedly. "I know, Ma." He sighed. "You know"—he looked hopefully at her—"I was hopin' maybe you could talk her into goin' to Doc Macklin."

Alice didn't answer, she was still thinking about how Mary Lou never showed up except to cause trouble. Finally, she asked, "What about her husband, where's he? Shouldn't we try to notify him…let him know she's sick?"

Well, that would be the normal thing to do, thought Aaron, *but nothing was ever normal in dealing with Mary Lou.* This was an idea he didn't care to explore however, and he hurriedly changed the subject.

"Ma, I gotta get back." He stood up and motioned her to stay seated. "Don't you get up now, I'll hunt up Norma and tell her goodbye."

Alice had never seen Aaron look so worried. She looked at him affectionately. What a wonderful son he was! He had been her rock and bulwark through the long illness of his father. He had never failed them in any way. She didn't want to fail him either. It was hard for her to get that worried about Mary Lou though. Even though she had helped raise her, being a generation away kinda took the edge off the worrying seemed like.

"Aaron, I'll go with you," she said decidedly. "I want to go home for a while anyway. I'm so tired of this town. A person can hardly get any rest with the trucks roarin' up n' down the highway. It'll do me good to have some peace and quiet."

Aaron smiled. He knew she always slept like a baby. He was noticeably relieved. He wasn't sure what she could do either, really. At least he felt as if he'd taken some kind of action.

Alice rose and went into the kitchen to tell Norma that she was going home with Aaron for a few days to visit with Mary Lou.

Norma hovered over her mother, reminding her to take her medicine, making sure she took enough clothes, reminding her not to do too much. "Now, Ma, these people are capable of taking care of themselves," she said. "You let them wait on you!"

Alice didn't pay too much attention. *My health is the least of my worries,* she thought to herself. *Life just isn't any fun anymore.* She sighed, thinking of Johnnie. The love of her life had gone ahead of her, and she was ready to go any time—longed for it, in fact. She would see Jesus, and her Johnnie would be there.

She missed him every day of her life. They were married when she was sixteen and he was twenty. She considered that the luckiest thing that ever happened to her. Or maybe it wasn't luck, perhaps it was God's grace. They were so different. She was tall and plain and reserved and Johnnie was short and stocky, full of laughter and emotion.

She smiled to herself, remembering. Funny thing was, much to her chagrin, she had grown taller than he after their marriage! He used to tease her about it—how he'd married her before she was full grown. He had never grown old in her eyes. Even during his illness and in the middle of his pain, he'd always had an affectionate smile on his face when he woke up and reached for her just as he'd done in all the years of their marriage.

"When will you be bringing her back, Aaron?" asked his sister.

She had reservations about her mother being so far away from her doctor. This was the last of her family, and she longed to hold on to her for as long as possible. She had to admit though that her mother had never been happy away from the country and her friends, what was left of them. Goodness knows she had tried to get her interested in the church in town and its social life. She wanted to go back home to die, she always said, to be with Dad, of course. Norma had a feeling that if she left, she might have a hard time convincing her to come back.

The ride home seemed endless to Aaron. He tried to still his mind, tried to pray, to push out the thoughts that intruded on his consciousness, but it was useless. What was he going to find in that upstairs bedroom? Maybe he shouldn't have left. Well, he couldn't guard Mary Lou the rest of her life, some action had to be taken.

His mother, seeing the worry on his face, tried to make conversation although normally she was a taciturn person not given to unnecessary words. "Remember the Johnsons that lived over there?" She pointed to a pile of rocks and a couple of half-buried pieces of iron alongside the road.

"We wrote back n' forth for years, then I just kinda lost track of them." She sighed. "When your dad n' I first came here there was a family on ever section of land, now there ain't nobody here. Hard life out here on the prairie, lot of folks just gave up n' went back. Not your dad though. The harder it was and the lonelier it was, the better he liked it."

She chuckled. "Last time we buried somebody, I forget who it was, upon the Windy Hill cemetery, the wind was blowin' n' the prairie dogs had dug in the graves, n' your dad, he said, 'I don't wanna be buried here.' I told him if it's a good 'nuf place to live, it's a good 'nuf place to be buried. He got a real kick outa that." She chuckled again at the memory.

"I'm real glad you and Johnny care about the land," she reflected. "Your dad worked so hard to build up this place. Course, we wouldn't have all this land either if we hadn't inherited money just at the right time. When people left, we were able to buy more land."

Aaron could not seem to concentrate on what she was saying. Of course, he had heard all the family lore a million times. When they arrived home, it was all he could do to keep from dashing into the house and checking Mary Lou's room. Instead, he patiently helped his mother out of the car and took her bag into her bedroom before he knocked on Mary Lou's door.

"Mary Lou," he said hopefully, "your grandma's here."

There was no answer, so he knocked again. Finally, he couldn't stand it anymore and so he went in and shook her. "Mary Lou, get up, your grandma's here."

She rolled over and looked at him. It seemed to him that her eyes were glassy, that she was not really seeing him. She made no move to get up.

In the meantime, Alice had entered the room and was peering at her from the foot of the bed. She too was shocked at Mary Lou's appearance. She looked like an old woman, an old sick woman. Mary Lou turned over and buried her face in the pillow without saying a word.

Alice motioned to Aaron to leave, and she closed the door quietly behind them. She took him by the arm and led him down the stairs to a chair and then sat opposite him.

"I think you're right," she said quietly. "Something is badly wrong with her. It's too late to do anything this evenin', but first thing in the mornin' we'll get her to town."

"How do we get her to go, though?" Aaron wondered aloud.

"Same way we get an old cow to town that don't wanna go," said his mother.

"In the meantime, I'm hungry, and I know you are too. I'll see if I can find something to fix," she said briskly.

"There's a pot of beans that Jake fixed," offered Aaron.

"Okay, I'll fix cornbread to go with it, if you got cornmeal."

"I don't think Mary Lou'll eat anything," he said.

"I wouldn't try to feed her," said his mother. "We need to eat and get a good night's sleep for all what we have to do tomorrow… and I want you to sleep too," she ordered. "Mary Lou is in the hands of the Lord, same as we are. I'm sure he has a plan and we need to be strong to carry it out."

Aaron began to feel the calm that his mother always engendered. Her great faith lifted his own faith and caused him once again to accept that there were things beyond his control.

3
CHAPTER

The following morning, he woke to the sound of birds chirping and water running. His mother was running water in the old-fashioned cast iron tub. He felt groggy, like turning over and covering up his head and not facing the day, so unlike his usual early morning exuberance. He liked to rise just as the sun was peeking over the prairie. He relished the coolness of the morning, the sound of the earth's awakening, the little sounds heard only in the deafening stillness of the dawn.

Even at that hour, Jake would have the coffee perking. In the summer they sat on the porch at the first light and Aaron would take up the Bible and read aloud while they savored their coffee. Then Aaron would send up the prayer for the day, and afterward they would discuss what needed to be done on the ranch. They always took this time no matter what else was going on or how busy they were. Although Jake never commented on the Bible reading or offered to pray, it seemed that it was as much a part of his day as Aaron's and he took care to see that he never missed it.

"You takin' a bath, Ma?" Aaron asked as he sauntered out to the kitchen and poured himself a cup of coffee. Baths were not something people out in the country took every day; water was too precious.

"No, Mary Lou is," she said.

He looked at her quizzically.

"If she's goin' to the doctor, she's got to have a bath," she said firmly.

Jake was fixing breakfast while Alice was setting the table. She stopped and went to turn off the water.

Aaron looked at the clock. It was late, almost seven. If they were going to town, he had to get out and get right at his chores. He looked apologetically at Jake. Too bad they had to miss their Bible reading, but Jake would have been embarrassed if he had said anything.

After breakfast, Alice went to Mary Lou's room. She didn't bother to knock. It looked as if Mary Lou hadn't moved since the last time she had been there, but she had heard her leave the house during the night and in the moonlight, she had watched her pacing in the yard like a caged animal. It was as if something was after her, like she was being pursued by a demon, which, most likely, thought her grandma, that's what it was.

She shook her granddaughter. "Mary Lou, get up, I want you to take a bath. We're taking you to the doctor." She spoke slowly and deliberately and with authority.

Mary Lou groaned. "I'm not going!" she shouted. "Get away from me!"

Alice put her hands on her hips. "You have a choice, you can either get up by yourself or I'm gettin' old Jake in here with a rope. We're takin' you and that's that!"

"Gran, please," Mary Lou changed tactics, "Gran, I'll be all right, just leave me alone!"

Alice was unbending. "Up, right now!" she said firmly. "Or it's the rope! You know me, Mary Lou, I never say anything I don't mean." She walked over and pulled up all the blinds, letting the strong sunlight into the room.

The glare made Mary Lou want to scream. Right then she hated the old woman enough to kill her. She knew she meant what she said. She had always meant what she said. In her growing up years they had always been at loggerheads, and Gran always won. She felt like getting up and running, but it was impossible to get away from the old lady.

She stood up and almost fell over as everything turned black. She was so weak from loss of sleep and not eating. She could not sleep at night. Only during the daylight hours was she able to get a little sleep.

Alice reached out to steady her. "Lay back down, Mary Lou. I'm gonna get your dad."

Aaron was just coming in the back door after finishing his chores when his mother caught him.

"I think you better go help her down the stairs, Aaron. She's weak as a cat." She went on ahead to be there and make sure he got her up and helped her down the stairs, because she knew Mary Lou would talk him into leaving her alone.

Between the two of them they got her downstairs and into the bathroom. Alice would have gone in with her, but she promised she would take a bath and put on the clean clothes she had brought with her.

Aaron was surprised when she came out in a little while with her hair combed and wearing clean, albeit very wrinkled, clothes. He was beginning to feel better about the situation than he had for some time.

He brought out the green-and-black Hudson automobile, which he had bought new and seldom drove, so that they could ride to town in comfort. Mary Lou obediently climbed into the back seat and scrunched up against the door, closing her eyes against the glare of the sun. This was the third time in just over two weeks that Aaron had made the long drive to town, which was a record for him.

It was still early when they pulled up in front of Dr. Macklin's office. But the doctor kept early hours and long hours in order to accommodate his patients, mostly farmers who came to town early to do their business and get back to their fields as soon as possible.

The Gerhardts had been going to the same doctor for over thirty-five years. In fact, he had delivered Mary Lou. They never made an appointment; they just went to town to see Doc, and he was always available to them.

Aaron went inside to talk to the doctor before bringing Mary Lou inside since it was a little awkward bringing a patient who claimed to have nothing wrong with her, and one of which they did not know what was wrong except that they knew something was terribly wrong.

Aaron detailed Mary Lou's symptoms for the doctor. He told him about the staying in bed all day, up all night pacing the yard in the dark. He told him how she never talked to them, just stared into space when they tried to talk to her. As bad as he hated to, he mentioned the possible drug use and the smell of alcohol. He took a deep breath and admitted that he was afraid she was going to take her own life! The two men chatted awhile before the doctor asked to see Mary Lou.

"Nice to see you again, Mary Lou." Dr. Macklin smiled kindly at her. "It's been a long time."

She was noncommittal.

"Can you tell me what's wrong, Mary Lou?"

"Nothing," she said, staring into space.

"Your dad said you had mentioned something about an ulcer," he volunteered.

She didn't answer.

Dr. Macklin had very little training in psychiatry, but he had been practicing medicine long enough to recognize a person in deep depression. She appeared to him to be in an almost catatonic state.

He tried again, "Mary Lou, do you take any medication?"

She shook her head.

"What about drinking, do you drink, Mary Lou?"

"No, no, no," she half-screamed the words. "Just leave me alone, I don't have to answer your damn questions, just leave me alone!"

For a minute he was taken aback by her violent reaction. "Mary Lou," he spoke firmly, "if you have an ulcer I can treat you for that, but I believe you have far deeper problems than that. From what I observe and what your dad has told me, you seem to be suffering from an emotional breakdown."

He observed her closely in order to determine her reaction. There was no noticeable reaction other than a slight slumping of her shoulders. She gripped her hands together, staring at them silently.

"Unfortunately, we don't have anyone in this town capable of giving you the help you need. In order to get the treatment you need, you will have to go to Pueblo or Denver. I can't urge you too strongly to go and as soon as possible." He paused, again waiting for her reaction. She continued to stare at her hands folded in her lap.

Outside of the reaction to the question about her drinking, Mary Lou seemed totally lost in the depths of her own mind. The doctor waited awhile to see if she had anything to add. Unable to see any use in pursuing the conversation further, he stood up. "Mary Lou, I will speak to your dad," he said, dismissing her. "Would you ask him to come in, please?"

The two men sat quietly; the doctor looking at Aaron, Aaron lost in thought. Absently twirling his hat in his lap, he stared past the doctor, staring out the window behind his desk into the bright sunlight sparkling on the leaves of the trees. The doctor had outlined the worst possible scenario, in case that, based on his observation, Mary Lou had suffered a nervous breakdown, it would mean intensive counseling, possible shock therapy, all taking place far away and costing a good deal of money.

The "money" part, he dismissed, he had plenty of that. The "far away" part, he admitted guiltily, for a moment seemed tempting. Off to a hospital to be locked away, counseled, and shocked, and coming out normal, ready to get on with life—he would give all he owned for that. However, even with his limited education and experience in such matters, he was pretty sure that would not be the case. Mary Lou had a sickness of the soul. He knew that. Only God had the answer.

The doctor had a feeling that Aaron was about to reject his recommendations. "You know," he said softly, "you told me you're afraid Mary Lou might want to kill herself?"

Aaron nodded.

"I think that's a distinct possibility."

"I was wondering about havin' her talk to David," Aaron mused.

"Your preacher?"

Aaron nodded.

Dr. Macklin felt impatient. He was a church-going man himself, but he had no faith in religion in such matters. Although, he had to admit, it did help some people. Alcoholics Anonymous, through a dependence on God, seemed to help alcoholics when nothing else worked. He had referred people there himself when he became aware of their problem. Perhaps that was Mary Lou's problem, he had no way of knowing.

He did not know what else to say; he wished he could guarantee that time in a mental hospital would make her as good as new. At one time he believed that. No more, he had seen too many failures. Too many patients after intensive therapy had come home and blown their brains out or had become one of the living dead. Of course, it wasn't always that way; some people were cured or improved enough to function.

"The only thing I can do is prescribe an anti-depressant… it might help. You will have to administer it though," he warned. "Otherwise, there's a possibility she'll use it to overdose." He looked straight into Aaron's eyes. "I strongly recommend that she see a doctor of psychiatry. I will write a referral for her to see a doctor that I highly recommend. Like you said, she could talk to David. I suppose he had courses in psychology in seminary. Frankly, though, I think from all that you've told me and from what little I've observed, she needs more help than he can give her."

He pulled out his prescription pad and began to write, while Aaron continued to stare out into the sunlight.

"Do you suppose she's depressed because she separated from her man?" Aaron wondered aloud.

"That could be part of it," the doctor said. "Sometimes people are depressed because of something that's happened, and usually they get over it, or sometimes they're depressed for no apparent reason, and that's the part we can't explain. I wish I had the answers, but I don't."

Aaron's shoulders slumped perceptibly. He had come here for answers, and the answers he'd gotten were the last thing in the world he'd wanted to hear. The doctor had mentioned months, sometimes years, of therapy—no quick cure. *Maybe no cure at all,* thought Aaron.

He rose and held out his hand for the prescription and the referral.

"I need to talk to Mary Lou about this," he said. "What if she don't wanna go?"

The doctor sighed. "She probably won't. Most of them don't."

"What do I do then?"

"The hardest thing you've ever had to do in your life," the doctor said sadly. "You may have to have her committed."

Aaron stiffened, staring at him. "How do I do that?"

"You will have to get a court order…with my help."

Aaron looked as if someone had struck him in the face. He was wide-eyed and speechless.

"Well," said the doctor, "you talk to her and then we'll plan the next move after that."

Aaron turned and walked out like a man in his sleep. He walked right past Mary Lou and his mother without a word and out the front door of the waiting room to his car. His breathing was heavy and labored, he felt that if he didn't sit down soon, he was going to faint.

Mary Lou and Alice followed him to the car. Mary Lou got in the back seat. She seemed lost in her own world, unconcerned about her diagnosis. Alice was dying to find out what the doctor had to say, but she figured she'd better wait until she had a chance to talk to Aaron alone. She knew it had to be serious. Poor Aaron, she thought, he looked as if he'd been struck by a bolt of lightning.

Aaron left town, not bothering with the prescription, driving faster than usual, trying to put as many miles between himself and the troubles he'd encountered, at the same time realizing he was taking his troubles with him. He had to talk to Mary Lou, his mother, God, think things out. Somewhere out there on the prairie was an answer. He had the greatest respect for Dr. Macklin, his doctor, his family doctor, but he couldn't accept his solution, not yet anyway.

Since it was not yet noon, his mother wanted to go by the cemetery. He felt annoyed. He wanted to go home, maybe saddle his horse and ride off alone, not sit in the hot car while his mother wandered about in the graveyard. But he dutifully drove on past the turnoff to home and drove to the church and on past to the graveyard where their family and friends were buried. He got out to help her out of the car and then decided to go with her. It was a bad time of the year for rattlesnakes, and since her hearing and sight were not too good she might run upon one without ever seeing it.

The graveyard was on a slight hill above the church. She often reflected how Johnnie would have loved the view from here. You could see for miles across his beloved prairie.

"The place looks good," she observed. "Somebody's pulled out all the weeds."

Aaron nodded approvingly. "That's David. He's a good man; we were sure lucky to get him for a preacher." He looked down over the church and the parsonage. "He sure keeps things lookin' fine around here."

Alice knelt at the grave of her husband, lovingly caressing the granite stone. *Beloved husband and father.*

Suddenly she looked up at Aaron. "What did the doc say?"

Aaron looked out across the prairie, not meeting her eyes. He said, "Mary Lou needed to go to Denver, needed to get therapy." He paused. "She might kill herself. If we don't take her, I mean, if she won't go, we might have to have her committed. Oh, he gave me a prescription for pills, said they might help some."

"Why didn't you stop and get the prescription filled?" she wanted to know.

"I don't know," he admitted. "He said they were dangerous…I mean, if we just gave them to her, she could use them to kill herself. It's hard to imagine how a pill could make you feel better when you're sick in your soul." There was a long silence between them, and then Aaron looked at his mother. "What if she won't take them? Do I force them down her like a sick animal? Ma," he said helplessly, "I've always had answers. What is the answer here, do I have my little girl locked up in some insane asylum somewhere, Ma? I know a pill is not the answer!"

She nodded. "You're probably right. I can't help you, son, only God has the answer."

"Well," she said, "finally, let's go home and talk to Mary Lou, maybe she can help you decide. Who knows, maybe she might want to go get help."

"I don't have much hopes of that, Ma."

He helped her to her feet and she moved on to her babies' graves saying a little prayer over each of them.

Somehow, this helped Aaron put things into perspective. *Look at Ma,* he thought, *she's suffered so much losing her little ones and her husband. But she was able to go on.* She was able to live again just as he had when his wife left. He would be strong and take things as they came, trusting in God. Maybe it was not that God would make Mary Lou well so that he could get back into his routine and comfortable life, but that God would be with him every step of the way.

And it's going to be a hard way, he reflected, especially if he had to try to commit Mary Lou. He hoped it wouldn't come to that.

Once they reached the house, Mary Lou headed for her bedroom and Alice began to prepare a little food for dinner. After they ate, Alice headed to her room for a nap.

Aaron waited awhile, trying to brace himself before he started up the stairs to Mary Lou's room. As usual, when he knocked, there was no answer so he let himself in and pulled up a chair at the side of the bed. He reached over and shook her awake. "Mary Lou," he said firmly, "I have to talk to you. I want you to listen to me."

He began, haltingly, stammering at first and then gained momentum. "The doctor said you were depressed, perhaps you had a nervous breakdown. It seems to me that you had lost your will to live. I'm afraid you might be thinkin' of takin' your life."

He left no time for her to answer but hurried on. "I have a prescription for pills that might help you. If that don't help you, there are doctors in Denver. You might have to stay in a hospital for a while, but I will be with you and help you all I can." He left no opening for her answer, and she made no effort to answer.

He paused. "I have another thought, maybe you could talk to our preacher, he's been in the war, been through a lot, sometimes he counsels people about their troubles. I don't know what kind of troubles, but we could try that first." He looked at her, really looked into her eyes for the first time, hoping that he might find in them some clue as to the direction he needed to take.

Strangely enough, she looked back at him, and then she smiled. "Dad, let me think this over and we'll talk about it tomorrow. Daddy," she smiled again, "I know you're worried about me, but it's not as bad as you think. I just need to rest now, Daddy. You'll see, I'll be down for breakfast tomorrow morning. We'll have a long talk then, okay?"

In a way he was relieved at her reaction, but somehow he knew he hadn't found the answers he was looking for and he felt a sense of trepidation. Why had she changed her tune so suddenly? There was little he could do though, except smile back at her. "That's my girl!" he said as he left the room.

It was funny, thought Mary Lou, suddenly she was able to think clearly for the first time in a long time.

As she had listened to her father detail the doctor's instructions for her treatment, she had felt a sudden calm. A strange peace came over her, she no longer felt trapped. Now she knew what she had to do and she could accept it.

They thought she was crazy, and they wanted to put her away, get help, her Dad had said, but she knew there was no help and she didn't want help anyway. She knew she was crazy and there was only one way to be free. She couldn't ever go back to California—to Larry. And she would rather be dead than live here, so there was no place for her, not in the world anyway. It was impossible to live in her head, there were too many demons there. There was only one way to escape her head—the pills. Were there enough of them to do the job? She wished she knew how many it would take. There was the alcohol. That would help, of course. People talked about the deadly combination—booze and pills.

It would be best, she decided, to wait until everyone went to bed. She did not want them to discover her before the pills had taken effect. Funny, she thought, when people killed themselves, they usually wrote a note. She, however, had no desire to write a note.

Actually, she was beginning to feel sleepy, but she knew she mustn't sleep. She might sleep through until morning and then it would be too late. *Who knows?* she thought, *maybe they're planning on having someone come tomorrow.* Her dad hadn't said anything about committing her.

She knew all about being committed. Larry had committed himself to hospitals and asylums several times, but then they had never been able to keep him. As soon as he sobered up, he left. She might not be able to leave. But then where would she go if she did leave?

No, she had made her decision, all she had to do was wait. She turned toward the window where the sun streamed through the lace curtain. It was slowly going down in the west, and she settled down to wait for the darkness. She tried not to think about her dad and what this would do to him. She felt he was the only person in the world who really loved her, but she had made his life miserable. He was entitled to a little peace. She thought fleetingly of Larry. Maybe he was already dead. The doctor said that if he drank again, he was a dead man.

She had learned to blank things out of her mind by focusing on something else, a spot on the ceiling or something. Now she tried looking straight at the sun and then closing her eyes and seeing the sun again. They told her when she was a little girl if she looked at the sun, she would go blind so she had tried never to look at it. Now, she thought ruefully, going blind does not really matter.

After a while, she reached for the pills and the alcohol, putting them safely under her pillow. It was dusk now, soon it would be over. The old folks went to bed early, not much longer to wait. No one came up the stairs to bid her good night, she was alone. She felt strong, she had made her decision and that alone gave her a feeling of control. The darkness crept into the room until she could no longer make out the patterns on the ceiling caused by the rain leaks.

It was time. She reached for the bottle holding it up in the dimness of the light. What was there? A pint, no, a half-pint maybe. Or maybe less. She took a long swig, and then another, gasping for breath as the whiskey burned like fire in her nostrils and throat. She wanted water, but no, the water might dilute the power of the drug, she would have to use the whiskey to down the pills. She took one pill and then another and another. She would not count them. She had to take them all.

Usually Alice slept the sleep of babies and old people, but for some reason, she could not sleep. This thing about Mary Lou troubled her. She could see that Aaron was deeply troubled. She had a hard time believing it was really that serious. In the depths of her memory, slowly emerging to the forefront was a woman she had not thought of in years. What was her name? Hannah something, she hadn't known her that well. She had had a nervous breakdown. What was that all about anyway? She racked her memory, but the details wouldn't come. She did remember one thing though, and the memory made her blood run cold. Hannah had taken a gun and blown her brains out leaving a husband and two small children!

Alice got out of bed and in the moonlight walked to the front room. Pulling aside the curtains, she peered into the night. The moon and a sky full of brilliant stars lit the yard almost as if it were daylight. Where was the familiar figure, pacing the yard in the moonlight?

Alice went to the table in the kitchen and lit the coal oil lamp. She then lit a candle and went up the stairs to Mary Lou's room. Something was propelling her up those stairs even though another part of her tried to tell herself she was letting her imagination run away with her and that Mary Lou would be furious at being awakened at this time of night.

When she opened the door and went in, Mary Lou seemed to be sleeping peacefully and then she saw the empty liquor bottle. *Oh, she's drunk,* she thought disgustedly. And then she saw the empty pill bottle. She picked it up and tried to read the label, but without her glasses she couldn't tell what it was. She reached down and shook Mary Lou who didn't stir. In fact, her eyes rolled open and they seemed to be set, like a dead person's!

Alice suppressed a scream. She was sure Mary Lou was dead. She went to the door and yelled as loud as she could. "Aaron." Fortunately, her son had not been able to sleep either. He was just drifting off when he heard her voice.

This was the moment he had been dreading and expecting. He knew immediately that it was Mary Lou. A feeling of cold terror almost immobilized him, but he threw on his pants and, barging through the door, he yelled, "Mom?"

"Aaron, somethin's wrong with Mary Lou. I'm up here, come here, hurry!" she yelled urgently.

Aaron flew up the stairs and into Mary Lou's room, where Alice stood over her holding the light.

"Son," his Mother's voice was quaking, "Mary Lou's took something. She's drunk that liquor…I can't rouse her…I don't think she's breathin'!"

Aaron started to shake Mary Lou, and then he knelt with his ear to her chest. It seemed he could not hear a heartbeat. He felt her pulse, maybe there was a faint pulse. He could barely feel it. He could smell the alcohol. What else had she taken? He saw the pill bottle, grabbed it, and read the label, but he didn't recognize the name of the drug.

All this time he had started to pray the prayer of the desperate. "Please, God, please, don't let her die, Lord, save her, Lord, please, Lord. Come on, Ma," he said desperately, "we have to get her to the hospital, we have to try."

He picked up Mary Lou as if she were light as a feather and literally ran down the stairs toward the door. Realizing he had to put on his boots, he laid her down on the sofa and ran to his room for his shirt and boots.

Like one does in the eye of the storm, Alice suddenly felt a calmness come over her. She reached for the bottle of pills to take with them. The doctor would have to know what Mary Lou had taken. She decided there was not time for her to dress, she would have to go in her housecoat and slippers. She would need clothes, but she had clothes in town. They did not have a minute to spare!

Aaron started to protest when he saw that his mother intended to go but changed his mind. He didn't have time to argue.

Alice quickly wet a towel to put on Mary Lou's head. She didn't know what to do, really, but it seemed to her the important thing to do was to try and wake her, if possible.

Aaron literally threw Mary Lou into the back seat with Alice climbing in behind her.

The car left the yard with a roar. Aaron would drive the car as fast as it would go, concentrating every sense on keeping the car on the road. Like a race car driver, he had to win the race, and that would take every power of concentration available to him. He asked God to ride with him, drive the car, in fact.

Meanwhile, Alice was doing her best to waken Mary Lou, yelling at her, even slapping her, and intermittently petitioning God, rebuking Satan, who wanted the life of her granddaughter.

Aaron tried to shut out every thought that Mary Lou was dying, in fact, might already be dead. He would not think, he would only drive!

Alice did have a thought, several times, that maybe this was the end of the road for all of them, especially when Aaron would fly across a ditch without seeming to touch the ground. But her job was to pray. She always admonished everyone to *keep prayed up* since you never knew the hour of the Lord's coming.

It seemed that God was with them because they never met or passed a car after they hit the highway. Soon they saw the lights of the town ahead and knew they had done the best they could. The hospital was conveniently at the very edge of town, and Aaron roared up to the front door, stopping with a squeal of brakes. It was only about ten thirty, the middle of the night for most folks since they retired so early.

The hospital was quiet as Aaron went bounding up the stairs, taking them two at a time with the dead weight of his daughter in his arms. Normally, a very reserved man, he started yelling as he hit the front door. "Get a doctor, I have an emergency here. My girl is dying! Hurry, hurry, please hurry!"

Suddenly, there was a flurry of activity as the sisters who ran the hospital took charge. Dr. Macklin was called, and he arrived, almost as worried and frightened as Aaron and his mother. Alice furnished the empty pill bottle, and then their task was finished. It was now in the hands of the doctors and nurses and God. Alice and Aaron fell to their knees in the waiting room of the hospital and began to pray.

Aaron asked God to spare Mary Lou, not just because she was his daughter and he loved her, but because, as he reminded God, Mary Lou had never been saved. He was worried about the state of her soul, and he knew the Lord must care about that also. He had always taken as a promise that God would pour out his spirit upon his seed and their seed. As it was, he could never have the assurance that Mary Lou would be there with Jesus. He had that assurance for himself, but what about her?"

And so he talked to God as one would talk to a caring neighbor, one who understood his hurts and fears. He reminded himself that Jesus was at the right hand of the Father, ever making intercession for him. Gradually, he felt his fear draining away, and he was able to release Mary Lou into the hands of the one who loved her more than he did and who alone knew the answer to the perplexing problem.

He was still deep in prayer when Dr. Macklin came in. The doctor touched their shoulders, and Aaron, who was seated, looked up and Alice rose from her position of prayer at the side of her chair. The doctor was amazed at the alacrity of the old woman. What an ordeal this must be for her at her age!

"Aaron," he began, "I'm pretty sure Mary Lou is going to make it. I can't say she's past the danger point though, she was nearly dead. I guess you found her just in time. I have no way of knowing how many of those pills she took. Fortunately, I don't think the bottle was full. You know, I think you could go and get some sleep now. You could go to Norma's house, couldn't you? I could call you if I needed you or if there was any change."

Aaron felt reluctant to leave, but he was concerned about his mother. He hated the thought of waking his sister in the middle of the night and give all these explanations. "Ma," he said, "I'm going to take you to Norma's and then I'm coming back. I want to be here in case Mary Lou needs me. Besides, I want you to tell Norma what all's goin' on here. I guess it's time the whole family knows what we're dealin' with here since it ain't likely to get any better…for a while anyway."

Alice nodded. She patted her weary son on the shoulder. "Whatever it is, you can deal with it, son. God will never give you any more than you can bear. I believe Mary Lou will get all right and that in itself is a sign. It's a sign that he is not through with her, and it will get better. Satan will not win this battle, you'll see," she said determinedly.

Aaron thought of the difference between his faith and his mother's. His was more like a quiet partnership, where hers always seemed more like a war, not against flesh and blood but against *principalities and powers*. And maybe that's what it was, or maybe a little of both, he thought.

The next morning, Aaron woke with a start. For a moment, he didn't know where he was, and then he remembered. For an instant the fear rose up in his throat, but then he knew that if anything had changed during the night, they would have called him. He inquired at the desk, and they informed him that the doctor would be in soon and then he could see his daughter.

He walked to the cafe in the bus depot several blocks away for a cup of coffee. The morning was alive with the sound of birds chirping, singing their heavenly melodies. The sky was crystal blue. Aaron breathed in the morning and felt better. It would be a scorcher again, but right now it was a typical summer morning. Somewhere, he heard a rooster crow, and all was right with the world. He was reminded of Peter and the cock crowing. Every time he'd heard the rooster crow, he must have remembered his shame. Perhaps from now on every time he heard the rooster crow he'd remember this low point in his life.

When Dr. Macklin arrived, he and Aaron went into the room where Mary Lou was lying, her eyes closed, an IV dripping into her arm. She looked so pale and quiet, not really alive, Aaron thought, but then she hadn't seemed alive for some time now. This was just another stage of her death; nothing had really changed.

Dr. Macklin read her chart, took her pulse, and then called her name sharply. Aaron was relieved to see her eyes open. He knew she recognized them when she quickly squeezed them shut again. The doctor motioned Aaron out of the room. "She's going to live," he said, "but now we have to discuss again what you are going to do with her. She will try this again, you know?" Aaron nodded. "Next time she'll probably make a better job of it. Now is the best time to commit her to the hospital where she can get the help she needs. It is easier to prove insanity if the person has just tried to kill themselves."

Aaron winced. It was hard to use the word insanity when speaking of his daughter. He simply couldn't think of her as insane in spite of what she had just done to herself. He knew now that when she had assured him that she would be fine, she had made up her mind to do what she had to do. Still, he couldn't bring himself to think of sending her away. He felt pressure from the doctor to do something when his instincts told him to wait. But wait for what? Wait for her to find another way to kill herself or live like a mad woman in the upstairs bedroom with him as her caretaker until he died and they finally took her away? But surely, that was not what God had in mind. Like Ma had said, Satan hadn't won the battle. God was still on their side.

"I'm sorry, Doctor, I'm not ready to make this decision this minute," he said decisively. "How much longer does Mary Lou have to stay in this hospital?"

"Well, she can probably get out in a couple of days."

"I will give you my decision before she leaves the hospital."

The doctor nodded. "I wish I could give you alternatives. I can't think of any."

"Well, you know, being a doctor, you fight against death. It's your enemy. But," Aaron said slowly, "there are a lot of things worse than death. I'm not going to let my fear of Mary Lou's killin' herself force me in to making a decision I'm not sure is the right thing."

Again, Dr. Macklin felt impatient with the implacability of this man. He nodded good day and hurried off, not willing to argue or press his point.

Mary Lou slowly opened her eyes, taking in the small hospital room, the IV dripping into her arm slowly restoring life, the life she didn't want. The last thing she remembered was taking the pills and drinking the liquor. Why hadn't it done the job? How did they find her and why? She knew they had gone to bed. They were not people who wandered around in the middle of the night. Both of them had always slept like they had died and gone to heaven.

Her heart sank like a rock in her chest. Now she was certain to be committed! How could she make her dad think she would be all right after this? He would do what he had to do to keep her from taking her life. That damn doctor, this was his fault. He was the one who had convinced her father that she needed to be locked up! She closed her eyes again, trying to think but unable to concentrate. Somehow, she needed to get out of there and quickly before they came for her. No use thinking about where she was going or what she was going to do after she left. The main thing was to leave as soon as possible!

She got out of bed, checking the closet, dragging her IV with her. "Damn," she swore. Her clothes were not there! No matter, just get the needle out of her arm and run like hell. She ripped the tape and yanked the needle out of her arm. Blood squirted. She had ripped her arm. She bit her lip, moaning softly in pain.

Suddenly, someone grabbed her shoulders holding her in a vise-like grip. She fought, but it was useless. It was her dad, and he was strong as an ox. She bit his arm, but he didn't relinquish his hold. She kicked with her feet, not daring to scream for fear of bringing the hospital staff.

About that time a nurse walked by, saw what was going on, and hurried off. In a few minutes another nurse arrived with a hypodermic poised to give a shot.

"Don't touch her with that," Aaron ordered. "Get out. I can hold her and I need to talk to her. Now, Mary Lou," he began quietly and decisively, "I can't believe that you're so far gone, that you can't listen to some reason."

"You're not gonna put me away in some nut house!" she screamed softly. "If you really cared about me, you would let me do away with myself. Can't you see how I'm hurting, or don't you care?" she cried.

"Mary Lou, I know you're hurting, I know that," he said. "But, Mary Lou, can I just say one thing? Will you listen to me, please?

She had finally stopped struggling, but there was no comment.

"What if, and I can't say for sure now, but what if you get to the other side and there is no peace and the hell you're in now is the hell you'll be in throughout all eternity? Just think about that for a minute."

She shook her head impatiently, "You know I don't believe in all that. It's just a pipe dream. There is no God, and if there is, he wouldn't care about me."

Aaron shook his head sadly, "Just 'cause you don't believe in him don't mean he don't exist."

Aaron picked her up and put her on the bed like a baby. He sat on the edge of the bed and took her face between his hands like he had when she was a little girl. "My little girl," he almost crooned, "I'm not gonna put you away because I don't believe it's gonna do you any good. If you're bound and determined to do away with yourself, you're gonna do it, but you can't run away, there's no place to go. There must be some reason you came home in the first place," he added. "I happen to believe there's a higher reason.

"Mary Lou, if you'll promise me to talk to David, our preacher, Now, he ain't no regular preacher," he hurriedly added, "he's had counseling experience, and he's been through a lot himself, he was hurt bad in the war." His voice drifted off, seeing the hard set to her mouth.

"If you could just give it a month," he pleaded, "talk to him. Mary Lou, let the land heal your heart, the wind and the prairie that you once loved." He saw that it was useless to plead in that way. "If after a month you ain't no better," he bargained, "I'll release you to do whatever you have to do, go where you want to. You may be locked up or dead, but you're in God's hands. I ain't gonna stop you." And he knew in his heart that he wouldn't.

He knew instinctively that it was her life to do with what she wished, but if she were willing to go that far, he had a month to cry out to God on her behalf. He knew that he had prayed before, but this would be different. This was a prayer that would demand his very soul with the urgency of it. For one thing, it would require letting go of all the resentments he had harbored on her behalf.

Suddenly he felt an overwhelming love for this poor waif of a girl. He had never felt such love before even though he claimed to love his children. He suddenly realized that this was not his love, but the overwhelming, all-pervading love of God for this girl. Suddenly in spite of what had looked like a hopeless situation, he felt a great peace come over him. This girl belonged to God, and he truly loved her with a love that was incomprehensible to the human mind and emotions.

This is holy ground, he thought, *I should take off my shoes and kneel in this spot.* But his humanity got the best of him, and even though Mary Lou had not acquiesced to the bargain, he looked at her and said calmly, "I'll find out when you can go and I'll take you home." It was a statement rather than a question.

Mary Lou did not answer. He was giving her a chance to try again. There was no point in running, out in the street with no clothes on. They would put her away whether her dad said it was okay or not. She turned over to go asleep just as the nurse came to replace her IV.

If Aaron felt calm and resolute, not so his mother and sister. His idea about taking Mary Lou home again did not set well.

"What did the doctor say?" asked Norma.

"He was not happy about it," Aaron admitted. "He was cussing up a blue streak, threatenin' to have her put away himself whether I agreed or not."

"Well, I should think so,'" said Alice. "Son, I usually respect your decisions, but I think this is just plain foolish. It doesn't make a bit a sense!"

"Ma." Aaron breathed deeply. "I'm not gonna lock her up in some insane asylum! She's not gonna get better, and she'll live there in misery the rest of her life."

"Well, what if she kills herself, what then?" his mother demanded.

"Well, maybe she's better off dead than living like that," he replied.

She didn't answer. That sounded like sinful talk to her.

"I'm gonna ask David to talk to her," he said.

Alice was incredulous. "What makes you think she's gonna listen to him?"

"Well," Aaron replied, "she didn't say she wouldn't. He has counseling experience, he was a chaplain in the war. What are they gonna do in the asylum, 'cept talk to her or shock her outta her wits?"

Norma spoke calmly to her brother. "Are you all right with this?" she asked. "Somehow, you seem so sure."

"Well," Aaron said, "this morning I surrendered her into God's hands. He loves her more than I do. It will be up to him whether she gets locked up or not. Right now, I just don't feel that's what he wants me to do."

Norma nodded. "I believe you're being led, Aaron. God will not let you down."

"I sure need the two of you to pray," Aaron said. "God has been awful good to us. I need him now. I know this won't be easy."

The morning was brisk and almost chilly, the wind starting to whip up when Aaron drove up in front of the church parsonage. It was getting close to fall, and then the first snow, the little dry snow that came first, whitening the brown prairie and then melting away. Aaron loved all the seasons. He loved the land with all of its changes.

4
CHAPTER

David Schwenk was just coming down the steps of the church when he saw Aaron approaching in his pickup truck. He was surprised. He normally never saw Aaron except at the Wednesday evening Bible study or at Sunday morning services. Aaron never missed either of these. He willingly braved snowstorms, windstorms, rain, and hail in order to study his beloved Bible. A good deal of the time, he and his faithful companion, Jake, were the only ones who came.

Managing the stairs was, for David, painful and laborious. In a more enlightened age ramps would have built for the handicapped. However, David didn't complain. He either worked around his injuries or in spite of them. David had been a rising star in his denomination. He had been assigned to his own church as senior pastor. Even though he was young, he was full of enthusiasm and love for his job. His congregation loved him, and he loved them. He was seventeen when he gave his life to the Lord, and shortly thereafter, he heard the call to preach. He hadn't been with the church too long when the war started. Soon after, he enlisted as a chaplain. At the time it had seemed a higher calling.

Near the end of the war he crawled up on the beach with the troops on an island that *might be or not be* inhabited. They no sooner arrived when all hell broke loose. David was ministering to the frightened, the wounded, and the dying when an explosion lifted him off the ground and slammed him into the ground. He never knew where the explosion came from. He was almost left for dead when someone noticed that he was conscious and called for a medic. David spent over a year in the veteran's hospital. His left leg was shattered, but somehow they had managed to save it and he was able to limp around with a cane. His left arm also was partially paralyzed, and he didn't have much feeling in his hand which was subject to tremors. He still had excruciating headaches as well as phantom *nerve* pain due to other operations where shrapnel had been cut out of his body. On top of that, he had a scar that ran from his hairline to the bottom of his chin causing his left eye to drop slightly. Before the war, he had been what was considered handsome with his dark hair and dark eyes and his boyish grin. All of that David considered as garbage as long as he was alive and serving his Lord.

As soon as he was able to move around in a wheelchair, he asked to see his bishop. "What are the possibilities of me being assigned to a church?" he asked.

The bishop was shocked. He did his best to hide his dismay. "David," he cried, "you're an invalid. How can you even think of pastoring a church with all the work it entails? Even strong men become worn down by the responsibilities"

"Somehow I must do it," David replied with determination. "Since I was a young boy I've known that I had a calling to preach the gospel."

The bishop shook his head sadly. "Perhaps when you're able, you can do some sort of evangelism, somewhat like an itinerate preacher. We could talk about it in a few months. After all, you've just now gotten out of bed and into a wheelchair."

"I will be walking soon," David was adamant, "and I expect to be assigned to a church."

The bishop left David with a heavy heart. Here was this young man broken in body but not in spirit, and he had nothing to offer him. It didn't seem fair. After all, he had done his duty and served his country, and now what?

After a time, the bishop heard that David was struggling to walk with a cane. He was amazed at the man's determination. He suddenly had an idea. There was a church that did not have a regular pastor. The congregation was quite small, and they had been getting by for several years with only a visiting pastor, one who served several small congregations which were too small to afford a full-time pastor. However, this particular church could afford a full-time pastor since the main congregant was very wealthy and a big contributor to the larger church and its ministries.

They wouldn't be too choosy either, he reflected, since their church was situated on a lonely windswept hill with a small parsonage which could accommodate only one person or maybe a couple with no children. There was a graveyard attached to the church with more people in it than people in the congregation.

There was a windmill and water had been piped into the house. There was propane for heat but no electricity. It had been impossible to find anyone willing to take the assignment. First, he would have to talk to the congregation to see if they would be willing to accept a crippled man as their pastor. Next, if they accepted David he would have to talk to him to find out if he would be willing to go there.

It would be a comedown from the church he had pastored before.

He asked the congregation to assemble. There were not enough people to warrant a special committee. The whole church was the committee. When he arrived, he found Aaron Gerhardt, his son John, and wife, Rosalie. There was Jake, Aaron's hired hand, and another older lady whose name he didn't remember. There were a few others he didn't know as well as a Mexican couple with their children. He assumed they were hired workers on one of the large ranches or maybe not. They seemed to be fluent in English.

He began to explain David's situation, the history of his service in the war, his long road to recovery, his determination to again preach the gospel. As he spoke, he couldn't seem to get a sense of what they were thinking or feeling. They listened carefully, not taking their eyes off him.

"Well, what do you think?" he asked finally. "If this man is willing to be your full-time pastor, are you willing to accept him even though he may have limitations?"

They continued to stare at him wide-eyed until he began to feel uneasy. He had no idea that he had just handed them an answer to their most fervent prayers. It was as if God himself had spoken. They hardly heard the part about limitations.

Finally, Aaron spoke, "If this young man is willing to come to us, we would be most honored to have him. We will do whatever it takes to accommodate him." There was no vote, no discussion. They turned to each other smiling joyously.

"Well, all right." The bishop breathed a sigh of relief. "You understand I still have to talk to Rev. Schwenk?" I couldn't talk to him until I had your approval." He began to have second thoughts as he looked around the diverse congregation. "Oh well." He sighed. "This is the best I can do."

He lost no time in talking to David. He explained the situation as it was—very small congregation, church and parsonage lacking in amenities. They could, however, due to Aaron Gerhardt and his devotion to God, afford a full-time pastor.

David broke in, "I don't care about the smallness of the congregation or the location of the church. I just don't like the idea of being some rich guy's pet pastor."

The bishop felt impatient. "I don't think you're going to find things that way at all. You will never find a more humble, Godly man than Aaron Gerhardt. Anyway," he said dismissively, "you think it over and let me know one way or another. Take as much time as you need. After all, the church on Windy Hill had waited a long time. They could easily wait yet another long time."

He was surprised when, in a few days, David called and asked for an appointment. He had decided to accept the appointment. He realized that he had been condescending.

And so after two years, here he was and he had never regretted his decision. The people of the church had loved him back to health and wholeness. As for being a rich man's pet pastor, the bishop had been right about Aaron Gerhardt. He had never met a man with more respect for God and his church and for his servant, the pastor. His daughter-in-law had done her best to make the parsonage into a pleasant home for him. People were always arriving with hot food. He lacked nothing.

As he approached Aaron, he was surprised to see his normally placid countenance had a worried look. He waited respectfully for Aaron to explain his unexpected arrival.

"I need to speak to you about my daughter," Aaron began.

David tried not to let the surprise he felt show. He hadn't known Aaron had a daughter.

"The thing is," Aaron began, "she's been in California. We haven't heard from her for a long time. She called and asked to come home because she was sick. I guess she lost her job and her man ran out on her." He paused, then hurried on. "The thing is, she tried to kill herself. We were able to save her, but I'm sure she's just waiting for a chance to try it again." He looked desperately at David.

David put a hand on his arm. "How can I help you, Aaron?"

Aaron looked at him. "I was wondering if you could talk to her…I know you said you had done some counseling."

David was shocked. "Aaron," he said, "I'm not qualified to counsel someone who is suicidal. In fact, I don't know of anyone in these small towns that have those qualifications. You may have to take her to Denver in order to get help."

"Well," Aaron said, "I'm not taking her somewhere to be locked up. There are worse things than death. She promised to a least talk to you to keep from bein' locked up." He looked hopeless.

David knew that Aaron would accept his decision not to get involved, but he wanted so much to help this friend, so dear to him, almost like a father.

"I could talk to her I guess," he said resignedly. "But I can't promise you a thing…I wish I could."

"I'll bring her over tomorrow," Aaron said. "I know that in the end only the Lord can help her. Maybe you could help her to see that," he said, hopefully.

David nodded. He felt nothing but apprehension. He had gotten too comfortable with his little congregation and his peaceful life here. It was as if a bombshell had been dropped in the middle of it.

The following morning, Aaron, true to his word, came bringing Mary Lou. He tried not to get his hopes up. After all, David hadn't seemed at all hopeful. He had spent an unusually long time in prayer. Finally, sometime before morning he had surrendered it all to the will of God. David sensed a calmness and a peace in his demeanor—so different from the day before.

David invited them into the parsonage which had a fairly large living area, sometimes doubling as a place for receptions or other special events. It was actually much too small for this, and in the summer they usually congregated on the grassy, shady side of the church where picnic tables had been set up. There were some, Rosalie in particular, who were urging the immediate building of a fellowship hall, especially since David's arrival. It seemed that his preaching was attracting a few new people.

David took a long look at Mary Lou who had sunk down on the nearest couch without an invitation. Her hair was wet and hung in strings, her face scrubbed as if someone had tried to make her presentable for her counseling session. David held out his hand, which she ignored. After David had said goodbye to Aaron, he took a chair opposite her. She seemed to him to be in a stupor. She sat with her eyes closed. He was at a loss to do or say anything.

After a while she opened her eyes, slowly becoming aware of her surroundings. She stared at David, suddenly aware of this man sitting opposite her. She had expected someone older, someone who looked like a preacher or her idea of one. And here was this boyish-looking man with a horrible scar running down the side of his face holding his withered left hand.

"What happened to you?" she blurted out.

David was so startled that he laughed involuntarily. Quickly he composed himself.

Not knowing what else to say, he said simply, "I was in the war. I realize my scars are enough to startle anyone."

After her outburst, Mary Lou again withdrew into her shell.

"Your dad tells me you tried to kill yourself," he began. "Would you like to talk about it?" he asked, knowing Mary Lou did not want to talk about anything.

"I can understand how a person might get to that point…just cash it in. But what about your family? Your dad especially…how is he going to feel? I guess everything would be over for you, or you think so anyway…but his remaining years would be filled with grief." He wasn't sure she was even listening. She gave no indication of it.

"Well, you just rest there, we're having our Wednesday evening Bible study and after that, your dad can take you home." *So much for our counseling session,* he thought. He hated to tell Aaron that it was no use.

Mary Lou fell asleep on the couch and David did not disturb her. He was thankful when it was time for the Bible study. Perhaps if only Aaron, and of course Jake, showed up they could include Mary Lou and have the study in the parsonage instead of the church. Otherwise, being around Mary Lou might prove awkward for everyone. He didn't know if anyone else in the congregation was aware that she was home except, of course, her family.

When it became apparent that only Aaron and Jake would be there, he suggested they include Mary Lou who unbelievably was still sleeping.

They were studying the prophet Jeremiah. *This is appropriate,* thought David. He thought it might be a comfort to his friend to reread the trials and tribulations of the prophet, who, though no fault of his own nevertheless suffered. He thought Mary Lou might also gain some perspective on her problems, whatever they were. Mary Lou, however, if she heard anything gave no indication of it.

Later, David took Aaron aside. "I was not able to communicate with your daughter in any way." Noticing Aaron's look of disappointment, David countered, "Can you tell me something about her? After all, I only found out a few days ago that you even had a daughter. If I may ask, where is her mother?" They had never discussed Aaron's single state, Aaron being a very private person.

"Her mother left when Mary Lou was a little girl. She left with a man she met at a dance." David could see that talking about the past was making Aaron uncomfortable. "She asked to come back, and I agreed…I felt the kids, especially Mary Lou, needed a mother, but… she never showed up. I don't know what happened to her. We never heard hide nor hair of her again. She came from a big family…but they all drifted away from these parts." He sighed, as if dredging up all the pain was too much for him.

"When Mary Lou finished high school, she married a fellow from town and they moved to California to get in the movies. I don't know what happened to him. She told me her latest man was a drinker that left her. I guess I don't know too much," he admitted. "I reckon I never wanted to ask, but now she's here and she's sick and I have to do what I can. I just wish I knew what that was." He looked hopefully at David. "When should I bring her back?"

Again, David felt like refusing to see her, but he found himself saying, "She can come whenever you have time to bring her."

And so the next morning there she was bright and early, looking the same as she had before. This time David was determined to get her to talk. Perhaps he would make her angry if nothing else. He forced her to look at him by saying her name in a loud voice. "Mary Lou, how do you feel about God?"

She looked at him through lowered lids. "There is no God." At last, a reaction.

"Just because you don't believe in him doesn't mean he doesn't exist," David countered. "Tell me, when did you stop believing in God?" No answer. "Was it when your mother left?"

"Please shut up about that," she said bitterly.

Finally, he was starting to get some reaction. "Why did your husband leave you? What is it about you that makes people want to leave you?"

Mary Lou raised her head and looked him straight in the eye. "None of this is any of your damn business!" she snapped.

"Well, something has caused you to give up on life. Life is good, life is exciting, life is worth living—"

"Well," Mary Lou finally shot back, "I don't see how you can say these things about life. You're all crippled up. You obviously could have found a better church than in this God-forsaken place. I don't see how you can say God is good, life is good. As far as I can see, God sure hasn't been good to you!"

Her words stung. He wondered if he should reply to them. Anyway, he did have her attention. "God is good to me! I'm alive, and in this God-forsaken place as you call it, I have met the kindest,

God-loving people I have ever met. It is a real privilege to serve them. No amount of money could buy the peace that I have found here!"

There was no answer.

Finally, David said, "All right, Mary Lou, your dad will be here soon. Would you like something to drink while you wait?"

"No," she snapped irritably.

David picked up his cane and dragged himself to the kitchen, more aware of his handicap than he had been for a long time. All of a sudden, he felt weary. *I can't let this woman's negative attitude rub off on me*, he thought.

So for the next few weeks Aaron brought Mary Lou sometimes daily, sometimes every other day, and sometimes only once a week. For the most part David did all the talking while Mary Lou was non-committal. Once he asked her, if she died what did she expect would happen to her afterward. She replied that she expected nothingness.

But David asked, "How do you really know that? What if you're wrong? Heaven is only promised to believers. What if there really is a hell. Are you ready to take a chance on that?"

"That is all a bunch of nonsense," she countered.

"But what if you're wrong?" David insisted. "What makes you all-knowing? Why do you possess knowledge that others, some much more intelligent than you or I, don't have?"

Mary Lou had actually never given much thought to such theological questions such as good and evil, heaven and hell. She had, of course, heard plenty of sermons, learned all the Bible stories in Sunday School, most of which had gone in one ear and out the other. It wasn't so much that she had rejected it, as she just hadn't given it much thought. She thought she knew plenty people who led successful fulfilled lives without giving any thought to religion. She wanted to be like them, except that, for her, it just didn't seem to work out. Her so-called career was a failure, as well as her marriages and love affairs. She couldn't even succeed in killing herself, she thought bitterly.

5
CHAPTER

Mary Lou was beginning to leave her room more, sometimes eating with the others. She had ceased her nighttime wandering. She didn't think about being better or worse. Maybe time was helping. At times she thought about suicide, but not as much. Besides, she felt under guard, her dad and "the old lady," as she referred to her grandmother, keeping a constant eye on her.

One morning Aaron asked her if she would like to ride with him. She'd always loved horses and riding. "Come on," he entreated, "I want you to go with me."

Finally, she followed him to the barn where she found two saddled horses ready to go. She hesitated; she had not been on a horse in a long time. Suddenly she felt a touch of fear. These magnificent animals were so full of life, snapping their heads back and forth. Aaron took the bridle of one of the horses and brought him to her.

"This is old sorrel. I bought him a few years back. He's a good solid horse and he's easy to ride. I want to give him to you if you'll have him."

To her surprise, tears welled up in her eyes. She took the bridle and buried her face in the horse's neck. She remembered the smell—the unique smell of horseflesh, the smell of the saddle. It did take her back to happier times, spending all day on her horse, exploring the countryside, the feel of warm sun on her body, the wind in her hair. Just being alive was enough. A small thought ran through her mind. Was it possible to get back to that?

"Where would you like to ride to?" Aaron interrupted her thoughts. Mary Lou was surprised. Aaron never rode a horse except for work; to him, a horse was a working animal. They never had more horses than was needed for working cattle.

"I'll follow you," said Mary Lou.

"Do you want to ride over and see John and Rosalie?" he asked.

She shook her head no.

"We could ride over to the parsonage and see David. It's quite a ways, I know."

"I see plenty of him already," said Mary Lou. "Let's just ride."

And so, they rode. They followed the creek bed for several miles before turning for home. Mary Lou's feelings alternated between a feeling of peace and irritation, the need to keep riding and the need to get back to her cave in the upstairs room.

When they reached the barn, Mary Lou jumped off the horse and ran into the house without a word.

Aaron was a little disappointed, but then he had been a little surprised that she had been willing to go at all. Maybe there was some improvement. He smiled to himself. The idea of giving her the horse had been a last-minute decision, and he felt it was a good one. He couldn't help but notice that she was touched.

Meanwhile, David was summing up his thoughts about Mary Lou. He realized that her mother's leaving had traumatized her, but that was years ago. She was evidently sick, or she wouldn't have attempted suicide. Evidently, she had not been faking it in order to get attention. She had very much wanted to die. But he couldn't help thinking that the majority of her problems stemmed from the fact that she was extremely selfish and self-centered. She seemed to care little about anyone's feelings, and she seemed to have no genuine love for anyone, including her father. It seemed to him that Aaron, out of guilt or ignorance or both, had never demanded much of her.

He could not see that he was helping her in any way. In fact, her feelings for him bordered on contempt. In spite of the fact that he hated to disappoint her father, he was going to have to end their counseling sessions. If he thought there was any possibility of helping her, he would be willing to do whatever it took, but there was not. He dreaded telling Aaron.

When he saw them approaching the next morning, he steeled himself, going over and over in his mind what he had decided to say.

He never had a chance to speak to Mary Lou. She went rushing into the parsonage to find her spot on the couch as if she had been trained.

Aaron too didn't give David a chance to speak. He was in fact smiling. He gave David a look of affection. "I think she's better," he said. "Yesterday, she agreed to go riding, and she's beginnin' to eat with us sometimes. She's not out runnin' around in the yard at night anyway."

David had his doubts about this being a big improvement. "Maybe she just needs time," he countered. "I honestly don't think it has anything to do with the counseling. She never says much of anything."

Aaron's face fell. "I guess you're getting discouraged. I don't blame you…I shoulda never asked you to do this in the first place. It was too much to ask."

"I would do anything in the world for you, Aaron. I just meant that, as I told you before, I'm not qualified." He continued, "Sometimes it seems to me that someone needs to turn her over their knee and let her have it!"

Aaron smiled. "It's too late for that."

"Yes, it is…unfortunately," said David ruefully. "Well, I'll talk to her today since she's here. But I think we have to explore other options."

"I can't think what that'd be," Aaron said resignedly. "What other options are there, do you know?"

David shook his head. "I'll have to think about it. His leg was beginning to pain him. He turned and hobbled off toward the parsonage.

Aaron left with a heavy heart. He had begun to hope, but he knew that David was right. Maybe there was no answer, no answer but prayer. Only God had the answers.

Meanwhile, David went in and sat in his usual chair opposite Mary Lou. He had stood up too long talking to Aaron, and he was in a lot of pain. Pain brought irritation, and he was in no mood to talk to an inanimate object.

"Mary Lou," he began, "I just told your dad that I cannot help you. I never could have. My counseling experience consisted of a course I took in seminary. I believe that you have some deep-seated pain, that you have been hurt deeply, that somehow you need to acknowledge that and perhaps work through it with an experienced counselor."

He waited for some reaction from Mary Lou. She remained noncommittal. "Actually," he said after a long pause, "my true belief is that you have a spiritual problem and that only God can heal you. I believe that he is the true healer. If you would turn to him and release your life into his hands, your life would be worth living again."

Seeing no reaction, he burst out with what he was really thinking, "I believe that you are a very self-centered, self-engrossed person who cares nothing about the feelings of others, even those who love you and want to help you. That is not going to change unless you will it to change and ask God's help. No one lives in perfect circumstances, but they are able to overcome with God's help. I have had plenty of experience in that kind of counseling, and I know it works."

He had said more than he had wanted to say or even thought of saying. He did, however, notice her eyes were open and that she was staring at him. He turned his head away, staring dejectedly at the floor, rubbing his leg which was throbbing.

Mary Lou stood up. "You're not well," she said, "I'll wait for my dad outside."

He said nothing, glad for the chance to be alone. He needed to take a pill and lie down.

Instead of waiting at the parsonage, Mary Lou started walking toward the road. As she plodded along, she was suddenly aware of her feelings. What was she feeling? It should have been relief that she didn't have to come back here anymore. Instead she felt a sense of fear. Had she found a sense of security in these weekly visits? What was her dad going to think? Perhaps he would have her committed after all. Why did she no longer think about suicide as much as she had before?

As Aaron pulled up beside her on the gravel road, he leaned over and flung open the door. Mary Lou could see by the look on his face that he had already spoken to David. He looked old, tired, and dejected. She wondered if David was right. Did she really care about him and his feelings, his worry over her, his love for her? If not, why not? They drove home in silence.

When they reached the house, Mary Lou resisted the urge to run to her room. Instead, she sat on the couch in the living room watching her grandmother preparing the noon meal. She managed to drag herself up and ask what she could do to help. If Alice was shocked, she managed not to show it. "You can set the table," she said brusquely. She didn't feel hungry, but she sat down at the table with her dad, Jake, and her grandmother. Happily, none of them wasted much time in table conversation.

Again, she resisted the urge to run to her room. "Dad," she asked, "could you saddle my horse? I'd like to ride"

Aaron hesitated. Did people kill themselves on horseback? he wondered. He should ask to go with her, but for once he decided to let go. Besides, he was bone-tired from all the emotion of the day. He could not watch her every minute of her life.

Jake got up. "I'll saddle the horse," he offered.

Mary Lou followed him to the corral, watching him saddle the sorrel. When he finished, he handed her the reins and she expertly mounted and waited for him to open the gate.

Jake hesitated, looking out over to the southwest. "I don't know, Mary Lou, it's startin' to blacken up over there."

"I'll be fine, I'm not goin' far," she lied.

"Well, okay." He shook his head resignedly and opened the gate.

Mary Lou started out slowly. The sun felt hot, but she savored it. She thought to herself, *I'll pretend to be a little girl again, back to when I knew nothing except this ranch. I'll ride to my favorite place.* She looked in the distance to the mesa where she had sat as a young girl. It had seemed as if she could see the whole world from there. She remembered how she had longed to be a part of that world.

She kicked her horse and broke into a gallop. She realized that if she were going to reach the mesa and have time to be there before dark, she would have to hurry. Behind the mesa were a series of canyons filled with straggly cedar trees. This part of the country was called the "little cedars," and beyond that were the "big cedars," which as far as Mary Lou knew ran on into infinity. The only way of exploring the place was on horseback. The trees were not of any use, except her family often cut one to use as a Christmas tree. Even if it was unshapely, it had a wonderful pungent smell which permeated the entire house.

Mary Lou was riding fast unaware of her surroundings when she heard it—a crack of lightning followed by thunder. She slowed the horse and looked up, a black cloud was advancing and fast. Mary Lou had a healthy fear of lightning. She had seen cows drop dead in an instant right in front of her when helping her dad move cattle. She had seen a haystack disintegrate within seconds as she sat by the window and watched. Again, the lightning flashed; this time much closer, close enough to cause sparks in the horse's hair. The sorrel jumped sideways almost upsetting Mary Lou. She clung tightly to the saddle horn. She realized that she and the horse stood out as a point of contact. There was no place to run, no shelter. Suddenly she felt fear.

"Oh god," she said aloud, "I may die here."

Again, the lightning struck even closer and this time the horse snorted and screamed in fear, bucking and then rearing on his hind legs. This time Mary Lou could not hold on, she flew out of the saddle and onto the hard ground. The horse took off in a dead run leaving Mary Lou clinging to the sod. She had seen lightning before but never like this. There was no lull between crashes, which to Mary Lou seemed to shake the ground.

"Oh god, oh god," she cried, "please make it stop."

The rain started coming down in great sheets, but the lightning and roar of the thunder did not stop. It was as if every raindrop itself was on fire. Mary Lou felt like a target, even worse, a wet target.

At last the storm moved on as fast as it had started. Little rivulets of water surrounded Mary Lou. Mary Lou felt as if every bone in her body was broken. She tried to move, to stand, but the pain forced her to lie still. She realized with a sinking feeling that no one knew where to find her and it was starting to get dark. "What can I do?" she cried aloud. "I can't even walk."

Suddenly a thought came to her. *I don't want to die.* David's words came to her mind. *What if this is not all there is?* She knew for certain that if she did die, she would take her misery with her. "So if one can't die and one can't live, what now?"

Meanwhile, Aaron had watched the storm moving in, hoping to see Mary Lou coming home. Surely she has sense enough to turn around and come back when she saw that cloud, he thought. He could see the lightning in the distance and hear the sound of thunder. Already it was starting to sprinkle.

"Did Mary Lou say anything when she left?" he asked Jake.

Jake shook his head. "Just said she wasn't goin' far. I told her it didn't look good out."

Aaron nodded. "When did she ever listen to a warning?"

He kept going to the window, peering out, willing her to come through the corral gate.

"Why don't you sit down?" said his mother. "You're going to wear out the floor."

He wondered how she could always be so calm. He tried to sit, but then he was up again and this time he cried, "Oh god!"

"What is it?" his mother jumped up in alarm.

"It's the horse! Oh no, Mary Lou's not on him…oh god, where is she?" He felt as if he might pass out, his face was ashen.

Even Jake looked worried, and now the rain was coming down and it was no passing shower. The huge drops hit the window like bullets.

"I've got to look for her," Aaron said decisively.

"Can't you wait till the storm passes?" asked his mother. "It'll be over in a bit. You don't even know which way she went. You can't see a thing out there."

But Aaron was already putting on his hat.

"I'll go with you," Jake volunteered.

"No, it'll take too long to catch and saddle two horses."

"But," Jake interrupted, "there's no help to it. If you find her and she's hurt, you can't handle her all by yourself."

Aaron nodded. Jake was right. "Let's go," he said.

Aaron saddled his horse and waited impatiently while Jake caught another horse, saddled it, and got ready to ride. He wished he had any idea which way she went. What if she got caught in a draw when she was thrown, she could easily drown, or what if she hit her head? He tried to put all these uneasy thoughts out of his head.

"Did you see which way she took off to?" he asked Jake.

"Well, I didn't watch her for very long, but what time I did see her she was headin' that way," he pointed in the general direction.

Fortunately, the rain was starting to let up and it was still light, but the sun was going down and it would soon be dark. How would they ever find her then? Aaron wondered.

After they had ridden out a ways, Aaron began to holler her name, hoping maybe she would hear and answer.

The prairie had never looked so vast, like looking for a needle in a haystack, he thought.

Worse yet, the light was fading fast. "I should have remembered to bring a flashlight," he said to Jake.

"I think I'll go back and get one," Jake offered. "It might help if I brought the dogs too."

"Do you think so?" Aaron asked hopefully. "Well, you go on, but I'll probably run on to her before you get back."

Jake wondered, unless she was hurt she could find her way back, she was young and strong. But if the horse threw her, then what? It could be bad. All his thoughts were for his boss, his friend, his mentor—he would do anything for him. He would have to put every effort into finding the man's daughter.

He tried to hurry toward the ranch, but the wet grass and mud held him up with his horse nearly slipping and falling at times. When he reached the house, he ran inside to grab a flashlight.

"Any sign of Mary Lou?" asked her grandmother anxiously.

"No," he said brusquely and hurried out whistling for the dogs who had taken cover under the porch in order to get out of the rain.

These were not tracking dogs, but he figured if Mary Lou were to make any sound at all, the dogs could hear her before they could. The dogs came eagerly in response to his whistle. One dog was a large white part hound with a yellow ear. He had been rattlesnake bitten so many times he was immune to the venom. If he were to see a snake a person had better get out of his way because he would fly into a rage, grab it, and shake it, and throw it over and over again until it was dead. On the other hand, he was very friendly and he loved people.

The other dog was squat and black in color. He was old and lazy and spent much of his time sleeping. Nevertheless, they both happily followed Jake and the horse.

Aaron had decided to stay in the same vicinity and wait for Jake. He wasn't having any luck running every which way and hollering.

Meanwhile, Mary Lou was still lying in the mud, her face pressed into a clump of grass. She knew her dad would be looking for her once he saw her horse. Darkness was falling fast, in fact the sun was gone leaving only a glimmer of light in its wake. Even though the lightning had moved on, she could still see the flashes in the distance one after the other. She was still filled with fear.

She knew she needed to stand in order to be seen. However, the pain was just too intense. She finally was able to sit up and call her father's name. "Daddy, Daddy," she screamed to no avail. Her ankle was throbbing inside her boot. Her right arm felt as if it were broken as well as her wrist.

She lay back down in the mud and the water to help lessen the pain. Soon it was dark, inky dark. Even the lightning no longer flashed in the distance.

Suddenly a sense of wonder came over her. *I wanted to die,* she thought, *I have just been waiting for a chance to end it all. I don't know what has changed, but when I came so close tonight I knew I wanted to live. I still don't know what I want to live for. Everything still seems useless. I know my dad will find me,* she thought confidently. *Maybe not tonight, but for sure tomorrow.*

Jake had been right about the dogs; they heard her call and they bounded toward her, happily licking her face and whining. Aaron and Jake were able to follow the dogs, trying not to lose sight of them.

Aaron, though not usually an emotional man, was filled with joy as well as worry at finding his daughter lying in the mud moaning with pain. He called her name while thanking God in his heart. At least she was still alive!

He dismounted and knelt beside her. "Mary Lou," he said gently, "it's Dad. How bad are you hurt?"

"Daddy," she moaned, "I want to go home."

"Mary Lou, I'll have to go back and get the pickup to bring you home. We need to get you to a doctor."

"Can't I ride back with you? I don't think I'm that bad, if you could just help me get up on your horse."

"Mary Lou," he was alarmed, "you might have internal injuries or a broken back...we can't just put you on a horse."

"Dad," she said firmly, "my back is not broken...I think I sprained my ankle and my ribs hurt, that's all. I want you to take me home!"

Aaron decided to take a chance. He really didn't know what else to do. If he tried driving the pickup, he would more than likely get stuck, it was so muddy.

It was all Mary Lou could do to keep from screaming in pain as Jake and Aaron lifted her on the back of Aaron's horse for the ride home. She was afraid if she screamed Aaron would be afraid to take her.

They were about five miles from the house, and it was slow going on the wet ground. Mary Lou bit her lip to keep from crying out each time the horse slipped or stepped in a hole, jarring her painfully. But she was determined to get home to her bed, and she had no intention of going to a doctor. She knew if she let on how much she was hurting, she would be going whether she wanted to or not.

It seemed they had been riding forever. It was so dark they could hardly see two feet in front. But they depended on the dogs and horses, which instinctively knew their way home.

Alice met them at the door. "Oh, thank you, Jesus." She breathed. "You found her. Is she badly hurt?"

"I don't know," Aaron said. "We have to get her to the doctor."

"I'm not going to a doctor," Mary Lou said firmly.

"Well, she's right about that," said Alice. "The creek here is running its banks. There's no way you could get over the crossing."

"Oh god, no," Aaron groaned. "We have to do something. But what?"

"Get her off that horse," Alice ordered. "I can figure out what's wrong. We don't know till we check her over. When I was young, we didn't run to the doctor for everything."

Again, Mary Lou felt she would pass out as they lifted her off the horse.

"Put her in the room off the porch. I see she's covered in mud."

As they helped her into the little room, which was the closest but hardly large enough for two people to stand, Alice ran to get warm water and a washcloth as well as clean clothes. Mary Lou had always used the room as a playroom when she was small, but there was a narrow bed and a chair.

"First, we need to get her boots off and check her legs and ankles," said Alice.

One of the boots came off easily, but as they tried to take the other one off, Mary Lou screamed in agony.

Aaron hesitated, but Alice was firm. "We have to get it off. Why people wear these things is beyond me." In spite of Mary Lou's moaning, he was able to get it off.

"Well," Alice said, "it's swollen for sure, but it might be just a bad sprain. I'll bandage it tight. We can tell more about it tomorrow." She pressed Mary Lou's ribs. Again, Mary Lou could not keep from crying out. "I don't feel any broken...could be just sprained too," she said as she moved Mary Lou's arms up and down. "They seem okay, everything's goin' to hurt for a while, no getting away from it."

"You all get out now, I'm gonna change her and try to wash off some of this mud."

There was more pain as Alice cut off some of her clothes with the scissors and pulled off the rest.

She tried to do what she could to help, but it wasn't much. At last Alice finished dressing her and washing her face, which was badly scratched and a little bloody.

"There's nothing I can do about your hair," she said. "It's full of mud, but I can't wash it like this."

"I know," said Mary Lou, "I will be better tomorrow. I've been thrown before."

"You don't know how bad you're hurt," said Alice, "and you're goin' to suffer tonight that's for sure, and we can't help you."

There was a little whiskey left hidden in a drawer upstairs, Mary Lou thought ruefully. It wouldn't do any good to mention that. She would just have to suffer, and she wanted to be alone with her thoughts.

Alice was obliging. She was tired and she had exerted herself far more than usual. Aaron was waiting anxiously for his mother and her diagnosis.

"We'll know more tomorrow," she informed him. "You get some rest."

"I thought I might sit up with her," Aaron volunteered.

"Absolutely not, she's hurtin', but she's not dyin'. You need to rest up for tomorrow in case we'll be able to get to town. You just pray, that's enough."

Aaron reluctantly agreed. He felt it would be impossible to sleep, but he was asleep before he even began his prayer.

6
CHAPTER

Mary Lou, of course, was in too much pain to sleep, but she knew she would be fine after a few days. In the meantime, she wanted to sort out her *new thoughts* as she had begun to think of them. The first one was that she did not really want to die and that she was deathly afraid of dying. She had seen hell yawning before her. The next thought was, how was she going to live?

She remembered David's words. *You are a self-centered, self-engrossed person incapable of loving anyone.* Was that true?

She let herself think of Larry. She was surprised that she could think of him without the usual stab of pain in her gut. Was that love? She had wanted to possess his body and soul. She wondered if she had ever really wanted him to get completely sober. He might have become less needy. He might have left her! In the end the alcohol possessed him and she lost him and she had wanted to die. Had she ever once thought about what might be good for him as a person apart from her? Well, that was in the past. She decided to give into her physical pain, her aching ribs and her throbbing ankle. Tomorrow she would think about other things.

The following day dawned clear and beautiful as if God had washed the prairie and watered the trees and wildflowers. Even though it was bound to get hot later, it was nice and cool for now.

Aaron could hardly wait to check on Mary Lou. He felt guilty about sleeping so soundly when she was suffering. His first thought was to hurry and get ready and take her to town to get fixed up whatever was wrong. He was surprised to see her awake and propped up on her pillows.

"How are you, are you okay, are you better?" He wasn't sure what to think. "We're getting the car ready for the trip to town, okay?"

"Dad, I am still hurting, but I know nothing is broken and I am not going to town!" She was adamant.

"Well, how do you know? You could be crippled for life," he countered.

"Daddy, Grandma was already in here and checked my ankle and she's sure it's only a sprain and so am I. You go on and do your chores." She looked him in the eye. "Daddy, I've given you enough trouble. You haven't complained, but I know it hasn't been easy. I'm going to make an effort to change. It's time I gave some thought to someone beside myself. You go on now."

Aaron left the room in a daze. What had suddenly changed? He had been wondering what to do about her. He was worried about his mother. She was cooking and cleaning up after Mary Lou as well as Jake and himself. He wanted her to go home where she could rest. Of course, she never complained. He had often thought about hiring someone. But of course no one would take a job so far from anywhere.

Mary Lou's words kept running through his mind. Was she leaving? Where would she go?

Alice, fully dressed, came into Mary Lou's room. "I figured out how we can wash your hair. I'll get a bucket and wash pan, and you can lean over the bed if you can."

"Grandma," she broke in, "we used to have some crutches, remember when John broke his leg?"

"Well, I don't know where they are," said Alice impatiently.

"Well, could you ask Dad to look for them? Go on, ask Dad, that way I can stand up to the sink."

Alice went to ask Aaron about the crutches. Sure enough they were gathering dust in a closet. With the help of Aaron, Mary Lou was able to hobble to the sink and get the dried mud out of her hair. When she was back in her bed, she looked at her grandma in her house dress. "Aren't you going to church? Today is Sunday, isn't it? You always go to church."

"I thought I would stay home in case you needed anything. It's all right, Mary Lou."

"Well, I'm going to church too," Mary Lou said firmly. "You had better get ready and bring me a pair of shoes."

When Alice had collected herself, she said, "Mary Lou, your foot is swollen, how can you wear shoes?" Actually, she was thinking that perhaps Mary Lou had hit her head on something. Even as a small child she had to be forced to get ready for church. It must be years since she had set foot in a church. "Are you sure? You know, you'll have to sit a long time and you're in pain?"

"I'm sure," again Mary Lou was firm. "When you're ready, tell Dad and Jake to come and help me."

When they arrived at the church, most of the people had arrived and were already seated. Brother John, Rosalie, Andrea, and the boys were filing into their usual pew. Rosalie and Andrea's faces broke into huge smiles when they saw Mary Lou and then turned to consternation when they saw her crutches.

There was no time to chat as the pianist had started the call to worship. Jake took his usual seat in the rear as Aaron and Alice took a seat with Mary Lou between them.

Aaron was ashamed of his thoughts. *Why is she here?* he wondered. *I guess I should be thanking God that she wanted to come.* Instead, he was aggravated that it had taken so long to get Mary Lou ready and out of the house and situated in the car that they had missed Sunday school. Since David taught the adult class, he especially never wanted to miss the lesson.

Alice was having her own problem with her thoughts. She was observing her granddaughter-in-law and her daughter Andrea. They were dressed alike in a soft lavender print. The dresses were, of course, modest in length with long sleeves and a white collar at the throat. Even if they wore gunny sacks, she observed, they would still be beautiful with their milk white complexions and their dark red hair, which curled naturally.

She couldn't help contrasting them with the granddaughter beside her. She had, apparently, brought not a single dress with her. At the present, she had on jeans which were frayed at the bottom and a plaid sleeveless top which was un-ironed. On one foot she had a well-worn moccasin and the other foot, the bandaged one, was bare. She told herself that she should just be glad that Mary Lou had wanted to come to church. It was wrong to be ashamed of her attire.

She remembered that when Mary Lou had visited from California in the past, she had always worn the latest styles. At that time, she had considered it showing off. How times had changed!

Mary Lou glanced around the church where she had grown up. She had been baptized here, married here. *Maybe I'll be buried here,* she thought. Her brother John and his family were seated contentedly in their usual place; John and his boys each with their cowboy hats in their laps, carbon copies of their dad. A Mexican family, father and mother and their children sat opposite. Counting her and her dad and grandma and Jake, there were about twenty-five people in all.

David sat on a chair on the dais. His cane beside him. She noted that he did not wear a robe but was dressed much as the other men in the congregation. Once or twice she caught him looking quizzically at her.

Rosalie moved to the lectern giving the few announcements and then asked the people to take their hymnals and turn to page 49. The church considered itself fortunate to have someone to lead the singing, which was a very important part of worship.

Mary Lou did not sing, but she did look at the words, the familiar words. They seemed to take on a new meaning almost as though she had never seen them before. She noticed that Alice and Aaron sang all the words in monotone with no change of inflection.

After the singing, David raised himself with some difficulty from his chair to give the sermon. For some reason he didn't understand, he felt strange preaching with Mary Lou there. He told himself that he was used to preaching to the choir and now for the first time he would be preaching to an unbeliever. After he prayed he pushed away these thoughts and preached with his usual confidence in the Word of God.

As soon as church was over, Rosalie and the children rushed up to Mary Lou. "What happened?" Rosalie asked anxiously.

"My horse threw me," said Mary Lou.

"Wow," the two little cowboys exclaimed, very impressed. "You got bucked off?"

Others came up to ask what happened wanting to know the particulars.

"Come on"—Alice took her arm—"you need to sit down and get off that foot."

There were picnic tables on the shady side of the church where the women were busy putting table cloths and food on them. This was a special time for the congregation, a time of socializing, a chance to catch up on one another's lives. This was a lonely country where many families lived quite a distance from one another. Soon it would be winter when some families would not be able to make it to church at all. When they did, they usually had to rush home to tend to their animals. Everyone kept an eye on the weather during the winter months.

David saw Mary Lou sitting with her bandaged foot propped on her other foot. He could see by the look on her face that she was in a lot of pain. He felt like avoiding her because he couldn't think of anything to say after their last encounter. Finally, he walked over and said, "Hi, Mary Lou."

"Hi," she said, without looking at him.

"Can I get you some food?" he asked.

"I'm not hungry."

"I'm sorry to see you in such pain. Are you taking anything for it?"

"No."

"When are you going to see a doctor?"

"I'm not, I don't need to, nothing is broken."

"Well, I hope you feel better soon." He didn't know what else to say. It was impossible to talk to her. He felt it would sound stupid saying the usual things—welcome to church, hope you'll come back, and so forth. He finally just walked away without saying anything more, glad of a chance to speak to some of the others who were waiting to speak to him.

Mary Lou wanted so badly to leave. Her foot and shoulder were throbbing with pain. She determined not to say anything as she could see how happy Aaron and Alice were to get together with their close friends as well as their family.

Why are they taking so long! she cried to herself. Then she told herself, *They have a right to enjoy themselves, I have no right.*

Reluctantly, people started to pick up their leftover food and prepare to depart for home.

Mary Lou was relieved to finally be leaving. All was quiet on the way home. Not a word was spoken, but that was as usual with the Gerhardt's. They could not express what a perfect day it had been with the blessed worship of God and the fellowship of other believers. They were filled with the joy and peace of the Spirit of God.

Mary Lou, also, in spite of her pain, felt a certain peace which she could not have explained. Was this life which she had always considered dull and boring beyond belief and which she had yearned half her life to escape…was this the real life? Was there actually more to this life than she had actually imagined? Why were these people so happy?

That night she lay awake for a long time, the words of the old hymns running through her mind. Some of the words of David's sermon came to mind: *God created us for himself. We can never be the whole person we were meant to be until we give ourselves to him wholly and completely—holding nothing back, keeping nothing for ourselves.*

How would one do that? she wondered. *What does that mean?* She still was not sure of God's existence. *How did these people know there really is a God? Did he show himself in some way? Does he want my life, my screwed up life?* Certainly, there was nothing left to want—even she didn't want it. Everything in life that she had thought she wanted was gone.

Mary Lou slept late, waking only when her grandmother came to check on her. "Grandma," Mary Lou asked as Alice checked her ankle, "how do you know there is a God? You haven't seen him."

"Well," Alice said, "I've seen him at work in my life."

"How is that, Grandma? Grandpa died and your babies died. Where was God?"

"Mary Lou," said Alice, "people die, we're all going to die, some young, some old. I've never felt the presence of God like I did in those hard times. I just knew he was near me, helping me to get through it." She paused, looking into Mary Lou's eyes. "When I was ten years old, I went to the altar and gave my life to God. I've never regretted it. I just believe...I don't have to see with my eyes what I know in my heart."

Alice was a little surprised, but then no one had ever asked her about how she felt about her faith. "Come on now," she said brusquely, "let's get you up. I saved you some breakfast. I know you must be hungry since you didn't eat a thing yesterday."

Mary Lou was surprised to hear her grandmother talk about her faith in such a personal way. She was such a private person. She knew her grandmother loved her, but she had never heard her say it. She realized that Alice was actually the only mother she had ever had, but she had never acknowledged it. She would have had to admit to herself that her own mother was never a mother.

Wednesday evening was Bible study and prayer. If Aaron had been surprised when Mary Lou decided to go to church, he nearly fainted when she informed him that she was going to Bible study. It felt strange to be going with her to Bible study. She was again shaking up his life only in a different way. David too tried not to show his surprise when he saw her. He noticed she didn't have a Bible, and he went to get one for her.

Mary Lou realized it had been many years since she had even seen a Bible, much less read one. She had once memorized all the books of the Bible in order to win a prize. The Bible study was held in the parsonage, just where she had received her counseling sessions. In fact, Mary Lou was sitting right in her usual seat. David was amused, smiling at the irony of it.

Mary Lou did her best to concentrate on the lesson. She was still in some pain from her injuries. Even so, it was hard to understand. The lesson was from the book of Romans, which seemed so familiar to everyone but her. She felt hopeless. *There are no answers here for me,* she thought. *How do I find a way to live?*

After the lesson, Mary Lou picked up her crutches and made her way to David who was still sitting in his chair with the open Bible on his lap. "I don't understand what people mean when they say Jesus died for my sins," she blurted out. "Why was that necessary, and why would he do that, and how is that physically possible anyway?"

David was surprised that she even had such thoughts in what he considered her *shallow mind.* "Well," he said, "that's a huge subject, and I don't think I have time to explain it. Your folks are getting ready to leave." He observed Aaron and Alice putting on their coats.

Mary Lou glanced at them and then back at David. "I want to know," she said adamantly.

"Well, let's see," he said, trying to put it in as few words as possible. "Suppose you hurt someone badly, sinned against them, I mean. And suppose you asked their forgiveness and let's say they forgive you, but the sin is still there, you still did it...nothing can erase it. This is where Jesus comes in. His dying erases the sin. His dying lets you off the hook. He's the sacrifice for your sin." He could see that she was still puzzled.

"Well, maybe you should think about your sins and ask yourself how to rid yourself of them."

"Maybe I don't have any." She smiled.

"Everyone does."

"Even you?"

"Yes, even me."

"Mary Lou, we're leaving," her grandmother hollered impatiently. "Hurry up!"

That night in bed Mary Lou thought about David's words: *Think about your sins.*

Reluctantly, she thought about all the people she had hurt. She thought about Larry's wife and his child, his son. She realized she had never given them much thought. Larry belonged to her. They were just intruders in their love, and since she had never seen them, she never thought about them. Mary Lou tossed and turned and closed her eyes tightly. When that didn't work, she tried to turn her thoughts to something else.

But the unwanted thoughts would not stop. What about his little boy? she wondered. How did he feel when his daddy didn't show up? Did he feel the same as she had when she waited for a mom that never came? Did he cry in the night the same as she had?

Mary Lou moaned aloud. It was impossible to stop thinking. How could she make up for these things? An apology would never make up for it even if she knew where they lived, which she did not. *I can't live like this,* she thought. Reluctantly, she thought that perhaps Jesus was the answer. But how? That was the great mystery. Finally, she fell into a fitful sleep.

The following Sunday she decided not to attend church. She begged off, saying she didn't feel well. The truth was, she had decided that life would be less complicated if she forgot about Jesus, heaven, hell, Satan, all those things that troubled her sleep as well as her waking hours. *If I don't think about it, it's not real,* she told herself. On the other hand, she had run out of things to think about. She dared not think about Larry. She couldn't daydream about having a glamorous, exciting life as she once had. All she had now was what she surveyed. She hardly recognized the person she saw in the mirror, the haunted eyes, stringy hair, dry complexion. The amazing thing was that she no longer cared. *I'm going to rot,* she told herself, *and I don't care and no one else does either.*

Aaron didn't know what to think. She had seemed to be getting interested in church and Bible study, then all of a sudden, she had made an excuse not to go. He resigned himself to the idea that it had been useless to get his hopes up.

Then, surprise, when Wednesday came, Mary Lou declared that she was going to the Bible study. Somehow, she felt compelled to go. *Perhaps,* she thought, *I just need to see other faces for a change.* If anyone was surprised to see her, they didn't let on.

When the study was over, Mary Lou again accosted David. "I would like to make an appointment to talk to you," she said.

David smiled wryly. "Appointment? I'm nearly always here. You can come by any time, have your dad bring you."

"I can come by myself," she retorted. "I can drive, you know."

"Of course, you can." He smiled. "Tomorrow's okay."

The following day she asked her dad if she could borrow the car. "I have an appointment to see David," she said.

Aaron was surprised. He had never heard of anyone making an appointment. He had never made an *appointment* in his life. If he wanted to see his doctor, lawyer, funeral director, no matter who, he just went. This was how country folks did things.

"Are you sure you know how to drive my car?" Aaron asked.

"Dad," Mary Lou answered, exasperated, "I drove all over the city, I'm sure I can drive ten miles on a country road."

"Oh sure," he laughed. "I'm sure you can. I'll get the keys." He didn't dare ask why she needed to see David. Hopefully, it was for the good.

When she pulled up in front of the parsonage, David was waiting on the porch. He smiled at her. "Maybe it would be cooler if we sat out here." He motioned to a couple of chairs. "Would you like something to drink?"

She shook her head and sat down in one of the chairs. She waited for him to sit down and then wasted no time saying what was on her mind. "I've been thinking about what you said. You know, about even if the person forgives you, the sin is still there?" David nodded. Actually, he'd forgotten. "I know my dad told you my man left me." David nodded again. Actually he did remember that. "Well," Mary Lou went on, "he was not my man. In fact, he was someone else's man. He was married and had a son. And he didn't leave me. I left him. I didn't want to, but his drinking got so bad I couldn't stand it anymore. I would have stayed, but I was so stressed out I lost my job and he didn't have one. So you see, I didn't really feel bad about the way I was living or about who I was hurting."

David was shocked. He thought of all the weeks he had tried to get her to say something, anything, and now here she was blurting out things he wasn't sure he wanted to hear. The whole thing was making him rather uncomfortable. He had to remind himself that he was a pastor and that this was his job. It was just that in his denomination people didn't do so much confessing.

Mary Lou continued, "This has been bothering the hell out of me. I mean…it never did before. Like I said, I didn't leave because my conscience bothered me. You mentioned asking the person's forgiveness. I don't even know where they live, so that's impossible."

She didn't wait for an answer. "What I need to know, does Jesus forgive a person who doesn't feel bad about what they've done? Or how bad do you have to feel? My pain has all been about losing Larry."

"Well," he said after giving himself a few minutes to digest all this, "you can't go too much on feelings. Feelings are subject to change."

"What does that mean?" she countered. "I want to know about how Jesus forgives, why would he, and how does he? I thought maybe you could explain all of this to me" she said hopefully.

"How does anyone explain all this without getting too theological and clear beyond her understanding?" He wondered how to begin. "Have you ever read the Old Testament?" he asked.

"Well, I know some of the Bible stories like Abraham, Joseph, David, and Goliath. I learned them in Sunday school a long time ago."

David wasn't surprised. He thought a lot of people ran around saying, "Jesus died for my sins," without really understanding the meaning—the sacrifice and the atonement.

"Well, as you know," he began, "God gave his people the Ten Commandments and other laws. He also set up a sacrificial system whereby people sacrificed animals in order to cleanse them from their sins. But the people kept on sinning. The blood of animals was no longer a sufficient sacrifice. In fact, God said, 'I despise your sacrifices.' So God himself came in human form and shed his blood as the once-and-for-all perfect sacrifice. He, Jesus, is the sin bearer for all of us. Those who choose to believe it anyway."

"How do I believe this?" Mary Lou asked skeptically.

"It's a choice you make." answered David. "There is no sin that you have committed that God can't forgive. He loves you; he created you. He not only forgives your sins, he forgets them, and finally, he will draw you to himself. Besides, I think you really are sorry about your sins, or you wouldn't be over here talking to me about them."

David paused. He had no idea if anything he had said had made a difference. He saw that she was just staring into space.

"Mary Lou," he asked, "do you know what the word *atonement* means?"

She shook her head.

"The dictionary says it means to compensate for, to make amends for, to do penance for. Mary Lou, Jesus did all that for you. He did for you what you cannot do for yourself."

"Could you write that down?" she asked.

"What?"

"What you just said…write the word and the meanings. It's hard for me to remember all this."

"Of course, but the best thing is for you to pick up your Bible and start reading it. I've just scratched the surface of all this. I feel I've left you with more questions than answers."

"That's another thing, do you have another one of those? I mean Dad and Grandma have their Bibles, but I don't know if there's an extra one."

"I have plenty of Bibles, and I will write the word and its meanings."

Mary Lou could see that it was a struggle for David to get up from his chair. She realized she had never heard him complain, not in church, Bible study, or any other time. She stood up to wait for him to return with the Bible and paper. She didn't want him to sit and then have to get up again.

"Thank you, David," she said formally. "I will think about all this and I will let you know if I have any more questions."

"You're welcome to stay longer and talk if you want to," he said graciously.

"No, I'd better get home. I should be more help to my grandma."

"Thanks again," she called back as she walked to the car.

When Mary Lou returned home, she found her grandmother busy preparing the noon meal. She looked quizzically at the Bible Mary Lou held in her hand.

"You know if I'd a known you needed a Bible, I could a given you one. I have several."

"Oh, I didn't know that. It's okay though, David said he has plenty."

"Are you gonna read that?" Alice asked.

"Well, I'm thinking about it, why?" asked Mary Lou.

"Could I give you some advice?"

"Sure."

"Well, if I were you, I'd start with the New Testament. It's not that I don't believe every word of the Old testament is God-given, but sometimes newcomers get bogged down with all the begets and wars and they throw the Bible aside and never touch it again."

"Thanks, I'll remember that. I do remember some of it, but not much."

Mary Lou took her Bible and piece of paper to her temporary room off the porch. Then she limped into the kitchen to help with dinner.

"You shouldn't stand too long on that foot," Alice admonished.

Mary Lou smiled. "It hardly hurts much at all anymore."

After dinner when she had finished helping clean up, she, along with Alice, retired to their rooms for their afternoon naps.

Mary Lou picked up her piece of paper—*amends, penance, compensate*. She went to the living room for the family dictionary. "Amends," she read, "payment made given for injury. Penance, sorry for having done wrong, payment for sin, compensate, make up for." It was easy to see, even for her, that she could do none of these things for herself. She picked up her Bible and turned to the New Testament. She was amused to see that the book of Matthew started with the "begets." She skipped over it and began reading. Soon she was asleep.

The following Sunday she was back at church. This time, even though she didn't sing, she followed the words closely. When David preached, she opened her Bible to the scriptures he used and marked them.

Meanwhile, Alice was thinking of how she could get Mary Lou into some decent clothes. Maybe the Lord didn't care how she looked, but she did.

There was the usual picnic after church, and this time Mary Lou helped herself to the food and sat down next to her niece and nephews. For the first time she felt guilty that she was almost a complete stranger to them, especially the boys. She could hardly tell them apart with their blond hair and blue eyes. She wanted to engage them in conversation, but she realized she had no idea what to say. She knew they were homeschooled, so she asked them what they were learning.

"Just stuff," they answered.

"What are you learning?" she asked Andrea.

"Well, for one thing, Mama is teaching me to sew. I really love it!" she cried. You know, Aunt Mary Lou, I'll soon be going away to Bible school. Mama says I'll need a whole new wardrobe! I'm so excited!"

Mary Lou stared at her. Here was her own flesh and blood who was leaving home, and she barely knew her! She had been so immersed in her own self-centered life that the other people in her life had been like shadows passing through. It seemed lately that every new realization was like a stab in the heart.

She sighed. "You know, Andrea, you are so lovely that it won't matter how you're dressed."

Andrea blushed. "I hope you can come over soon now that you're better. I'd like to show you what I'm making."

"I'll be there soon," Mary Lou promised.

The following day Alice finally got up the nerve to speak to Mary Lou. "Mary Lou," she began with her hands on hips, "I have talked to your dad and asked him to take us to town." She hurried on, "I want to go to Penny's and buy you a new dress and shoes. Now I'm not going to take no for an answer! We'll go first thing in the morning!"

Mary Lou had been aware of her grandma's disapproving looks and that she had been embarrassed by her appearance. She hadn't given it much thought, but maybe it was time to address the situation. "Grandma," she pleaded, "I know that Dad has a Penny's catalog around here somewhere. Can't I just order something from there? I hate going to town!"

"Well, I doubt it'll come before next Sunday."

"People are used to looking at me the way I'm dressed anyway."

"I guess so," Alice relented. "Maybe you could order two dresses. I'll pay for them. I have nothin' better to do with my money. I'm not gonna need it much longer anyway."

"In that case, why don't you order one too, Grandma?"

"Absolutely not!" Alice snorted. "I already have two nice dresses."

Mary Lou laughed as she went to get the catalog. It seemed as if two was the magic number.

Opening the catalog brought back memories of the young girl who had spent hours poring over the catalog. She had cut out the beautiful clothes she had planned to wear someday, nothing homemade for her. She had picked out her silverware, her linens, her appliances, everything she would need for elegant living. All of these she had cut out and pasted in a scrapbook.

How ironic, she thought as she sat at the old oak table, surveying the well-used oil cloth and the well-worn linoleum, *here I am and what do I own? A worn-out suit case full of worn-out clothes. Strange,* she thought, *I don't find that terribly depressing. Anyway, maybe I can enjoy picking out a new dress and shoes.*

She picked out a simple green dress and a black one with shoes to match and gave the catalog to Alice to fill out the order. Alice added some hosiery and undergarments to the order. She felt pleased with herself. You never knew with Mary Lou how she was going to react when asked to do something, even if it was for her own good. Now, she could attend church without embarrassment over her straggly granddaughter. *Perhaps,* she thought, *if she gets new clothes, she might be persuaded to do something about her stringy unkempt hair.*

After the noon meal was cleared away, Alice sat down to read her Bible. Mary Lou decided to join her. She brought her Bible and sat down opposite.

After watching Mary Lou read for a moment or two, Alice said to her, "Ask the Spirit for understanding in your reading."

"What spirit is that? What are you talking about?"

Mercy, Alice thought, *for all her years growin' up in the church, this girl knows nothin' about God or the Bible. No wonder she ended up in such a mess! How can I explain this so she has any idea what I'm talkin about? In all my days I never had to explain such things.* "Have you never heard that God is three persons in one?"

Mary Lou shook her head. "I don't remember."

"Well," Alice hurried on, "God, Jesus, and the Holy Spirit are all one God." She turned to the book of John in her Bible and read that when Jesus went away, he would send the comforter, the Spirit of Truth who would be a teacher.

"I'm not there yet in my reading. How do I accept this? It sounds far-fetched, strange."

"Well," said Alice calmly, "you accept it by faith at first…then it just becomes a part of you, and gradually, you come to believe that it makes sense. Even if Jesus were here in the flesh, he couldn't reach everyone. But his spirit can reside in the heart of everyone on earth who believes. Oh," she said abruptly, "I'm probably not explainin' it right, I ain't no preacher!"

"Grandma," Mary Lou said calmly, "could you just give me those verses and where they are so I can mark them. I have so much to learn, but I'm beginning to realize that I really do want to learn."

Praise the Lord, Alice thought as she proceeded to look up the verses.

The following Sunday, Mary Lou wore her new green dress to church. Her grandmother was so proud. Her hair wasn't fixed, but it was straight and clean and shiny. The green matched her eyes. Most people noticed, but they didn't say anything, not wanting her to think that they noticed what she usually wore. The exception, of course, was Rosalie and Andrea.

"Oh, Auntie, you are gorgeous!" gushed Andrea.

"Oh yes," Rosalie agreed. "You look so pretty!"

Mary Lou was pleased. "Thank you," she said quietly.

David said nothing, but it was obvious that he noticed. He was also pleased to see her at Bible study. It was amazing how suddenly she was asking a myriad of questions. She always brought a notebook and wrote everything down. He was used to giving a Bible study to people who knew every inch of the Bible, who probably could have given the study themselves. *Actually,* he thought, *it's refreshing.* In his prayers he asked God to help her in her quest to know him.

So far, she had certainly not given any indication that she was ready to make any *decision*. Well, that would be up to the Lord; he would do his best to lead her in that direction.

And then, several months later during church, a miracle of sorts happened. It was during the hymn singing as Mary Lou sat between her dad and grandma listening to their monotone that her beautiful voice rang out. She could no longer just read the words, something within her just had to sing, “Holy, holy, holy.”

The congregation listened in amazement. Her dad and grandma were plainly shocked. They too stopped singing and stared at her. And then she stopped singing as suddenly as she had started.

When the hymn was finished, Rosalie, who was leading the singing, could not let this *miracle* pass. In her mind with her Pentecostal background they had witnessed a movement of the Holy Spirit. Raising her arms, she began to praise the Lord, thanking him for the gift that the sister had just used to glorify him, the blessing that had been received for the people’s edification. There were some shouts of amen and hallelujah!

As Rosalie went on and on in her praises, Mary Lou felt only embarrassment and an urge to run.

Later, after the last prayer and amen, Rosalie accosted Mary Lou. “Mary Lou, that was so beautiful. I was wondering if you would consider leading the music? I mean, my voice is adequate, but yours is so powerful.”

“No!” Mary Lou interrupted, I can’t do that. At least not now. I’m just not ready to put myself up there, I’m sorry.”

“Well, I understand,” said Rosalie. “Perhaps sometimes you could do a special song. You know, a solo?”

“I don’t know about that either.”

“Well,” Rosalie persisted, “pray about it. You have a special gift that was given to you by God, you know.”

Mary Lou had never thought about praying about any decision. You either did it or you didn’t. *Maybe that’s why all my decisions were bad,* she thought ruefully. It did feel good to sing though. She had never realized how beautiful the hymns were. It was ironic though that all the years she had spent singing in honkytonks and now she was afraid to sing in church. Well, then she had always had something to take the edge off. A few drinks made all the difference.

She did not know how to respond when people came up to her and complimented her on her beautiful voice. They wanted her to know how they had been touched by her singing.

Mary Lou was glad when it was time to leave. If God was in her singing, then she was unaware of it.

Life went on as usual. Mary Lou tried to be more help around the house, insisting that Alice rest. They became close in a way they never had in all of Mary Lou's years of life. She began to realize that maybe she had unknowingly resented her grandmother for taking her mother's place. Perhaps she had withheld love as punishment. She hoped it wasn't too late to make up for it in some small way.

She took time to talk to her dad, trying to show some interest in the things that interested him. She was surprised to find that, for a cowboy, he had a wide range of interests as well as knowledge on a lot of subjects she had never given much thought. She realized that her interests were narrow and her knowledge on most subjects nonexistent. For instance, she had never voted, never taken an interest in politics or government.

She had no idea that in terms of land and cattle, her family was very wealthy. Their belief was that they should make money in order to give money. Aaron knew that when John inherited what he had, he would carry on that tradition. Part of him wanted to disinherit Mary Lou, believing she would squander the Lord's money. Still, he didn't have the heart to disinherit her completely. It was hard to know what to do, and so he did nothing.

7
CHAPTER

Summer passed and suddenly it was fall. For the church, it was time for the yearly revival. This was a time when an itinerant preacher was invited to come and speak to the congregation as well as, hopefully, whatever unsaved people who could be persuaded to come. The church at Windy Hill was located on the highway between two small towns. Before the revival, ads were put in each of the local newspapers announcing the arrival of the evangelist and time of the services.

Since Rosalie was one of the main pillars of the church, she usually did the work of finding someone, usually someone of her persuasion, which meant there would be a lot of singing and shouting in the Spirit. Alice called them "fire and brimstone" preachers.

Nevertheless, it was a time that everyone looked forward to. In the years that it had become a part of the church's calendar, it had been well-attended. For the congregation it was to be a time of soul-searching and repentance. For others who might be persuaded to come just to see the goings-on or to please a family member or friend, hopefully it was a time to win some unpersuaded soul into the Kingdom of God.

It was not, as some believed, a time to fill the church coffers or to increase membership. Every effort was made to make it a holy event. The congregation was asked to bathe the days in prayer beforehand. Even each child was given a time to pray asking God's blessing. Special music requested by the evangelist was practiced. It was to start on Sunday morning and continue through Sunday and Tuesday evenings. There was to be a potluck on Sunday evening in the parsonage living room, which meant that David had to move his papers and books into his bedroom. The preacher and his wife was to lodge with John and Rosalie.

Mary Lou could see that her dad and grandma were excited about it. There was talk of finishing the chores early to be sure to be on time. Her Aunt Norma planned to come and spend the whole time with them. She was shocked to see that her dad, who was always so quiet and reserved, take his hat in hand and go to town to invite some of the people he did business with to his church for the revival. It seemed he did this every year. She wondered if any of them had ever shown up. She was sure that they probably listened respectfully at least, since he was a long-time valuable customer.

Could I ever do something like that? She wondered. *Could I ever humble myself, could I ever care enough about someone else's soul enough to humble myself?* She knew for sure that she wasn't there yet. In fact, her reason for going to the services she had to admit was to observe the goings-on. With Rosalie in charge, it was sure to be different.

When they arrived at the church it was gratifying to find that there were more than the usual crowd there. The small parking lot was full, and some cars were even parked out on the prairie.

"The Lord has blessed us," Alice said. "I'm sure he has great things in store for this meeting. He's answered our prayers!"

Seeing the joy on their faces, Mary Lou too felt a surge of excitement and expectation.

In fact, by the time they arrived, the church was so crowded, they had to sit separately.

During the music Mary Lou had a chance to observe the evangelist and his wife who sat on the dais with David. She noticed that he was rather chubby with a round face and curly hair. In contrast to the rancher's usual attire of jeans and boots, he wore a rather ill-fitting suit, which could have used a pressing. His eyes were closed and he was tapping his foot to the music. His wife sat beside him staring at the people. She was bird-like thin. She wore a dark colored dress, which had seen better days. She was not singing or clapping.

Mary Lou felt a pang of shame for judging their clothes. After all, if it hadn't been for her grandmother's generosity she wouldn't have anything decent to wear. She supposed that when you traveled from church to church depending on collections or *love offerings* as they were called, you couldn't have much. Certainly, she didn't have anything to give them. If they had to depend on people like her, they would be in bad shape.

The worship music and the prayers went on longer than usual. Rosalie had somehow persuaded a violinist whom no one had ever seen before to come and accompany the piano. Mary Lou loved the sound. It seemed to provide an almost haunting sound to the hymns.

At last, David made his way to the lectern and introduced the man whose name was John Martin. He, in turn, asked David to pray for him before he spoke. David asked the Lord's blessing on Brother Martin. He asked the Holy Spirit to give wisdom to the brother as he spoke and to open the ears of the assembly to hear the Word of God in a new and a fresh way. He prayed for the congregation that they might be expectant for God to do a new and wonderful thing in their lives.

Mary Lou tried to take David's word to heart, not to be distracted by her surroundings and especially unworthy thoughts.

Pastor Martin gave a short history of his life, where he came from, the crisis in his life that brought him to the Lord, his call from God to bring revival to the church. He then began a rather lengthy sometimes loud exhortation punctuated by shouts of amen and "preach it, brother" from the congregation.

What is wrong with me? Mary Lou wondered. *Why am I not getting into this like the others?* She decided it probably had to do with her cynical attitude.

Later at the potluck, as Pastor Martin was getting acquainted with the people, he saw Mary Lou standing against the wall trying to look inconspicuous. He came over to her and asked her name. Then he looked directly into her eyes long enough to make her uncomfortable. *He knows me*, she thought. *He knows who I am, who I really am!* She tried to look away, but she couldn't.

Finally, he said, "The Lord has a word for you, Mary Lou. You were saved for a reason, you will bring my Word to Spanish-speaking people." He smiled at her and walked away.

Mary Lou was dumbstruck. When she had recovered she thought to herself, *I don't know where they got this fellow, but he belongs in an asylum.* She made up her mind to avoid him as much as possible. However, he made no attempt to single her out after that.

After the Sunday service, Mary Lou was very quiet on the ride home. She went straight to her room without a word to anyone. Later in the darkened room, in spite of herself, she could not stop thinking about what the man had said even though she told herself it was all gibberish. God didn't speak to people in this day and age, especially to her.

She couldn't help thinking about it though. Did he mean she was saved from the lightning storm? She tried to laugh. She didn't know a word of Spanish. The only Spanish-speaking people she knew was the family at church, and certainly they didn't need anyone to tell them about God. They were far more devout than she would ever be.

She thought about making an excuse to get out of the Monday evening service, but something seemed to propel her there. Perhaps curiosity. One never knew what might happen next. The service was similar to the Sunday evening service except that after the worship they took time for testimonies. Mary Lou couldn't help but be touched by people's admissions that they had been in a backsliding state before the revival and that they had made a new commitment to the Lord. Even some of the men had tears running down their cheeks. Some asked for prayers for forgiveness of their sins, sins of commission and omission. There was so much rejoicing, praying, and testifying that it was pretty late by the time Brother Martin gave the message. However, no one seemed to care. In fact, they seemed reluctant to leave.

Tuesday evening was more of the same. Everyone seemed to know that this night was special. If you hadn't been *touched* by this night or if you hadn't made your decision, well, prayerfully this was to be a night of miracles.

Pastor Martin chose a scripture from Luke. He talked about a man with a great harvest who had to build even more barns to hold it all. How smug he was, thinking he had it made for life, he could eat, drink, and be merry. But God had a message for him: "You fool, tonight you will die and then who will get all you have accumulated? Some people," he went on, "are holding back not just riches but the life God had created for himself. What are you holding back? What if tonight you die? How many of you want to eat, drink, and be merry just a little while longer? My friends," he spoke with authority, "tonight is decision time! You are not promised tomorrow!

As he continued his exhorting, Mary Lou couldn't keep the words *you fool* from running around in her brain. *You fool. You are a fool!* She glanced at Jake in his usual spot in the back of the church. She thought about how much they had in common. Neither of them had ever gathered anything into barns, but they had their pride, tattered though it was. How did she know she had tomorrow, or even tonight?

Had God saved her for a reason? Of course not, not her. Brother Martin had finished his sermon and was deep in silent prayer. The music was playing softy. Suddenly, it was as if she had been propelled out of her seat. She stumbled down the aisle hardly realizing what she was doing and fell against the railing of the altar. She realized she had started to cry for the first time in many years. She was aware that David had his hands on her head and that he was thanking God for her deliverance.

Meanwhile, Alice and Norma were clutching one another with pure joy. "Praise the Lord." Alice breathed. "I have lived to see this day!"

Aaron was crying unabashedly, fumbling for his handkerchief. "Was there ever such a God as the one they served?" he thought. *How can I thank him, where are the words?*

Of course, there were others who had seen the light and there was much rejoicing over them as well. But for the Gerhardt family there was only one, a true miracle! Even David felt that probably Mary Lou was the greatest miracle. He had to admit that he had had his doubts about the power of even God to break through to her. Sure, he knew that she had been searching. But still he sensed a spirit of cynicism and unbelief that seemed impenetrable. How had he ever doubted what God was able to do?

Soon the evening was over. Brother Martin and his wife had to leave early in order to make their next assignment.

8

CHAPTER

For several days after the revival, Mary Lou moved about in a joyful daze. After a while she began to wonder what it had all been about. What had really changed? She did the same things she had always done. It seemed that even her Bible reading was going stale. Finally, she asked her grandmother, "What does God expect of me now?"

Alice was a little taken aback by the question. "What do you mean, what does God expect of you?"

"Well," Mary Lou said, "it seems like nothing has changed."

"What is supposed to change?"

"I don't know, I just feel as if I should be doing something different."

"Like being a missionary or something?" She paused a minute. "Look, Mary Lou, most women in the Bible, with the exception of a few, never did anything spectacular. Deborah led an army…Mary birthed the son of God, but even she probably spent most of her time cooking and cleaning. In fact, I think she was a little bewildered by it all." She thought for a minute. "All I ever wanted to be was a wife and mother. Course I helped out in the church and with the neighbors when it was needed. I never felt God expected more of me."

"Well, I don't have any family to do for," said Mary Lou.

"Mary Lou, why don't you pray and ask God what, if anything, he has in mind for you to do. I know one thing," she said firmly, "your dad needs you here and certainly the church needs you. You need to be getting on your knees more. Just surrender it all to him."

A few days later, Aaron asked Mary Lou if she would like to go to the rodeo the following evening with him and John.

"Sure," she said, anxious to get out of the house.

It was dusk when they arrived at the fairgrounds. The smell and sound of the animals, the smoke of the barbecue, the laughter of the people reminded Mary Lou of when she was a child and attended the fair and rodeo with her dad and brother. Something they did every year. It had all seemed so exciting.

When they arrived, people were just beginning to arrive. The bleachers were beginning to fill up fast. Aaron picked seats near the ground as he didn't like sitting up high. John sat next to him and Mary Lou sat on the other side of John.

They were surprised to see David arriving on crutches. Most of the time he used his cane. Mary Lou felt a pang of sadness wondering if his injuries were getting worse.

His face lit up when he saw them, and he struggled to climb up to them. Aaron started to scoot over, but he hobbled over them in order to sit on the other side of Mary Lou. He said hello to Aaron and John and then turned his attention to Mary Lou.

If Mary Lou could have pointed to a time when her life changed forever, this would have been it! She was stunned; it seemed as if time stood still and the only thing she was aware of was David beside her. Everything she was looking at the time was imprinted on her brain forever.

"I didn't know you liked rodeos." David turned to her with a smile.

"I didn't know you did either." She felt tongue-tied. *What is wrong with me?* she cried to herself. She felt as if David's leg which was almost touching hers was burning a hole in her leg.

"My niece is competing in the barrel racing," he replied.

Oh, he has family. But of course he does. She wished she could get up and move. She was being overwhelmed with feelings she didn't understand. She felt like a school girl with her first crush.

David was saying something about the revival and how God had moved in people's lives. Mary Lou tried to pay attention. *How can I sit here and not make a fool of myself?* she wondered.

Fortunately, David's sister and her husband spotted him and asked him to come and sit with them as it was about time for his niece's event. So once again, he stumbled over them and left.

Mary Lou tried to shut down her mind and enjoy the rodeo, but it was impossible.

That night she was unable to sleep. *I am going crazy,* she thought. *There is something wrong with me. Was the reason I gave my life to Jesus was because I had the hots for the preacher? I am not like these other people.* She cried. *I cannot change! What works for them can't work for someone like me.*

After several days of being in misery, which she tried to hide, she determined that she needed to speak to someone. The only person she could think of was Rosalie, the last person she ordinarily would want to talk to about anything.

The next morning after her chores were finished, she saddled her horse and left for Rosalie's. It was a bright beautiful fall day. Pretty soon it would be turning cold and then the snow would fall. *Another year passing,* she thought, *another year older.* The thought was depressing. What has it all meant?

She tried to hurry her horse along. She wanted to talk to Rosalie before John and the boys came home for dinner. One thing she had learned about this horse was that he hated going anywhere, but he loved going home. It was hard to get him out of trot going. But returning to the corral he ran as if he were in a race. It was hard to hold him back. She wondered if her dad had investigated his temperament before buying him. In spite of his faults, she had grown to love him. She was pleased to see that he had a stubborn personality like hers.

Rosalie and John had a fenced yard—something her dad didn't have, allowing the animals to come to the front door if they had a mind to. Rosalie had done her best with the dry land, planting morning glories, zinnias, and marigolds. They had lots of elm trees, berry bushes, and a huge garden which was about picked out. Mary Lou was amazed at how beautiful it was. She wondered how Rosalie had managed with so little water from a windmill and the small amount nature managed to squeeze out. If the wind didn't blow there was no water from the well. Of course, she observed, the wind did blow most of the time.

The dog's barking alerted Rosalie and Andrea to her arrival. They were so excited to see her since they seldom had company, living so far from their neighbors. Nothing would do but for Andrea to show her aunt the clothing she and her mother were making for her to take to Bible school.

Mary Lou noticed that even though the material and the print was different, the pattern was basically the same—long sleeves, high neckline, and below-the-knee length. However, she exclaimed over the fine workmanship and the beautiful material. "I'm sure you'll be the best dressed and most beautiful girl in the school," she declared. "I just hope I get to see you in one of these outfits before you leave."

Andrea beamed. "Of course, Auntie. I'll see you at church for sure. I have two more Sundays."

"Well, come over anytime. You don't have to wait till Sunday."

Mary Lou felt like crying out, "Don't go, I want to know you, so many years have been wasted and I never knew or cared how precious you are, and now it's too late to make up for lost time." Instead she hugged her tight and then she asked if it would be all right to talk to her mother alone for a minute. "I just need to ask her something, okay?"

Rosalie cut in, "Come in the living room. Would you like something to drink? Andrea, could you make some tea, please?" She ushered Mary Lou into the living room and onto the couch and sat beside her, turning to face her. "Did you have a question for me?" she asked.

Mary Lou wasted no time getting to the thing that was bothering her. "I think I'm in love with David," she blurted out.

Rosalie was noticeably shocked. "Mary Lou," she cried, "what about your husband?"

"Well, actually I have no husband, we were just living together." She seemed unaware of how shocking this news was to Rosalie.

"Does David know about this?" Rosalie dared to ask.

"No!" Mary Lou turned to face her. "He must never know either! Please, I need to talk to someone about this, don't say anything to anyone, not even John!"

"Of course not!" She was trying to digest all this, wondering why Mary Lou had possibly wanted to tell her all this.

"Besides"—Mary Lou leaned back on the couch—"this is all beside the point. What I need to know...and the reason I'm telling you...well, you know the Bible and you're almost like a minister." She faltered, not knowing quite how to express herself in what she was about to say. "You see, since I realized how I feel about David, I'm wondering if I'm really in love with Jesus, and maybe the reason I went down to the altar was because I was trying to impress David and maybe I'm not really saved at all?"

Rosalie had picked up her Bible, which was lying next to the couch. She had not opened it; it was as if she was just holding it for support.

Meanwhile Andrea brought the tea and left it, seeing that it might be better if she left.

"Mary Lou," Rosalie finally answered in a firm voice, "what we're talking about here are two separate issues. First of all, it is no surprise that you're attracted to David. After all, he has been your mentor, your counselor...I'm sure a big influence on your spiritual life. As for not being saved, you laid yourself on the altar and you can't take yourself back. You made a commitment, and it had nothing to do with David. I'm sure you weren't thinking about him when you made the trip to the altar. This relationship with Jesus is a relationship which has to do with your eternal destiny. What you're going through right now has to do with feelings, and feelings are subject to change."

Mary Lou didn't answer, she was trying to digest what Rosalie was talking about.

"Another thing," Rosalie added. "This does not surprise me that you are going through this; you were safely in Satan's camp and he doesn't want to let you go. He will put any idea he can into your head to convince you that what happened to you was not real and that you are not saved at all. You're not the first new Christian that this has happened to."

Anything having to do with Satan was a new idea to Mary Lou. She wasn't sure of his existence nor of how much influence he had on her. She seemed to make plenty of mistakes without his help.

"Finally," Mary Lou spoke, "I guess I have a lot to learn. I went to church a good deal of my life, and apparently I never learned anything. I think I'd better concentrate on my Bible reading and study and try to forget about David.

"Concentrate on prayer, Mary Lou. You really are talking to a person, you know. God will help you, trust me."

Mary Lou got up to leave. "I'd better get back and help Grandma with dinner. Thank you, Rosalie. I will think about everything you said. I'm sure you're right about everything you said and, believe me, I'm going to try to follow your advice. I have to."

"You're always in my prayers," said Rosalie.

They begged her to stay for lunch, but she insisted she had to get home. She needed time to think.

To say that Mary Lou was still confused was an understatement. She was sure of one thing: David must never know how she felt about him. In her mind he was a pure saintly person and she was… well, she was used goods. Besides, how could she trust her feelings anyway? Not long ago she was so in love with Larry that death itself seemed better than being without him. And now she was sure that she was in love with David.

"What is wrong with me?" she cried. "All my family is so stable and sure of their place in life with their faith in God. Maybe it's my mother's side of the family. Maybe that's where the darkness comes from." She was surprised that she could think of her mother without the usual mix of anger and sadness.

As soon as she had unsaddled her horse, she went straight to her room and got down on her knees beside her bed and began to pray to an invisible God. She remembered something else that Rosalie had said: "Have faith in the faith of others while your faith grows." Mary Lou thought about the faith of her dad, her grandmother, David, Rosalie. Could they be wrong? It didn't seem likely. David, for instance, was a well-educated man. Why would he choose to believe a lie? "I choose to believe what they believe," she said aloud. "I choose to believe the Bible."

9
CHAPTER

Life went on as usual except that Mary Lou was still troubled about her feelings for David. They seemed to get stronger as time went on. She started to notice how much pain he was in much of the time. However, he gritted his teeth and carried on. Sometimes she felt this longing to hold him in her arms and comfort him. She began to think that perhaps she needed to make changes in her life.

Meanwhile she began to experience new insights into her spiritual life as she prayed and read her Bible. One night as she was watching her dad wrestle with his grandsons on the floor of the living room, she was amused to see how he loved acting like a kid again. Mary Lou was amazed at how strong he was for a man in his sixties. The boys were loving it too. Mary Lou was thinking how adorable they were and how in a way she wished she had children when she remembered with stab of pain, *You aborted your children! Oh god,* she thought, *why did I think of this?*

She rose abruptly and went out into the night. She let herself remember how frightened she had been when she had missed her monthly period. Finally, she had confided in a friend that she worked with. "My mother can help you," offered her friend. "She helps lots of people." She remembered drinking the concoction her friend had brought her and the hot baths fearing that this was an old wives' tale that would never work. She remembered the relief she felt when she saw the flow of blood. Relief was all that she had ever felt. From then on she had known what to do.

I had forgotten, now I know that I not only committed adultery, but also murder. I murdered my children! But how was I to take care of them? I had no husband, no steady job, I could barely take care of myself. She was trying to justify herself. Then it came to her what her real sin had been. The answer came down through the ages woven through the Bible standing out like a thread of a different color—man's rebellion against God, the root of all other sin. She had not loved God, had hated the mention of his name, that was her real sin. From that stemmed fornication, adultery, lies, murder, hatred, all the things for which she could never make amends. And suddenly she knew in the depths of her heart why Jesus had to die for her! She understood the atonement! He had made amends for her! She could never explain it with her mind; it would be enough that now she knew! Heavy tears welled up, coursed down her cheeks unchecked. Her heart felt heavy, almost as it were too heavy for her to bear. "Jesus, Jesus," she whispered, "the name above all names, I do love you and now I know why!

Weeks passed, months passed, Christmas came and went. Mary Lou was growing in her faith and awareness. She was taking over many of her grandma's duties and trying to be as helpful as she could be to her dad. However, the winter months were long and cold and there wasn't as much to do, and so outside of reading a lot of time was taken up with napping.

The mailman came when he could get through and brought the weekly paper as well as the rest of the mail. Mary Lou looked forward to reading the paper although there wasn't much in it. It was then that she saw the ad: "Apt. for rent, single man or woman." An idea began to form in her mind. And so the first chance she got, she asked her dad and grandma to have a seat, she needed to talk to them.

Aaron felt apprehensive. What was this about? he wondered. He was sure it wasn't good.

Mary Lou got right to the point. "Dad, I want to move to town and get a job."

She saw his face fall. He had been expecting bad news and he got it.

"Dad," she hurried on, "I know what you're thinking, and you're wrong. I have changed. In fact, I love it here with you all and the church. I have found peace, but I just don't want to live off you for the rest of my life. It's time I took responsibility for myself."

"Well, I could pay you for what you do around here," said Aaron, hopefully.

"Dad, you don't owe me anything!" she exclaimed. "I can never repay you for what I owe you. I don't ever want to take a dime from you! But I'll still need your help to find a job. I know you know a lot of people. And, I can't find a place to live without your help either. I'd have to ask you to pay the rent until I get a job and get paid."

Everyone was quiet for a few minutes trying to digest the meaning of all this.

"Daddy," Mary Lou broke the silence, "I really want to do this. This is not just a whim. I need this, I really do!"

Again, they were silent.

Finally, Mary Lou got up and started for the stairs. "I'm going to bed," she said. She turned and faced her dad again. "Please, think about it."

Aaron and Alice sat staring at one another. Alice was the first to speak. "I think you ought to let her go," she said. She paused for a few minutes, letting her words sink in. "I think you ought to help her. She's still a fairly young woman and she has a life to lead. What kind of life is it for her, here with you and me and Jake?"

Since Aaron didn't answer, she continued, "I suppose you think she'll go back to her old ways? Maybe she will, but I don't think so. Besides, if she does, you can't hold on to her. She's a grown woman."

"She sure has a way of upsetting things," he observed.

"Yes, she does," smiled Alice, "but maybe things need to be upset once in a while."

Aaron rose. "Well, Mom, it's my bedtime. Yours too, I reckon."

As he left, Alice was thinking back to the time Norma has informed them that she wanted to leave the ranch and move to town. She had gone away to school, and after graduation they had expected her to move home and hopefully say yes to a young man who had expressed an interest in her. Even though "town" was only forty miles away, it was still hard to see her go since they didn't make the trip that often, sometimes not for months at a time.

Anyway, they had helped her buy a big old house, which she had turned into a boarding house for young ladies. It took a while, but she had repaid them.

Sometimes, she felt bad that Norma had never married and had a family. But, she figured, she had been a mother to so many country girls who had had to leave their families in order to attend high school. It had been a safe place to leave them with someone to look after them.

The following morning after chores and after breakfast, Aaron was ready to talk to Mary Lou. He had an idea. "Maybe you could rent a room from your aunt…if there's one available."

"No!" Mary Lou was adamant. "Maybe you can't see it, but that is not the same as getting on my own. I have found this ad in the paper. It's for a single woman, and the rent is cheap. I want to go look at it! There's another ad too for a housekeeping supervisor at the Brand Hotel. I know you know the owner. Daddy, you can speak to him for me, please," she begged.

"That's also a bar and restaurant!" Aaron looked aghast.

"I know," Mary Lou said calmly, "but just because it's there doesn't mean I'm going in there. In the first place, by the time I pay the rent I won't have any money to drink or eat out!"

Aaron knew that it was useless to continue arguing even though he had a bad feeling about the situation. "I still have to have more time to think about this," he said.

In spite of his misgivings, that evening he informed her that he had thought it over and for her to get ready to go to town the following morning after chores.

Alice said she planned to go too. She could visit with Norma while they did their business.

Mary Lou was torn between feelings of sadness and excitement. She had been at peace here. What if she was making a mistake? Could she trust herself out from under the protection of her family and the church? Well, she would never know until she made the break.

After breakfast she dressed herself in her green dress, brushed her hair, and surveyed herself in the mirror. She felt she looked so plain. She wished she had brought a lipstick. When she left California, the last thing on her mind was her appearance, and she hadn't thought much about it since.

Alice and Aaron were waiting by the door when she came down the stairs. "You look nice, Mary Lou." Alice looked at her approvingly. Alice did not approve of face painting.

As they approached the town limit, Mary Lou suggested they look at the apartment first since it was early.

"I think you better see about the job first," said Aaron. "Why would you be settin' up here in the apartment with no job?"

"Well, you're right," said Mary Lou. She realized she was putting it off because she was apprehensive about her chances of getting the job. After all, her only work experience was singing in bars. She had stopped referring to them as "clubs."

After they dropped Alice at Norma's, they drove to the hotel. Aaron parked and waited for Mary Lou to get out of the car.

"Daddy," she said plaintively, "I want you to go with me. I need you to put in a good word for me."

Aaron had to think about that for a moment. What if this turned out badly? He checked himself. He was doubting the power of God to redeem his daughter.

As they entered the front door of the lobby, they met the owner, John Hershy, coming down the hallway.

He and Aaron had gone to high school together. While Aaron was a country boy, John had been raised in town. After high school he had gone away to college and, after college, had lived in the city for a while. He came home to run the family business after his father died. He and Aaron had become slightly reacquainted over the years as Aaron was a member of the Cattlemen's Association, which held their meetings in the banquet room of the hotel. Other than that, except for knowing about one another, there was not much contact.

He and Aaron shook hands, and after the usual inquiries about health, family and business, Aaron introduced Mary Lou. Not knowing what else to say, Aaron forged ahead. "Mary Lou is interested in the job you advertised."

If John Hershy was surprised, he tried not to show it. First of all, he wondered why a daughter of a man he knew to be extremely wealthy would even need such a menial low-paying job. And then it seemed odd that her father would be the one to speak for her. So far, she hadn't said a word. However, the job was still open and no one else had applied.

"Do you know what this job entails?" he asked.

"Well, all I know is what the paper said," she answered.

He explained that after the maids finished their work, she would inspect to make sure they were clean and in order. That wouldn't be much of a problem since the women he had now were very experienced. However, they came and went and sometimes there were a lot of problems. He also needed someone to run the switchboard during the day, part-time. "Do you have any questions?"

Mary Lou bit her lip. "I suppose someone would train me?"

"Oh sure, I'll take you through the rooms and show you what I mean by 'being in order.' Martha, the night operator, will show you the switchboard. There's not much to it. The pay is not much…fifty dollars a week."

There was silence while they all looked at one another. Finally, John Hershy said, "The job is yours if you want it."

"I want it," said Mary Lou.

"This is Thursday, can you start Monday?" he asked.

Mary Lou looked at her father. Everything was transpiring so fast, he was having a hard time taking it all in. Finally, he nodded in acquiescence.

"Well, then, I'll see you on Monday." He shook her hand and then Aaron's. "It's good to see you again, Aaron. I'm glad to see you looking so well. A lot of our old classmates are either dead or in bad shape. Stop in and see me whenever you're in town and you have time. I'm nearly always here. We go back a long time, your dad and I," he said to Mary Lou.

Back in the car, Mary Lou gave a huge sigh of relief. "Thanks, Dad," she said. "You know I feel like a person just beginning to live again, like I'm taking baby steps."

Maybe that's true, thought Aaron. *She is newborn, born again.*

"We better get over and see about the apartment," said Aaron, "be something if you had a job and no place to live." The apartment was located on the north side of the tracks. The railroad ran straight through the middle of the town, so there was a north side and a south side. It was an unspoken fact that the wealthier people lived on the south side. However, there was no special stigma in living on the north side. In fact, some fairly prominent people lived on the north side.

They pulled up to a house that was old but well-kept. It was two-storied with a large front porch. It seemed to be the only one on the lot. Mary Lou was disappointed. She really didn't want to live in someone's home. Nevertheless, they were greeted at the door by a small bird-like older woman.

"We came to see about the apartment," explained Aaron. He introduced himself and Mary Lou explaining that she was a single woman interested in looking at the apartment.

"Oh yes, come on in." She led them through the living room and kitchen into the backyard. There, behind the house, was a full basement completely finished except for the house. Mrs. Hall, that was her name, explained that after her husband died, she was unable to afford to build the house, so she rented out the basement.

"Would you like to see it?" she asked. Mary Lou nodded. There was a small ante room over the stairs which led down into the basement. There were no partitions except for a makeshift one partitioning the bedroom and bathroom, which were very small rooms. The bedroom had enough room only for a bed and a nightstand. The bathroom had an old-fashioned tub with a small sink over which there was a small mirror. The kitchen was in one corner, which consisted of a small stove, refrigerator, table and chairs, and an old-fashioned cabinet containing a few pots and pans and a few cracked dishes. Against the opposite wall was a couch and chair; both of which were fairly worn but clean.

There was a lot of empty space covered in linoleum, also worn but clean. "A person could have dances in here," observed Mary Lou. The rent was cheap and affordable on Mary Lou's salary.

Aaron looked dubious. However, he was reassured when he noticed the good lock on the door and the small above-ground windows also looked secure. Mrs. Hall's assertion that Mary Lou would not be able to entertain gentlemen friends, as well as no drinking and no parties and so forth, reassured him further.

He himself would never dream of living such a bare uninviting place, and he fully expected Mary Lou to refuse to live there. But to his surprise, she seemed very happy with the place.

"If it's okay with you, Dad," she said, "I would love to live here!"

"It's two months' rent in advance," said Mrs. Hall. "Another thing," she added, "dishes, pots and pans, and beddings are all furnished. But if you have your own things, I'll take these out."

"Oh no!" exclaimed Mary Lou. "I don't have those things."

"Well, fine. Also, if you need to wash, you can use the washer and dryer on the back porch."

Mary Lou could not believe her good fortune—a job and this wonderful place to live all in one day!

As soon as Rosalie heard about Mary Lou's leaving, she immediately got in her car and hurried to the church to talk to David about having a going-away party for her after church.

David was noticeably shocked when she told him. "Why is she leaving?" knowing that as he asked it was none of his business. He couldn't imagine Wednesday evening Bible study without her and her incessant questions. And then there was her singing. Everyone, especially him, looked forward to her beautiful solos whenever she could be persuaded to sing one. It was hard to contain his disappointment.

Rosalie looked at him strangely. *Maybe he cares for her too,* she thought.

However, he managed to get ahold of himself and said, "Of course, we must have a going-away party for Sister Mary Lou. I'm sure everyone is gonna miss her. Do you think there's time to notify everyone? It's so soon. By the way, did she say why she's leaving?" Again, he couldn't help asking.

"Well, she said that it's time she got out on her own and stopped living off her dad. That's all I know. And don't worry, I'm on my way to notify everyone now since it's such short notice. Another thing, I hate to ask you to move your stuff out of the living room again. One of these days soon." She sighed. "I hope we will start building a place for fellowship. We need to bring this up at the next board meeting."

David nodded. He was anxious for her to leave so that he could sort out his feelings. He was surprised at himself for caring so much. Most of the time that he had known Mary Lou she had been the bane of his existence. He determined to put aside his feelings, pray for her, and wish her all the good God had in mind for her. The reason she had given for leaving made perfect sense. It was in keeping with her conversion to step out and trust God instead of her wealthy father to care for her.

Sunday morning Mary Lou rose early and, after prayers, went to the barn to say goodbye to her horse.

The dogs came to join her out of the warmth of their hole under the front porch. She knelt to pat and hug each of them, her dear companions during her nightly wanderings when she had been so sick. She would miss them so much as they always accompanied her when she rode across the prairie.

Surprisingly, Barney, her horse, came to the fence in response to her whistle. Usually, he played hard to get and had to be chased down when she wanted to ride him. *Maybe he knows that I'm leaving,* she thought. *How precious these animals are. Their love is so unconditional and how in tune they are to one's pain.*

She spent as much time as possible there beside the fence stroking her horse's neck and surveying the prairie and the hills beyond. Soon the snow would be melting, and the prairie would be green again, silvery green, the tough old sod. She noticed the white-faced cattle down the hill at the water tank, bunched together to keep warm.

I really don't want to leave here, she thought sadly. *I have found peace for the first time in my life. But I know I must go.* She turned and walked resolutely toward the house.

Since she had to be at work the following morning, the car was packed and ready to leave right after church. When they arrived at the church, to their surprise they found that everyone knew that she was leaving.

Leave it to Rosalie, thought Alice.

Rosalie announced that there would be a reception for Mary Lou in the parsonage immediately following the service.

When David gave the sermon, Mary Lou had a hard time concentrating on his words. She couldn't believe that she had made a decision that would take her away from him every Sunday. He waited until the end of his sermon to announce what everyone already knew, that Mary Lou was moving to town. "We will miss Mary Lou," he said. "She has played such a big part in the life of this church in the time she has been here. We will never forget her beautiful voice, which has enhanced our worship. I have seen so much growth in her, her eagerness to learn God's Word. Mary Lou is truly a Godly woman, and I am sure she will bring those qualities to the workplace and wherever she chooses to worship.

"Mary Lou," he addressed her, "could you come and kneel at the altar? I would like for the congregation to come and lay hands on you as we pray for all of God's blessing on you and your new endeavor."

Mary Lou knelt at the altar and the congregation gathered around laying hands on her as David prayed. For the first time she felt the presence of God in her and around her. She could not explain it, but she suddenly felt loved and forgiven, truly forgiven. *God loves me.* She smiled to herself. And suddenly she was unaware of those around her. It was just her and the God of the universe. "I believe," she whispered to herself, "and I don't want to leave this place and this moment."

When she arose from the altar she had the feeling that surely everyone must have noticed that just for a moment she had been somewhere else. But of course, they hadn't. Although, some did notice that she had a glow about her. One who did notice was David. Later at the reception when he had a moment alone with her, he mentioned it.

"I had a feeling that something special happened to you when people were praying for you?"

She smiled and nodded.

"I have to tell you," said David, "I have seen that look before. I have seen it on the faces of dying soldiers as they passed over from this life to the next. It may never happen to you again, but don't lose the memory of it."

It was a lovely reception. Mary Lou basked in the love and good wishes of these good people. Everyone gave her a card or a little gift even though this had been an impromptu occasion. Rosalie had raided her daughter's "hope chest" for a beautifully embroidered set of tea towels for Mary Lou's new home.

Aaron was anxious to get to town and get Mary Lou settled and get home before dark, and so they left while people were still lingering at the church.

"I'll probably call on you soon," David told her.

Others also promised to visit and begged her to "get home as often as you can." Mary Lou prided herself on never crying. However, she had tears in her eyes as they drove away.

Since Alice had never seen Mary Lou's new abode, she was shocked at how plain and uninviting it looked. "This looks like a barn," she said with her usual bluntness. Nevertheless, she had brought bed clothes, towels, soap, and everything she could think of that Mary Lou might need, including food for the refrigerator, which was barely large enough to hold it.

Aaron gave her money to have a phone installed in case she needed anything. He reminded her that there was a phone at the parsonage and that David could always get ahold of them in case of emergency.

She hugged each of them in a special way she never had before, and they realized it, the change in her feelings for them and theirs for her.

Jake had missed church and stayed home. He rarely went to town unless he absolutely had to. Mary Lou used to wonder if maybe he was wanted for something somewhere. Alice too refused to stay in town with her daughter. "I want to go home," she told Aaron. "Spring is coming, my favorite time of the year in the country."

And so Mary Lou was left alone. She had mixed feelings about it. Part of her liked feeling independent and part of her felt the emptiness of the place.

"I know now that I am never alone," she reassured herself.

10
CHAPTER

Mary Lou was up early Monday morning as she was afraid of being late to her new job. She took time for prayers and Bible reading asking God to help her do a good job. Even though the town was small, everyone drove a car even small distances. This was in the day before it was fashionable to walk for health's sake. Mary Lou, however, had to walk the eight blocks to the hotel.

When she arrived at eight thirty, half an hour before her starting time, the restaurant was open for business. The bar was dosed until ten. Since she had no idea where the office was, she stood awkwardly in the door of the restaurant until one of the waitresses approached her. "Can I help you?" she asked.

"I'm supposed to see Mr. Hershy," she replied.

"Oh sure, I'll get him." She went to the kitchen and came out with John Hershy, Mary Lou's new boss.

"Good morning, Mary Lou," he said kindly, noticing that she looked nervous and unsure of herself.

He was a busy man without time for the usual amenities and so he asked her to follow him and he took her to one of the hotel rooms where he proceeded to show her how the bed was supposed to be made, how the bathtub and sink were to be immaculate, how many towels, how many rolls of toilet paper, everything that made up an inviting room, one that would attract people looking for a place to stay.

He explained that some guests were regulars who knew that his hotel was a decent place to stay.

As he had said before, the maids he had now knew their job well, but they came and they went and some he had hired were lazy and tried to get out of changing the sheets and scrubbing toilets and everything else. Her job was to inspect and report to him. She was not to fire or reprimand but to let him know about these things. What with all his other responsibilities he did not have time to inspect toilet paper.

She was also to be in charge of supplies to make sure they did not run out. He showed her the supply cabinets with a list of what was to be there at all times.

"Okay," he said, "now that we've gone over all that, are there any questions?"

Mary Lou shook her head. It didn't seem too hard. There were only twenty rooms not always fully occupied.

"Okay," he said again, "Martha, the night operator, has stayed over to teach you the switchboard."

Martha seemed nice enough and was very helpful in showing her how to take incoming and outgoing calls. Again, she didn't feel that it was too complicated. After all, she had had some experience years before which she preferred not to bring up. Mary Lou was amused at how Martha treated the job as if it were a matter of national security and that there was not, nor had there ever been, a job as important as the switchboard at the Brand Hotel.

Later, Mary Lou got to know the current maids at the hotel. There was Lupe who had been there the longest. Since she had six kids and an alcoholic husband, this job was extremely important to her. There was Janet, tall and gangly, missing her front teeth. Mary Lou could not guess her age. She observed that she was probably not as old as she looked and had probably led a hard life. There was Jody who also had a large family and who was supplementing her husband's meager income. The other two were young and unmarried and filling in the time until they could find a husband or at least a better job.

Some of them made extra money by helping out in the restaurant and bar for special occasions like weddings or meetings.

Mary Lou enjoyed the camaraderie of the people she worked with. She was surprised, however, to find herself uncomfortable with their conversation in the break room. They thought nothing of sharing their most intimate moments with their husbands or their lovers. It seemed that some of them thought nothing of being unfaithful themselves or the fact that their spouse was unfaithful. They recounted every detail of their husband's drunken brawls. They recounted beatings and all manner of mayhem with the police being called, seemingly constantly. Mary Lou wondered how they could live that way, but then she remembered, *Yes, you can live that way.*

She was more than surprised to find that Mr. Hershy's wife was not really his wife. It seemed that his real wife was in an insane asylum and that he would never be able to divorce her as long as she lived. She told herself that there was no reason for her to judge. As the Bible says, "Such were some of you." *And probably worse too,* she thought.

Even though the work was not hard, by the time she finished and walked home she was tired. After fixing herself something to eat and cleaning up, she was glad to drop into bed.

11
CHAPTER

The weekends were hard, especially Sundays. The first Sunday she thought she would die of boredom and homesickness. She longed to find a church, but even though there were churches on nearly every corner, she was cautious. She knew she had had a bad reputation, and even though her affair with a married man had happened a long time ago she also knew that people in small towns had long memories and they loved to gossip. She was trying to make a fresh start, and she felt it was a good idea to be as inconspicuous as possible.

One evening as she was walking home from work, she passed a small church near her home that she had not noticed before. They were playing and singing gospel music loud enough to raise the roof. She walked past but, on impulse, turned and went back. She made a decision to go in and seated herself in one of the back pews. She observed about twenty-five people singing and praising God. She closed her eyes, silently enjoying the praises of the people, lifting her own heart in praise. She felt tears welling up in her eyes in gratitude. *Oh, how I need this worship*, she thought.

When the service was over, the pastor and his wife greeted and welcomed her. His name was Alfredo and her name was Barbara. He was third-generation Mexican and spoke Spanish as well as English. Barbara was not Mexican, but she also spoke Spanish. Both had been born and raised in the town. They had known each other since Kindergarten, both having attended this same church. They had been "bus children," children who are picked up by the church bus every Sunday morning. Children whose parents seldom if ever attend church but are perfectly willing to see their children go off to church every Sunday morning. Most children eventually drop out, finding other things to do with their time. However, Alfredo and Barbara stayed involved during their teenage years into adulthood. Eventually, they were drawn to one another through their common love of the Lord and their wish to serve him.

Alfredo was dark, stocky, and muscular from working in construction in order to supplement their income. Barbara also had to work. She was a substitute teacher in the public school. Since the congregation was small and, for the most part, poor, their pastors were what was known as "bi-vocational." Barbara was tall with reddish brown hair. She wore glasses and would have been considered plain were it not for her sparkling blue eyes and infectious smile.

The congregation consisted of some elderly people who had been born and raised in the church as well as other Spanish-speaking people; some of whom were migrants and quite a few migrant children who were picked up by the bus. Their parents sometimes worked on Sundays, and it was a place for them to go which was safe as well as a place to hear the Word of God.

Mary Lou was invited to join them. They had church on Sundays as well as a prayer and praise service on Wednesday evenings. Mary Lou was thrilled. She just knew she had found what she had been longing for. She felt as if she had known Alfredo and Barbara forever. They were so friendly and full of joy.

Saturday morning Mary Lou sat on her couch wondering what she could possibly do with the long day stretching out before her when she heard a knock at her door. She was startled. *Who could that possibly be?* she wondered.

When she opened the door, she was really startled. There, smiling at her, was David. She almost forgot to ask him to come in, she was so surprised.

"Don't worry," he grinned, "I introduced myself to your landlady and explained that I was your pastor. She gave me permission to visit you."

"Oh, come on in," she exclaimed, feeling as if she were going to faint.

He declined her offer of the one easy chair and the couch. "I need something I can get out of easily," he explained. He also did not want coffee, water, or tea. "I just had breakfast…or maybe it was lunch." He smiled.

As Mary Lou sat opposite him, she had to resist the urge to just sit and drink in the sight of him. "What brings you to town?" she asked.

"Oh, I come here often," he said.

"Really, what do you do here?"

"Well, I go to the nursing home to visit people I know who used to attend church and then I visit some I don't know. Same thing at the hospital. Some people like to be prayed for, and if they don't have a regular pastor, I'm available. If there's anyone in jail, I visit them. Today there were two."

Mary Lou was impressed. There was so much about David's life that she was unaware of. "What were they in jail for?" she asked out of curiosity.

"Mostly public drunkenness, disturbing the peace, those things. By the way," he added, "for some reason those people are happier to see me than anyone else."

"Well, I suppose when you're desperate is when you're most anxious to hear about God," Mary Lou surmised.

"What about you, Mary Lou?" he asked. "Are you happy here?" He looked around. "My," he said, "we could have church here."

Mary Lou laughed. "I was thinking dancing. Yeah, I'm happy enough. I like the people I work with…and I have found a church."

"Really, where?" He had a strange feeling of regret. He would not admit to himself that he was hoping she would be unhappy here and return home.

Mary Lou told him about the church and the fact that it was small, which she liked. It reminded her of his church, she added.

Without saying anything further, he said that he must be going and with some effort stood. Somehow, he didn't want to discuss further her new life and her new church.

When Mary Lou stood to see him out, he turned to her and asked if they could pray together. He held out his hand and took hold of hers. She felt her hands tremble involuntarily. She bowed her head and did her best to concentrate on his words all the while realizing that she loved him even more than she had previously been aware of. *This is such a dilemma,* she thought to herself. *Where do I go with these feelings?* No matter how much she prayed, God did not seem to have an answer for her.

Everything else in Mary Lou's life seemed to be going well. Her employer, Mr. Hershy, seemed pleased with her work. He asked if she would mind training to be a cashier in the restaurant. "If I can ever get a crew together that I can trust, I can take more time off. As it is, I'm tied down here every day of the week." He appreciated the fact that she was always on time and never missed work. He reflected that he hadn't thought much of her when she came in with her father. In fact, if it hadn't been for her dad, he wouldn't have hired her at all.

Another thing that pleased Mary Lou was that her grandmother had decided to move back to town to live with her Aunt Norma. She had really preferred to stay on the ranch, but Aaron had insisted that she was better off in town where she could be close to her doctor.

Alice hadn't said anything, but she had had a couple of spells where she had found it hard to breathe. She realized that if anything happened to her, her son would never forgive himself.

As for Mary Lou, it was great to be able to walk over to her aunt's house from work and have lunch with her grandma and aunt. She loved to listen to Alice complain about the dirty air and the roar of the trucks which kept her awake at night. "Besides," she complained, "there's nothing to do here. I'm just sittin' here ready to die."

"Now, Mama," said Norma, "you know that isn't true. There's plenty to do here, especially work." Norma smiled indulgently at her. "Anyway, as long as you're complaining, I know you're alive and well."

One thing that really displeased Alice was that Mary Lou did not attend church with them. She called Mary Lou's church that "holy roly church."

However, Mary Lou loved the informal atmosphere in her church as opposed to the more formal worship service with a choir and litany and large attendance.

One Sunday after church, Barbara stopped Mary Lou and asked her if she would think about teaching children's Sunday school.

"I don't speak Spanish," Mary Lou offered weakly.

"Well, they all speak English, they go to school here, and they're not all migrants either," countered Barbara.

"What would I teach them? I'm not all that familiar with the Bible yet myself."

"We have materials. All you have to do is read it. Besides, the main thing is to show them love. Let them see Jesus in you." Mary Lou looked dubious. "I see Jesus in you, Mary Lou."

"You do?"

"Yes, I do." She paused. "Maybe you could try it, and if it doesn't work out, you're certainly not obligated. Mary Lou, you'll never grow in your faith until you start giving out what you're taking in."

Mary Lou nodded. "Okay, I'll try it, but not having been around kids much or hardly at all, I wonder if this is a good place to start giving."

"You'll be fine." Barbara laughed. "Be sure to pray about it."

And it was fine. Mary Lou had no trouble loving the kids. Most of them were poorly dressed, and some were not too clean, which wasn't surprising due to the conditions under which they had to live. But they were eager to learn the lessons that Mary Lou had pored over and over again. She realized that this was about the only thing she had ever done for anyone other than herself. Of course, she had sung a few solos in church, but that had not taken too much effort.

The next time David visited he was thrilled to hear about Mary Lou's teaching Sunday school and especially her enthusiasm as she talked about the children. He invited her to lunch, and she suggested they go to the restaurant where she worked. They laughed and talked long after they had eaten their food. Mary Lou was wishing the day would never end. But of course it did, and she was left with a yearning in her heart more than ever. Maybe it would be better if he never came, she thought, but then she couldn't bear the thought of that either.

Life went on in a way she once would have considered boring but which she now relished. Her routine of work, church, and visits with family gave her a peace unknown in her entire life.

12
CHAPTER

At the Santa Fe railroad station, it was time for the afternoon train to arrive. The stationmaster left the coolness of the depot and went out into the hot afternoon sun to watch it arrive in case someone might need help unloading luggage.

This day only one person got off the train. The stationmaster eyed him curiously. Even though it was hot as blazes, the man wore a wrinkled, ill-fitting suit as well as a hat pulled down over his ears, which looked as if they had both been slept in for days. He had only a small bag for luggage, not large enough for a change of clothes even. He went right into the station followed by the stationmaster.

"Can I help you?" asked the stationmaster.

"Do you have a phone book?" the man asked.

"Well, yeah, I do. Who're you lookin' for?

The man really looked at him for the first time. "Could I see it please? he asked firmly.

"Oh sure, here it is." He pulled out a dog-eared phone book.

"Thanks." He turned the pages until he found who he was looking for.

"Can I help you find an address?" His curiosity was about to get the best of him.

"No," the man said curtly and left.

Mary Lou was relaxing in her apartment on her day off. She had finished her few chores when someone knocked at her door. She could not imagine who it would be unless it might be her landlady.

When she opened the door, she came close to fainting. It was if someone had come back from the dead in order to haunt her.

"Larry," she gasped, and finally when she had recovered enough to speak, "what are you doing here?"

"Can I come in, Mary Lou? It's hot as hell out here."

"Oh, of course, come in." Her mind was racing along with her jumbled thoughts. What about her landlady? She was not supposed to have male company. What could he possibly want and what was wrong with him? He looked terrible; she hardly recognized him as the man she had once known and loved.

He plopped down in a chair, breathing heavily. He took off his suit jacket and his hat and threw them on the floor beside the chair. "It's so damn hot here. I nearly died walking over here." He gasped. "Do you have anything to drink?" He acted as if he had just seen her yesterday.

Mary Lou rushed to the refrigerator for cold water. "How in the world did you find me?" she cried.

"Well, I looked in the phone book, and of course I knew where your hometown was."

"Why did you come here?" she wanted to know.

While she was waiting for an answer, Larry was taking time to get himself together. He pulled a handkerchief from his pocket and began to cough into it, deep hacking coughs which seemed never ending.

"What is wrong with you?" Mary Lou asked, alarmed.

"I'm dying. I'm a dead man," he said, gasping for air.

"What do you mean, why aren't you at home under a doctor's care?" This seemed surreal to her, like a bad dream.

"I came to make amends," he said when he finally caught his breath and looked at her.

"Amends, what are you talking about!"

"Mary Lou, it's true, the doctor says I don't have much time left. After you left, I proceeded to drink myself to death. My liver is shot, my stomach...is...pickled, I have emphysema. God knows what else." He paused, a shadow of sadness crossing his face. "Anyway," he continued, "I thought about you and the shabby way I treated you. I could have written a letter, I suppose, but I wasn't sure you'd get it. But then," he paused and breathed deeply, which caused him to start coughing again after which he said, "the truth is, I just wanted to see you one more time. I do love you, at least as capable as I am of loving anyone. I wished I could have been the man you deserved."

Mary Lou was silent, staring at him, not knowing what to say. This was all so unexpected, so strange.

Finally, she said to him, "You don't owe me an amends. I walked into everything with my eyes wide open. In fact, we both owe an amends to the people we hurt."

"Well, that's one thing you need to know," he said. "Remember when you would mention marriage and I would tell you that my wife wouldn't give me a divorce?"

She nodded.

"Well, the truth was, she had divorced me long before you left. In fact, she was already married to someone else."

Mary Lou was shocked. "Why would you lie to me like that? What was your reason?"

"In my fucked-up mind I thought I needed you, but I didn't want to marry you," he said matter-of-factly.

Mary Lou looked long and hard at him, really seeing him for the first time. Finally, she spoke, "Why are you here, really?

"Well," he said, "I'm on my way to Nebraska to see the attorneys about my trust, make sure it's all in order when the time comes. But," he implored now with his eyes, "please believe me when I say that I want and need your forgiveness. Please, Mary Lou, it's important to me."

Mary Lou shook her head. "Well, you have it. Forgiveness, I mean. What I mean is, I still don't feel there's anything to forgive. I was just as screwed up as you were, maybe more.

The conversation was interrupted by another fit of coughing, which again was alarming.

As soon as he could compose himself, he finally took time to look around at her surroundings. *This is a depressing place,* he thought. But as he gazed at Mary Lou, he saw that there was something different about her. She looked healthy and there seemed to be an inner glow about her, a sense of peace.

When she left him, she had looked old and beaten down, as if all life had been drained from her.

"Are you working?" he asked.

"Yes, I am," she said. "I'm the housekeeping supervisor at the hotel here in town."

He looked amused. "I can't imagine you having anything to do with housekeeping."

"Well," she said defensively, "I'm the supervisor. Besides, work is work. I'm lucky to have a job since I never trained for anything."

"What about your singing?" he asked.

"There are no jobs for singers in this town." She paused. "I only sing in church."

"You go to church now?" He was surprised.

She nodded. Meantime she was thinking that she didn't remember that Larry ever worked. She knew that he came from a wealthy family somewhere in Nebraska. She also knew that he had a trust fund from some family member who died and left him a good deal of money which was doled out to him giving him enough to live on. When she first knew him, he was involved at different times with different people in schemes to make a lot of money. These all came to nothing, awash in a sea of booze. Of course, at the time she had agreed with everything he said as to why these things never worked out—the person was undoubtedly a crook, misrepresented himself, not someone he wished to be involved with over time, on and on again as he poured himself another one and another.

Suddenly, the coughing started again; this time deeper and even more violent.

She sat there helplessly not knowing what she should do, if anything, when suddenly he threw his head back against the sofa and passed out, a trickle of blood running down the corner of his mouth.

"Oh god, oh god!" She gasped. She ran to him and shook him, calling his name over and over to no avail. She ran and got a towel, wetting it and pressing it to his forehead. Nothing was working; he wasn't responding.

In the middle of this she heard a knock at the door. She had mixed feelings of relief and fear of who it might be, feelings she realized were wrong. She needed help and quickly.

She opened the door and saw David standing there with a smile on his face until he saw the panic and fear in her eyes.

"What's wrong?" he asked anxiously.

Mary Lou nodded toward the sofa.

David didn't ask any questions. He went immediately to Larry and picked up his wrist. He shook his head. "This man is in bad shape. We need to get help immediately." He went to the phone and called the hospital. Since there was no regular ambulance service in town, the hospital took care of transporting people when needed.

David turned and looked at Mary Lou. "They're on their way," he said.

"It's Larry," said Mary Lou dispassionately, feeling she owed David some explanation. "He's dying. He said he came to ask for forgiveness and make amends."

David searched her face wondering what her feelings were. Her face was blank, unreadable. He knew she had once tried to kill herself because of her love for this man. Would this crush her spirit? he wondered. Would her newfound faith in God sustain her?

In no time two men from the hospital came with a stretcher, putting Larry on it and hurrying out the door. They could see that there was no time to waste. David assured them that they would be right behind them.

"Mary Lou, come on, I'll drive you to the hospital," David offered hurriedly.

Actually, Mary Lou didn't want to go. "What could I do there, what help could I be?" as she tried to find an excuse not to go.

"Come on," David urged impatiently. "You're the only one that can give them his name and any other particulars they may need."

He picked up Larry's coat, searching through the pockets. "Fortunately, here's his wallet. Hopefully, it has his address or something," he said, handing it to Mary Lou.

Mary Lou never said a word on the way to the hospital. She couldn't believe this was happening. She knew she no longer had any feelings for Larry, although she certainly didn't want him to die. She wondered if she was supposed to be responsible for him even though they had never been man and wife.

Nevertheless, she dutifully answered all the questions the sister in-charge asked as well as she could.

She found a driver's license in his wallet, which helped. As far as next of kin to be notified, she had no idea. She realized that she had lived with a man for a long time without knowing even his mother's last name or his father's. She vaguely remembered that his parents had divorced and remarried. She had no idea whether he had brothers or sisters, let alone their names. *What if he dies?* she thought with a sinking feeling. *Who would I notify?*

She and Larry had lived in a cocoon with their passion for one another and his for booze with little thought for the outside world, including his wife and child.

I am no longer that person, she reminded herself, *that person was insane. I have been restored, I have received a miracle!* Suddenly, she found herself wishing that Larry also could find that same miracle.

If only it's not too late. Lord, she prayed, *give me a chance to tell him about the miracle. It's a gift I could give him if he's willing to receive it. If he lives, then I know you want me to tell him. It's in your hands.*

All of this went through her mind as she was sitting at the desk attempting to answer questions. She felt as if the sister was looking at her with a good deal of suspicion since the only information she had was what she had gotten off Larry's driver's license. *Maybe she thinks I'm a hooker or something,* thought Mary Lou.

Soon, she saw David coming toward her. He had been talking to the doctor.

She smiled at him, which surprised him. She had seemed so cold before.

"The doctor says they will be taking tests to determine how to treat him. He also said it doesn't look good," he said solemnly.

"I think he'll make it," she said.

He looked at her strangely, wondering what had happened to her to make her so confident.

"Mary Lou, I have to go," he said hurriedly. "I have someone I must see. I'm already late. I'll take you home."

"I think I'll stay a while," she said. "I can walk home, I'm used to it."

"Mary Lou, if you need me, you can call me. I'll be here as soon as I can. In fact, call me and let me know how Larry's doing. I'll be praying for him and for you," he promised.

After he left, Mary Lou went into the small chapel to pray. She realized that she was now glad that Larry had come. There was unfinished business between them, and now she had forgiven him, and she hoped there would be a chance for her to ask his forgiveness and make amends to him. This would be a cleansing of both their conscience.

Finally, she left her phone number at the desk in case of any change in Larry's condition and walked home. That night she slept well.

When Larry woke up, he was surprised to find himself in the hospital. It took him a while to get his bearings and remember what he was doing there.

Why did I get off in this God-forsaken place in the first place? he wondered. *I have important business to attend to and I need to make sure I get there on time.* There, meaning Nebraska, where he'd been born and raised.

It had been many years since he'd left there and headed for California to make his fortune. The reason he'd never been back was that he had never sobered up long enough to make the trip. *It was the curse,* he thought. *The alcohol, his father had died from it as well as his uncles and several of his cousins.* They had all inherited money, lots of it from the great-grandparents and grandparents. Money from wheat, cattle, speculation; everything they touched seemed to turn to gold. He had managed to run through his share of it with nothing to show for it.

He still had his trust fund from which he received what he considered a paltry sum each month but which kept him off the streets, the rest going for liquor.

He had. to sign papers to make sure that in the event of his death, the money went to his son. Also, he wanted to see his mother whom he hadn't seen for at least twenty years or more. She had remarried after divorcing his father. She had married into a family with even more money and prominence.

He had managed to "borrow" thousands of dollars which, of course, he had never repaid. Finally, she had stopped sending money and he had stopped contacting her after the money dried up. He didn't know if saying he was sorry was enough, but he felt he should try. The doctors hadn't given him any outs. "Get your affairs in order," they said.

As for Mary Lou, was he really here to make amends or did he just want to see her one more time?

He had met her, where else, in a bar. It was a fairly high-class place, more so than the places he usually hung out. She was singing, he couldn't remember what. But he remembered thinking how incredibly beautiful her voice was. They were immediately attracted to one another, both with a neediness that neither could satisfy. Nothing could keep them apart, not his marriage, which he never worried about anyway; it was there and always would be, not his child and his half-hearted attempt to be a father.

Mary Lou was just divorcing her second husband who, she told him, had turned out to be a bum and a two-timer whom she had never loved in the first place. At the time, they were fighting over who was going to pay for the divorce, neither of them having any assets to worry about dividing.

These were loose ends which had nothing to do with their passion for one another which was immediate and all-consuming.

Deep inside, perhaps he had never admitted it even to himself he had considered Mary Lou somewhat beneath him. After all, he had been raised in the city in a prominent well-known family, maybe not always known for the right reasons. His father, for instance, had had an affair with a floozy who was also married, which in those days was big news. The ups and downs of the love triangle was recorded in the newspaper for all to read with their morning coffee.

Mary Lou, on the other hand, was raised on a farm in the middle of nowhere. In other words, a hick. She too had looked up to him "as a man of the world," which he took as his due. However, alcohol had taken him down and her with him. Since he was going right through her hometown, he couldn't resist the urge to see her one more time. He had stopped, and here he was in the hospital, which he planned to leave as soon as possible even if it took his last ounce of strength. As for Mary Lou, he could forget any guilt he had felt about her. Even though she was living poorly, she seemed happy and not at all happy to see him for which he was a little disappointed even though he knew he shouldn't be.

When Mary Lou woke up, she began to have second thoughts about talking to Larry about God and his eternal destination. He had always seemed so sophisticated and worldly. How would he react to her attempts to talk about spiritual matters? Part of her wanted to forget it, maybe not even go to the hospital. Perhaps he had left, or maybe he was already dead. She knew these thoughts were wrong, and she knew what she had to do. In the church they talked about *witnessing*. She had never witnessed to anyone, and no one had ever witnessed to her. Being in the church most of her life maybe they thought she would just receive everything through osmosis.

As soon as she finished work, she headed for the hospital trying not to wish that he would be gone or asleep or in a coma. She hated herself for these ungodly thoughts, but they were there, and she couldn't deny them. As soon as she arrived, she propelled herself directly to his room. His eyes were closed, and he was breathing heavily. She observed him for a few minutes before saying his name. She determined that if he didn't wake up, she would leave. But he must have heard her, for he turned his head to toward her and smiled.

"Mary Lou, I was hoping you'd come."

"How are you feeling?" asked Mary Lou. "You look better," she lied.

"Well, I'm the same. I refused to let them take any tests; I've already seen the best doctors, I know what my prognosis is. I'm sure these people have nothing new to tell me," he said bitterly.

Mary Lou took a deep breath. "Larry, I have something to say to you," making her voice as serious as possible. "I'm asking you to please hear me out."

"Well sure, what is it?" he asked.

"You tell me you're dying. I'm wondering how much thought you've given to God and the hereafter?" She hurried on. "Remember when you went to AA and they talked about God as you understand him? I was wondering, how do you understand God? Who is your God?"

Larry stared at her. "I never gave it much thought. Hmm, maybe that's the reason I never stayed sober," he said ruefully.

Suddenly, he was the old Larry with the amused look on his face. "I'm curious, Mary Lou, when did you turn preacher?"

"Are you mocking me?" cried Mary Lou, becoming angry in spite of herself.

"Actually no," he assured her. "I knew there was something different about you the minute I saw you. I'm glad you've found something for yourself. As for me, I've lived every minute of my life for myself without much thought of anyone else. It doesn't seem right to go whining to God at the last minute."

"That's where you're wrong," said Mary Lou excitedly. She told him the story of the thief on the cross who had asked Jesus to remember him when he came into his kingdom and Jesus said, "Today you will be with me in Paradise." "Don't you see, this man had only moments to live, and yet when he believed that Jesus was who he said he was he was saved for all eternity. That's all you have to do…believe!"

"Well," he said skeptically, "that's easier said than done. I'm sure there's more to it than that."

"Of course, the man surrendered his life to Jesus when he believed."

Larry still looked skeptical. She began to feel as if she were treading water upstream.

"I didn't have much to offer God either," she continued, "but what little I did have, I surrendered it all, and I have found the blessed gift of peace and much, much more."

Again, he looked long and hard at her. "I'd gladly accept hell if I could just hold you in my arms again."

"Larry, that's blasphemy," she cried. "You should be thinking about your eternal life."

"I always thought our love was beautiful and pure, certainly nothing to be ashamed of," he said nostalgically.

"What planet were you living on?" she cried unbelievingly. "We were living in adultery, we aborted our baby. These are terrible sins worthy of hell. We can never be forgiven except through Jesus's death on the cross. We cannot pay for our own sins!"

She realized she was becoming defensive and angry, which in her mind was not the way to lead someone to Christ.

About that time the nurse stuck her head in the door to announce that visiting hours were over.

"Larry, I'm leaving," she said reluctantly. "I'll be back tomorrow if you want me to." She managed to smile at him.

"Mary Lou," he said, "I'm going to think about what you said. By the way, your preacher friend came by today. Is there something going on between you two?"

"Absolutely not!" she snapped. "Why in the world would you say that?"

"Well," he said, "he was visiting you when he found me."

"Larry, he visits a lot of people. He was my pastor when I lived in the country. I seldom see him anymore. You're just lucky he passed by. I was in such a panic I didn't know what to do."

"I love you, Mary Lou," he said.

"I love you with the love of Christ," she said decisively.

As Mary Lou walked home, her heart felt heavy. "Well, so much for my plan. Maybe God has other plans." She knew she had to see Larry again. Somehow, she had to convince him. She thought about how he had looked lying there with his eyes closed as if he were already dead.

The next evening, she hurried to his room with all the persuasive things in her mind to say to him, when to her surprise, he wasn't there!

Oh no, maybe he died, and they took him away! She rushed to the nurses' station and asked with fear in her voice what had happened to him.

"He left," the sister said.

"What do you mean, he left? He's dying!" cried Mary Lou.

"I know that he's a very ill man, but he got out of bed, put on his clothes, and left."

"Couldn't you stop him?" She was nearly hysterical.

"No, we couldn't," she said firmly. "He's a grown man, and he had a right to check himself out if he wished. He paid his bill in full and left."

Oh no, oh god, Mary Lou cried to herself. *He left because of me. . . I was unkind to him. I sounded so self-righteous. I know I did! Now it's too late to say I'm sorry. I should have asked someone else to speak to him, someone who knows what they're talking about. Now it's too late.*

That evening David called to ask about Larry.

"He left," she said. "He just got up and left! I feel so bad, I tried to talk to him about the Lord before it was too late. I ended up getting angry and defensive. I never mentioned love or forgiveness. I went back today to apologize and try again, but he was gone. I feel so guilty."

"What did he say?" asked David.

"He said he'd think about it."

"Well if he said he'd think about it I'm sure he will" said David. After all, if he left the hospital under his own steam, he's still alive. Even though he's a very sick man, only God knows how much time he actually has left. Besides that, I spoke to him about the Lord when I visited him, and he didn't seem too unreceptive."

"Well, that makes me feel better," she said. "I'm glad to know that. I can't thank you enough, David, for all your help during this whole ordeal."

Meanwhile, David was struggling with his own unworthy feelings of relief that Larry had left. He told himself that he just didn't want Mary Lou to get hurt again by this man. He needed to pray for both of them, he told himself.

For weeks Mary Lou could not get Larry out of her mind no matter how much she struggled to put the whole ordeal behind her. She went over and over the things she had said to him. Guilt began to consume her. How could she have said those things to a dying man? She began to dream of Larry dying alone, crying out for help. One recurring dream she had, where she swore she was awake, she heard someone knocking at the door. When she opened it there was Larry. His face looked like the pictures she had seen of death masks. He stared at her with eyes of burning coals. She screamed and screamed for help, but no one came. Her tossing and flailing finally awoke her.

Realizing it was a dream but so real that her heart was pounding in her chest, she realized that she needed to talk to someone. She couldn't go on like this.

She thought of Barbara, her pastor's wife. She taught the women's Bible study that she attended. She was a very devout woman but also, in her opinion, very practical and down to earth.

The first chance she got, she stopped by the parsonage and asked Barbara if she could speak to her.

"Of course," said Barbara. "What's on your mind?" She ushered Mary Lou into the kitchen, seated her at the kitchen table, offering her a cup of coffee. She sat opposite her and waited for her to speak.

As bad as she hated to bring up her past, she knew she had to if she wanted Barbara's advice. So she started at the beginning, telling her about Larry and her relationship to him and his unexpected visit.

She went into detail about her visit to the hospital, what she had said to him, and what he had said to her. After which, to her consternation, she began to cry.

"I flung his sins at him," she sobbed, "I was angry, he was dying, and I never said a word about love or forgiveness, and now I have so much guilt and I can't tell him how sorry I am." She tried to stop crying, sniffing and wiping her eyes with her sleeve.

Barbara found a Kleenex and handed it to her. "Mary Lou, get ahold of yourself," she said sternly. "Look at me!" She took Mary Lou's face in her hands. "Listen to me! Mary Lou, this man is standing on the precipice of hell. He deserved to hear the truth, and you told him the truth! He was trying to romanticize sin. Hell is paved with the philosophy of 'you're okay, I'm okay, we're okay.' No one is okay without God no matter how good they look on the outside. He said he'd think about it, and I'm sure he will. What he does with it is up to him and God. Besides, you gave your testimony, that's all we can do."

Mary Lou wiped her eyes and sat there taking in what Barbara had said. She knew Barbara and she knew how blunt and honest she was. If she had felt Mary Lou had made a mistake, she would have said so.

"Besides," Barbara said, "if God had wanted you to say anything else, it seems he would have given you the opportunity. Come on now." She smiled. "Put this behind you and get on with your life. How do we know but what God planned this whole thing. Maybe he knew you and Larry had unfinished business. Forgiveness was offered by both of you and accepted. You should have a clear conscience. Yes," she said with wonderment, "I can see God's hand in this!"

Could that be true? Mary Lou wondered. Maybe she and Larry did have unfinished business. He had said that he came to make amends, and he had and she had offered forgiveness. At once she felt a deep sense of peace in her soul. Only God was responsible for Larry's eternal soul! What a blessing!

13
CHAPTER

And so, Mary Lou's life gradually returned to normal. Somehow, she had managed on her meager salary to save enough money to buy a used car. This meant that she and her grandmother could spend some Sundays in the country visiting her dad and of course attending church with family and friends. Seeing David and listening to him preach was almost more than she could take though. It seemed as if every day she loved him more and of course she had no way of expressing those feelings, no place to go with them. Sometimes she felt it might be better if she stayed away, but she had no excuse for that. Alice was always so excited to go.

Also, she had developed a close relationship with some of her coworkers. She talked them into letting her pick up their children for Sunday school and church, hoping that they too might decide to come.

She made a special effort with Janet. She saw in her what she herself was rapidly becoming had she not changed her life when she did.

Sure enough, Janet began to confide in her what her life had been—the drinking, the drugs, the abusive relationships. She had very little money to live on as the job didn't pay much, but she was managing to stay sober although it wasn't easy. She had managed by the skin of her teeth for more than a year. Gradually, Mary Lou was able to talk to her about the one who forgave her and loved her unconditionally. She finally agreed to attend church with Mary Lou where she found love and acceptance. Everyone who knew her began to see a change in her. Every time Janet smiled, which was seldom, because of the gaping hole where her front teeth were missing, Mary

Lou knew that it shouldn't bother her, but it did. After all, one looks at the heart, she told herself. The more she thought about it, she decided to ask Alice for the money to have Janet's teeth fixed. She inquired and found out how much it would cost and finally got up the nerve to ask for the money.

She explained Janet's situation to her grandmother, how she had had a hard life and now she was going to church. "Grandma," she said, "her front teeth were knocked out and she doesn't smile and when she does it looks terrible. I so want to do something for her." She looked at Alice to see if there was any sign of sympathy. There wasn't any that she could see. *Oh well, I've nothing to lose,* she thought. "Grandma," she hurried on, "Grandma, I want to get her teeth fixed, but I have no money. I was wondering if I could borrow the money from you. I would have to pay it back in small amounts."

It seemed to take forever for Alice to answer. Finally, Alice asked, "Do you know how much it costs?"

Mary Lou gave her the amount.

"Mary Lou," her grandmother smiled at her. "I'm real proud of you for thinkin' of someone like this. I know the Lord wants this poor girl to be able to smile. I'm proud to give you the money. I have no need of it, and one day it'll be yours anyway."

Mary Lou was so overcome with gratitude she ran to Alice and knelt and threw her head in her lap. "Oh, Grandma, thank you so much. I just love you so much!"

Alice was a little taken aback by all this display of affection. She herself loved deeply but was not used to showing it so overtly.

Now that Mary Lou had the money, she wasn't sure how to approach Janet. She didn't want to embarrass her or have her feel that she owed her.

After thinking of all the stories she might make up, she decided the best way was just to be truthful. If Janet turned her down or hated her, well, so be it. So the first time she got her alone, she came right out with it. "You know, Janet, if you had your front teeth you would be so pretty. Now, I have some money and I want to give it to you to get your teeth fixed," she said hurriedly, without giving her a chance to speak. "I talked to the dentist and he told me how much it costs and he'll be glad to make you a bridge." She paused, holding her breath, waiting for a reaction.

All of a sudden, Janet's face crumpled. Her whole body began shaking with heavy sobs.

Mary Lou began to panic. *Now what have I done? My big mouth! Oh no, the poor girl!*

Finally, she lifted her head and looked at Mary Lou. "I don't know what to say." She sniffed. "No one has ever done anything like this for me, not in my whole life. You don't know how much this means to me. I've never had a friend like you. I've never known anyone like you!"

"You need to thank the Lord, Janet, not me. The old me never thought of anyone but myself. Anytime I can be used by him to help someone else, I'm glad to do it. I was afraid I might embarrass you. I'm so glad you can accept this gift thankfully."

"Oh yes!" cried Janet. "Maybe someday I can do something for someone else."

"I'm sure you will," Mary Lou assured her. "I see you growing and changing so much, it's so amazing!"

It seemed that life couldn't get much better! Once again, it was Christmas and Mary Lou took it upon herself to produce a Christmas play starring her Sunday school class. She scrounged costumes and taught them the Christmas songs. As she watched them perform the night before Christmas, she was so proud. *These are the children I never had*, she thought, adoring their shining faces, the black-eyed, brown-haired, as well as the blue-eyed blondes.

She invited Alice and Norma to the program. They were so proud of her. They still could not get over the miracle that had happened in her life.

And so, another winter passed and it was springtime again. She realized in amazement that she had been home for five years! Time had passed so quickly! Even though she was now forty, she felt young and full of life. She was hardly ever ill, and for the first time in her life, she looked forward to each day, anxious to see what the Lord had in store for her. She was always anxious to tell someone about God's love or to pray with someone. It seemed that her job always brought opportunities to testify what with the hotel and even the bar. She knew that a lot of people went to bars because they were lonely.

In the middle of this peace, Barbara dropped a bombshell. One Sunday she asked Mary Lou to stay after church, she wanted to talk to her.

"Alfredo and I are leaving," she said abruptly.

"What do you mean, you're leaving?" Mary Lou was startled.

"The church is sending us to Mexico to plant a church."

Mary Lou was shocked and dismayed. These people were like family to her.

"What about Kate, what about her school?"

"She will go to school there," Barbara said calmly. "In fact, that will be one of my duties, teaching children. We need to start a school."

She could see that this information had hit Mary Lou hard. She looked absolutely crestfallen.

"Why don't you go with us? We're going to need lots of help." Barbara had not thought of this before, but now that she had it seemed like a wonderful idea. She realized she probably shouldn't have mentioned it before checking with someone, she wasn't sure who.

"Well, in the first place, I can't leave, and besides, I don't speak the language." She paused. "I can't imagine what you would need me for."

"We're going to need all the help we can get. We not only are going there to preach and teach, we're going to physically build a church!"

"You're going to build a church, how?"

"Well, as well as being a preacher, Alfredo is in construction and with the help of the people there we're hoping to build a church."

"Oh my," said Mary Lou, "that's a huge undertaking."

"I know," said Barbara. "There was a family there, but she got sick and they had to come home. They lived in a trailer until they built a house. Hopefully, it's livable." She sighed.

"When are you leaving?" Mary Lou asked with a heavy heart.

"In about a month," answered Barbara. "We have to get supplies together. Mary Lou, think about it. I know you want to serve the Lord. Maybe this is something he has in mind for you, or maybe it's not. He'll let you know if you keep an open mind. As far as the language is concerned, you'll pick it up. You'll have to if you want to talk to anyone. I'll help you," she promised.

She looked at Mary Lou affectionately. "I guess one reason I want you to go is for my sake and Kate's. I consider you one of the best friends I ever had. I'm selfish, I guess. I know it's going to be lonely for me."

Mary Lou reached for her, and they hugged long and hard. They both had tears in their eyes when they drew apart.

Mary Lou promised she would think about it, but she knew without a doubt that this would be something she wouldn't, couldn't, do.

Mary Lou just could not wrap her mind around this, which for her was very bad news indeed. She just could not imagine what the church would be like without Alfredo and especially without Barbara and Kate. Just when life was going so well, suddenly there were changes and not for the better, she thought bitterly.

That evening in her Bible reading she happened to read about Paul and the man from Macedonia begging him to "come over to Macedonia and help us." *But,* she thought, *that was in Biblical times, nothing like that happens these days.* Then she remembered the evangelist and his words to her about her ministry to Spanish-speaking people. Did this man have a vision? She remembered that she had considered him to be a crackpot. *How does God speak to people these days?* she wondered. *Maybe he speaks through other people.*

But what about my job, my apartment, and most of all, my family? They were very devout people, but they weren't prone to running off to some foreign country with no training and not even able to speak the language.

*D*ays passed and Mary Lou tried to put this idea out of her mind. Finally, she decided to put out a fleece to see what would happen. She would start with her family. She had been invited to come home the next Sunday for a celebration of her dad's birthday.

As she drove the long drive home it seemed to go by more quickly than usual since she was nervous about telling them the news. She brought Alice and Norma, and as she drove in the yard she saw that the whole family had gathered. She was thankful it was just the family. It seemed her dad had celebrated that morning at church with all his friends.

He was pleased to see her with his mother and sister. *Life doesn't get much better than this,* he thought. *All my family together. How Good the Lord is!*

Rosalie had brought her usual spread for all to enjoy.

Mary Lou waited until everyone had retired to the living room with their coffee and cake before she took a deep breath and announced that she was glad that the family was all present as she had a matter to discuss with them.

Aaron felt his heart jump in his chest, trying not to imagine the worst. Why did his daughter always do this to him? he wondered. Nothing ever stood still for Mary Lou. Maybe it was nothing, he prayed, nothing too important.

As usual, Mary Lou was blunt and to-the-point. "Alfredo and Barbara are going to Mexico to build a church, and they want me to go with them!"

Rosalie was the first to speak. "Oh, Mary Lou, a missionary! How wonderful! Who would have ever dreamed!"

Brother John just shook his head. To him it was just another of his sister's wild ideas.

Alice, however, was not happy to hear this latest news. "This is crazy!" she said sharply. "You'll likely get sick and die down there. I hear you can't even drink the water. It's that holy roly church you're goin to! Anyway," she charged, "people are supposed to go to school to be missionaries, learn the language, and all that."

Meanwhile, Aaron sat with his mouth open. Of all the things that had run through his head, this surely was not something he ever would have imagined in his wildest dreams. He couldn't think of a thing to say.

For a time, there was dead silence. Finally, Norma asked, "How long would you be gone, Mary Lou, and when would you leave?"

Mary Lou shook her head. "First of all, they have to get permission for me to go. They will be leaving in about a month. She, Barbara, said I could come back whenever I felt like it. I won't be receiving any money, but she promised they would see that I got home. I don't think I can stay too long anyway since I have to get a visitor's pass or something like that…I forgot what she called it."

Aaron was finally able to get himself together. "I guess you're just asking our advice? I reckon you don't need our permission, you're forty years old," he said, rather sadly. "I kinda hate to see you go. Are you sure this's God's will for you? Have you prayed about it?"

"I've done nothing but pray," Mary Lou said simply. "Believe me. I'm happy with my job and my apartment. I love the church and I can't bear the thought of leaving all of you. But I can't get it out of my mind that God does want me there. I don't know what for… maybe to carry bricks." She smiled.

"Well," Alice said resignedly, "I still think it's a bad idea, but like your dad said, you're old enough to know whatever you think is good for you."

"I think it's wonderful," intoned Rosalie. "Please let us know when you're going. I'm going to talk to David about having a sending-off service for you. All missionaries have a sending-off, you know."

Mary Lou decided it was useless to tell her that she was not really a missionary and that a sending-off would be rather embarrassing.

"Please don't say anything till I give you the word that I'm really going," she begged.

They all agreed they wouldn't say anything since it was possible she might change her mind or perhaps she wouldn't get permission to go.

The three women were quiet during the ride to town. Mary Lou thought she sensed Alice's disapproval, but when she turned to let her out of the car, Alice turned and leaned in, telling her that her prayers were always with her no matter what she decided.

"Thanks, Gran, that means so much to me," she said, tearing up. *How can I leave her*? she thought. *Will she still be here when I return?* So many hard things to think about.

14
CHAPTER

Rosalie sat in her car, admiring the new addition to the church. It was not quite finished, but it would do to have her sister-in-law's send-off party there. The church had grown to nearly one hundred people since David had been there. It was no longer feasible to crowd into the parsonage each time they wanted to have a special event, and Rosalie was great on special events. If it hadn't been for her, the new addition would never have happened. She had done everything except physically build it herself. They now had a fellowship hall and two new Sunday school rooms.

She hoped she wasn't too early to see David. She knew how he suffered and how he rested as much as he could to conserve energy for the important things. They had finally hired someone to clean the parsonage and keep up the yard and the graveyard. The idea of losing David was more than anyone could bear to think about. They had taken him into their hearts. He was family.

She was happy to see him sitting on the porch of the parsonage. "You're up early," she called as she got out of her car.

"These mornings are too good to miss," he replied. "I need to take advantage before the heat starts."

"You're here early," he noted. Rosalie was one of his favorite people. He knew she aggravated some people; they felt she was too bossy. But he knew her to be one of the most devout people he'd ever known with a heart full of love for everyone she met. He'd never known her to say an unkind word about anyone. The only thing was, that if she felt there was a solution to a problem, she felt it should be taken care of without a lot of conversation.

"You're going to be so surprised when you hear what I have to tell you," she burst out.

"What is that?" He smiled. With Rosalie, everything was the most exciting thing that had ever happened.

"Well," she began, "I've been waiting to tell you until we found out for sure, and now we know. Mary Lou is going to Mexico as a missionary!"

David was dumbstruck, he didn't know what to say. He felt he should say something, but he couldn't. He just stared at her.

Rosalie felt an overwhelming desire at that moment to play matchmaker. David didn't seem very happy about the news. Maybe he had feelings for her that he wasn't aware of? She quickly put these ideas out of her mind. What if she were wrong? Besides, she had been sworn to secrecy.

"She's going with her pastor and his wife to help build a church down there. We don't know how long she'll be gone. Anyway, what I came to see you about was to ask you if we could have a sending-off service for her.

"Well," David said, "she's not being *sent* from this church. Wouldn't that be a little odd?"

"I don't know what the rules are," she said impatiently, "but she's been a part of this church since she was a baby. Looks like we could do something to send her off. It wouldn't have to be too formal. At least, we could have a reception after. I know people will be thrilled to hear about the work she is going to be doing."

"What work is she going to be doing?" asked David.

"I'm not sure. I know they plan on building a church and a school. I suppose there'll be plenty for her to do."

"Yes, I imagine so," said David, hoping he didn't sound too skeptical. "I tell you what," he continued, "I'll think up something appropriate for the service and you handle the rest, okay? By the way, does Mary Lou know about this?"

"No, not yet, I wanted to speak to you first. I'm sure she'll be tickled."

David doubted that, knowing Mary Lou, nor did he doubt that Rosalie would have her way.

David was still flabbergasted. Mary Lou never ceased to amaze him. Just when he thought he had her figured out, she decided to do something like this. At first, he was inclined to think she wouldn't stay long. The conditions there were probably pretty primitive, something she wasn't used to. But then she had surprised him when she left her dad's house, moved to town, and got a job. He'd had to revise his opinion of her as a spoiled "Daddy's girl." He did not want to admit to himself that even though he didn't see her that often, he did look forward to seeing her whenever he had a chance. He admired her honesty and he enjoyed her sense of humor.

Anyhow, since Rosalie was intent upon having a send-off ceremony, he needed to think of something appropriate to say.

Meanwhile, Mary Lou was having a hard time trying to think of something to say to her boss. It would be hard to tell him she was leaving. He had been very good to her, giving her a raise and trusting her with more and more responsibility.

Finally, she mustered up the courage to tell him about her mission to Mexico. At first, he'd thought she was talking about a short-term mission, and he said that even though it would be hard, they would find some way to manage until she returned.

To her dismay, she had to inform him that she had no idea when she would be returning except perhaps for a visit. He was visibly upset. "I finally found someone I could trust to handle things when I am not around and now you tell me you're leaving for good!" He shook his head. "This is not good!'

Mary Lou was surprised. She hadn't realized she was such a valuable employee.

"You know," she said, "someone who could take my place and do just as good a job would be Janet."

"Janet," he snorted. "Janet was the town drunk."

"Well," Mary Lou said calmly, "whatever she was, she no longer is. She attends my church faithfully, and she's taking on responsibilities there. If you took a chance on her, I'm sure she wouldn't let you down."

"I don't know," he said warily. "I'll think about it. Anyway," he sighed, "I see you've made up your mind about this Mexico thing. I guess all I can do is wish you well. From what you've told me, it seems like it is something God has laid on your heart."

Mary Lou was surprised. She had never heard Mr. Hershy mention God. She felt the urge to hug him, but he had never encouraged such familiarity, so instead she held out her hand. "I just want you to know," she said, "I've really appreciated this job and you and all the people working here. It's not easy for me to leave."

He nodded. "Thank you," he said simply.

Telling the other employees and some of the customers was almost as hard. Some of them had become like family.

The girls had a little party for her on her last day. They gave her cards and little gifts and teased her about coming home with a handsome Mexican husband. She laughed and assured them that it would never happen. They were always trying to fix her up with someone they knew. She couldn't tell them that her heart belonged to someone she could never have.

Another hard thing was giving up her apartment. This was her home where she paid the rent giving her a sense of independence she'd really never had. It seemed she'd always depended on someone else for her livelihood in some way or other. Again, her landlady was extremely sorry to lose her. "It is hard to find decent tenants," she said wearily. Mary Lou had been the best one she had ever had. She urged Mary Lou to visit whenever she came home.

Mary Lou planned on vacating her apartment and going back to the ranch to be with her dad until time to leave. She would take Alice with her.

Coming home to her room, the same room in which she had tried to take her life five years ago, she reflected on the changes in her life.

"I don't have to go there and I won't have to," she exulted, her whole being filled with joy. She buried her face in her musty pillow and fell asleep.

The next morning, she was up with the sun. She observed that it was going to be a gloriously sunny day. *I want to go riding while it's still cool,* she thought as she came down the stairs. She saw her dad sitting at the table pulling on his boots. He had a fresh cup of coffee.

"Mary Lou," he exclaimed, his eyes lighting up at the sight of her. "You want some coffee?"

"No, Dad, I thought I'd catch my horse and go riding."

"So early?"

"Yeah, before it gets too hot."

"Well, I doubt if today'll get too hot. See if you can catch Jake to saddle him for you. I think he's down by the windmill."

Mary Lou stood on the porch looking for Jake. The ranch had two wells powered by windmills, one for the house and one for the cattle. There were two large tanks for the livestock which stood on a slight hill which allowed one to run into another with any excess water running into a fairly large pond. There was manmade dams on other parts of the vast ranch which were full or empty depending on the rainfall. Her grandfather had had the dams built to ensure that their cattle always had water in this dry land.

Mary Lou decided she could saddle her own horse, but Jake saw her coming and hurried toward her. "You goin' ridin'?" He had anticipated her wishes. "I'll get the horse."

"I hate to bother you," she said kindly. "I appreciate it very much."

He was taken aback by her new attitude. In the past she had always treated him as an unwanted servant or, worse, as someone who didn't exist.

Mary Lou rode slowly. She wanted to savor every moment of this beautiful day and her beloved prairie, the smell of sage and cedar, and the vast acres of buffalo grass. As soon as she was away from the house she began to sing to the Lord, her voice soaring in songs of praise. When she had run out of the hymns she knew, she began to make up words of her own. She rode farther than she had intended, and it was starting to get warm. She decided she would savor the heat and love it as part of God's creation and not something to be avoided.

She also decided that she would treasure every moment with her family. *Why am I feeling this way?* she wondered. *It's not as if I'm leaving forever. When am I coming back?* She realized this was all sort of open-ended. No specific time had been set for her return.

Sunday morning dawned bright and beautiful, soon to get hot. This was to be Mary Lou's big send-off, and she was dreading it. She certainly didn't feel as if she fit the classification of "missionary." She imagined a missionary as someone who went to a foreign country and led the natives to Christ while curing their diseases.

Anyhow, she tried to fix herself up so as to look as presentable as possible—same green dress as always, she still only owned two dresses, except that Barbara had made long skirts for both she and Mary Lou.

It seemed that where they were going women who wore pants were looked down on. Mary Lou felt that if they had to do manual work it would not be easy with skirts that came almost to the ankles. She herself practically lived in pants or jeans. It occurred to her that her grandmother had worked hard all her life and had always worn a dress, never pants. Whatever, she wanted to do what was proper.

When they arrived at church the place was full of cars. There was no parking, so people simply parked on the prairie in every conceivable manner. Mary Lou had been told that the church was growing. People who were serious about their faith wanted to hear this passionate young preacher. David knew all about death and hell; he had lived it. He didn't bother with platitudes. He felt that the decisions people made regarding God, Jesus, heaven, and hell were deadly serious and that these decisions had to be made before it was too late. He had seen a lot of young men who had never really lived, alive one minute and dead the next.

After the morning Sunday school, David asked Mary Lou if she would mind saying a few words after he introduced her. She really didn't want to. She knew very little about the mission she was soon to go on. What her role would be, she had no idea. But she agreed to say a few words.

After David gave the sermon during which Mary Lou hung on every word, David looked back at where she was sitting with her dad and grandmother. He began, "We are pleased to introduce our special guest, Mary Lou Gerhardt, whom most of you know since she grew up in this church. Mary Lou accepted Christ as her savior at this very altar. We haven't seen much of her since she moved to town where she has been attending another church. God has put it on Mary Lou's heart to go and serve him in Mexico. When this opportunity arose, she knew that he had opened this door for her to go and help build a house of worship for his people.

"I would like for Mary Lou to come and kneel at the altar, and then I will ask the congregation to come and lay hands on her and pray and ask God's blessing on her and the place she is going as well as the people there that she will be ministering to. But first, I would ask Mary Lou if there's anything she would like to say."

Mary Lou stood up feeling completely tongue-tied. She took a minute to ask God to speak through her. "For some time," she began, "ever since I accepted Christ as my savior, I've felt there must be something he wanted me to do. After all, I'm a single person with no obligations." She paused. "When this opportunity came up, I really felt it was something God was putting in front of me. These people need a church and a school. I have no idea what my duties will be until I get there. I know I'll have to spend some time learning the language."

She paused, wondering if it would be appropriate to testify. She decided to plunge ahead. "I just want to thank all of you here who have blessed me since I came back here. Even though I was raised here in this church, I had no connection to Jesus, the Bible, or any church. I have to admit that I was in a very bad place mentally and physically, but today, with your love and the grace of God, I feel amazingly strong and able to serve God in any way he sees fit."

Someone, she assumed it was Rosalie, shouted, "Praise the Lord," and then some others joined in with "Praise the Lord and thank you, Jesus."

David beckoned her to come and kneel at the altar, and then he asked the congregation to come and lay hands on her and pray. As the people gathered around, David took the holy oil and made the sign of the cross on her forehead. He then prayed, "Lord, we ask your blessing on Mary Lou as we send her off to do your will in building your church. We ask you to keep her strong, to put a hedge of protection around her, keeping her from harm, either from disease or people that might wish to hinder her mission. We ask you to protect those who are going with her. Bless the people she will be ministering to. In Jesus's name, we ask it. Amen."

Mary Lou felt surrounded by God's love through these dear people who were blessing her mission. It was such a profound moment, she wished it never to end.

Afterward everyone walked to the new fellowship hall, which was finished except for plastering the walls. Rosalie was so proud of it. She could hardly wait until the walls were finished and painted.

As usual, there were tables filled with every kind of good country food. People came up to Mary Lou and assured her that they would be praying for her. They let her know how brave they felt she was for going to a strange country among strange people.

Finally, to her delight, she saw David approaching her. *It would be nice to be alone with him for a moment without interruption,* she thought. Suddenly it dawned on her, *When will I see him again? Why am I leaving him? I may never see him again!* The thought horrified her.

"Mary Lou," he said warmly, "I certainly never expected you to do anything like this! I don't know why though. It seems you always are expected to do the unexpected. God has made so many changes in your life, I'm amazed."

'Well," said Mary Lou, "this is all sort of embarrassing. After all, I'm not really a missionary. I can't even speak the language. I think Rosalie sometimes gets carried away."

"No, she doesn't!" he broke in. "You are going on a mission… that makes you a missionary. This is a sacrifice, and you deserve to be recognized for it! Just remember, I am always praying for you," he said as he walked away.

"Thank you," she called after him. "I'll need it."

15
CHAPTER

That night Mary Lou had trouble sleeping. She was leaving the next day, Monday. Her dad would get up early and take her to town along with her grandmother.

Aaron was having trouble sleeping also. He just couldn't feel comfortable with the idea that Mary Lou was going to what he considered a dangerous heathen country. After all, he didn't really know the people she was going with either. He wanted to give her some money, but he wasn't sure it would be any good where she was going. And what if she got sick, or just wanted to come home, what then? How remote was this place? He determined that he would find out about all this when they got to town. There was no way that he would just drop her off. However, this was just for his peace of mind, there was no stopping Mary Lou. She could still unsettle him even if she had been saved and sanctified.

When they got to town very early, Alfredo and Barbara were still packing the van the church had bought for their use. Mary Lou felt almost like backing out when she saw some things they were bringing such as a galvanized tub, wash pans, and even a wash board. She recognized these things used on the ranch until they had gotten water piped into the house with propane gas and finally electricity. Alice, when she saw them, was rather amused. They were certainly familiar to her! *My poor granddaughter,* she thought. *Well, hard work never killed anybody, at least not in this family.*

Alfredo assured Aaron that anytime Mary Lou wanted to come home, the church would make sure she got there. As far as money, he didn't see as how she would need any where they were going. Their church, the denomination, was fairly well-established in the cities, just not in the part of the country where they were going. They would see to their needs.

And so Aaron and Alice, fighting back tears, kissed and hugged Mary Lou, who was crying unashamedly, goodbye.

Alfredo and Barbara were packing the van to the ceiling leaving barely enough room for Mary Lou and Kate in the one back seat.

Mary Lou brought one suitcase. She had plenty of toothbrushes and toothpaste as well as jars of face cream, comb, brush, and her clothes. She was wearing her heavy shoes and carrying her coat.

Barbara assured her that they would have plenty of water for bathing and washing dishes. She was to find out that was not always the case.

Just before they left, Aaron had pressed five hundred dollars fastened with a rubber band into Mary Lou's hand. "Just in case." He envisioned her perhaps having to bribe someone to save her life or perhaps to help her leave the country.

They got a late start, and so it was dark the second day by the time they reached the border. It seemed to take forever for them to inspect everything, the letter from the church as well as their identifications. They went through the van and checked all the supplies. Mary Lou began to feel as if they were not going to get through, but Barbara assured her that this was always the case since they had been through here several times when they went to visit relatives.

Mary Lou felt surely they would stop somewhere to spend the night, but no, it seemed as if they would keep going. Any sleeping would have to be done sitting up in the van. She was extremely uncomfortable because each time Kate fell asleep, she leaned heavily against her.

Finally, she was able to fall into a deep sleep, and when she awoke, she found that they were parked and Alfredo and Barbara were asleep in the front seat. She tried to fall back to sleep, but it was impossible. It was so dark out she could see nothing.

I feel as if I'm on a ship sailing nowhere, she thought, *I'm beginning to wonder if this was a good idea. Even if this was a good decision for them, what about Kate? What do I really know about these people anyway?* She was letting her mind run wild. *Alfredo is my pastor, but he hasn't said two words to me. He is driving like a man possessed stopping only when he finds a private place for someone to relieve themselves, which unfortunately is a bush or a draw. I'm hungry too,* she thought. *The food Barbara brought is about gone. Fortunately, we still have water.* She tried to remember some of the Spanish words she had learned. *In case,* she thought, *I might have to get out of here. Oh, I am so unprepared!* she lamented. As she was letting all these gloomy thoughts take over, suddenly Alfredo jerked himself awake, started the van, and took off into the night again.

In spite of her trepidation, she was able to fall asleep again. When she awoke it was morning. Although there was still no sign of civilization, the beauty of the sunrise gave everything a new look and raised her spirits. *God is in charge!* she mused. *I'm like the children of Israel, always longing to return to Egypt when the going gets rough.* Also, Barbara's smile and her cheery "Good morning" threw a new light on the situation. *Everything would be fine,* she assured herself.

The terrain started to change and become more mountainous. She knew that they must be getting close because as she had been told, the people there worked in the mines. The closer they got to their destination the worse the roads became. Some of the roads were not even on the map Alfredo had been given. Even he was becoming concerned about becoming hopelessly lost.

Finally, they did arrive at their destination just after dark the following day. Unfortunately, there didn't seem to be anyone there to greet them. No one seemed to be stirring in the small village. It seemed to be deserted. Since Alfredo couldn't think of anything else to do, he drove down the dusty street and honked his horn. He didn't feel as if this was a very good beginning. However, he knew that he, his family, and Mary Lou were near to collapsing if they didn't find a place to stay.

Suddenly, people came out of their houses and surrounded the van. Since they were chatting in Spanish, Mary Lou had no idea what they were saying. Soon, however, they were being led to the house that had been the home of the former missionary and his family. To Mary Lou it looked like a shack, but at this point she didn't care.

Since it was dark it was hard to tell too much about it. They were grateful to see that at least it did have a cement floor. There was a small kitchen which opened into a fairly large living room. There were two very small bedrooms but no beds. They would have to sleep on the floor with the pallets they brought until, Alfredo promised, he would build a frame to get them off the floor.

Although they were practically dead from lack of rest, there were amenities to be followed. The people brought a lamp and they brought food. Even though they hadn't been properly notified, they apologized for the lack of preparations.

Alfredo and Barbara offered their own apologies while Mary Lou tried to smile and nod in agreement, while all the time thinking, *If I don't lie down, I'm going to die!*

The minute her head hit the pillow she was asleep even though she would have sworn she would never get any sleep lying on a bare floor with the possibility of spiders and no telling what else.

She woke the next morning with Barbara gently shaking her. "I'm going to school now," she said. Kate was beside her and they were holding some of the supplies they had brought—paper, pencils, a small blackboard and some books.

"Alfredo is busy looking for lumber to fix the beds. He needs to see what else has to be done to make this place halfway livable."

Mary Lou wondered what she was supposed to do. "If you want, you can get dressed and come with us," Barbara offered.

Since Mary Lou had slept in her clothes, she hurriedly smoothed down her skirt, pulled her hair back in a ponytail, and went with them. She would have liked to have washed her face, but she didn't see any sign of water or a place to wash up.

She observed that the morning was beautiful, but it showed signs of getting hot later. She felt she had on far too many clothes for hot weather, but she resolved to follow Barbara's lead. When they reached what was presumed to be the school, they were overwhelmed to find at least forty-five children sitting on the ground under a lean to. There were two teenage girls on hand in order to help keep order. They introduced themselves as Esperanza and Noella.

Barbara had hoped for a wall to hang her small blackboard, but there wasn't one. She really didn't know how to begin. She knew she had to do the best she could since all little eyes were looking on her expectantly. It seemed they were so happy to have a teacher and a school that behavior problems were practically nonexistent.

Mary Lou, even though she couldn't understand what Barbara was saying, looked at her with admiration. *She really knows how to make the best of a bad situation,* she thought. She had no doubt that the school would be successful.

Barbara, meanwhile, determined that whether anything else was built, her school would be finished before winter set in.

Meanwhile, Alfredo had taken some lumber from the church to put together some beds. He realized that there was no way the church could be finished with the amount of supplies that were there. Somehow, he had to get word to the church that he needed a lot more lumber as well as other supplies to finish it.

In the days to come, Mary Lou realized that she was three generations away from back breaking work. It fell to her to tidy up their abode. Her job was made more difficult by the fact that there was not enough water. Water was hauled in from some distance and each family had an allotment. Rain barrels caught some rainwater, but not enough. They had a pan for washing their face and hands, a bucket and a dipper to drink from. This water had to be boiled on a wood burning stove. Fortunately, as they were on the edge of the mountains there was plenty of wood, but it had to be gathered and chopped.

She had to wash their clothes on a washboard and hang them on a fence to dry. The fence in back of the house was built to enclose their chickens who had to be fed and their eggs gathered. The chickens had belonged to the previous missionaries, and the parishioners had faithfully taken care of them until the arrival of the new missionaries. If they wanted to eat one of them, someone had to catch it, whack its head off with a hatchet, scald it in boiling water, pluck it, and cut it up. At first Mary Lou refused to do this, but soon she had to. Barbara and Alfredo simply did not have the time for domestic duties what with the school and church duties. Mostly, they ate beans. Mary Lou lost weight becoming lean and brown.

There was a formal welcoming committee the next evening after their arrival. There was food especially prepared for the occasion and speeches of welcome, which Barbara did her best to interpret some of it for Mary Lou's benefit.

It seemed there was already a small core of believers. And so, thought Mary Lou, someone else has planted and Alfredo and Barbara will water. She determined she would do whatever she could to help. She was humbled by the piety of these simple people, their gratitude at having someone to minister to them as well as someone to teach their children as most of them were basically illiterate.

Of course, there were those in the village who were lazy, who spent their time drinking and causing trouble. Alfredo had faith that these too could be reached by the love of Jesus. Even though she couldn't understand much of what he was saying, she noticed that he preached with a passion she hadn't noticed before. She admired this young man who grew up in a town where Mexicans were looked down on. And yet there were some people who saw his potential and they reached out to help him accomplish his goals. Consequently, he was able to finish college and Bible college in order to finally become ordained. After all that, after he was finally ordained; the denomination he chose was not known for its wealthy parishioners and he had to continue working while at the same time pastoring a church.

Now, here he was, pouring out his soul in order to bring the gospel to the poorest of the poor. It was frustrating for him, however, since he wanted to finish the church. He was unable to do so due to the lack of labor and materials. Also, it was hard to ask people to labor for nothing after they had already labored for hours doing back-breaking work for which they received little pay. On top of this, the tools they had to work with were primitive compared to what he was used to.

Barbara too was concerned about her school and what she would do when winter came with no enclosed space. All of them, however, including Mary Lou, felt a sense of purpose, determined to trust in the Lord's provision.

In the evenings Alfredo led his family and Mary Lou in Bible reading and devotions in English. He was concerned about Mary Lou's spiritual life, because, even though she was picking up the language, most of what was said, she didn't understand.

One day Barbara mentioned to Mary Lou that some of the young people, those that were not working, would like to learn English. "You could teach them and in turn they could help you with some of the work around here."

"How could I do that?' she questioned.

"Well, you have your English-Spanish book, which you are learning from. All you have to do is reverse it."

Mary Lou was dubious. "Come on, Mary Lou," Barbara urged. "You could use some help around here; goodness knows I haven't any time to help. Besides that, the girls love you. I'll set up a lesson plan for you. It'll help you too. You could make it for an hour to start."

As usual, Barbara was right. So many of the ones not quite old enough to work all day in the mines had nothing to do except cause trouble among themselves.

The first day they started by learning the English words for the things they used every day. After that, they worked up to short sentences. They were so thrilled to be learning a second language and so proud of their teacher who was so playful and full of laughter.

Mary Lou also was full of joy. At last, she felt she was doing something really worthwhile. Although she knew the chores she did freed up Barbara and Alfredo to do the work of educating and spreading the gospel, it seemed that what she was doing was so menial. It was also an opportunity to teach practical things like cooking and housework to her charges.

Winter was approaching and no work had been done on either the school or the church. Due to Alfredo's efforts more people had joined the church and there were no facilities in which to hold services. Previously, it had always been nice enough to hold services and other events outside. He and Barbara organized picnics and games. Alfredo had even put together baseball teams. He tried to make church not only a worship time but also a fun time in order to involve all the community.

Now, they would have to be very creative. They decided to use their living room and have as many services as needed in order to accommodate everyone. The same thing would have to be done for the school. Barbara would have to teach in batches. It was inconvenient, but somehow it worked.

Finally, it was spring again and then summer and a year had passed since their arrival. One day, Barbara announced that they would be going home on furlough.

"Why?" Mary Lou asked. "Me too?"

"Of course." Barbara laughed. "We're not leaving you. This is not a safe place for a young single woman. Not everyone is a Christian. There are some unsavory characters here."

Mary Lou thought ruefully about all the unsavory characters she had known while singing in bars. Besides, she didn't consider herself "young" anymore.

"We'll only be gone a month. You and Kate and I will be going home. Alfredo is going to church headquarters to try and get answers on when we're going to get the materials we need in order to finish the church. We have a thriving congregation here, we need a church building and a school," she added.

Mary Lou was conflicted, part of her wanted to go home and see her family, but part of her felt really sad about leaving her class as well as others she had become close with. *Oh well, I guess it won't fall apart in a month. After all, these people likely won't be going anywhere.*

As Mary Lou prepared her meager belongings for leaving she began to feel excited. She hadn't received much mail since leaving. Actually, she wasn't sure she had received all of her mail as the mail service was very poor. She had received letters from Alice and a very long one from Rosalie detailing all the news about the family and church members. She was disappointed to find not one word regarding David in any of the pages. *What if he isn't there anymore?* she wondered with a sinking feeling.

Meanwhile, using her broken Spanish, she assured her students and friends that she would soon be returning. She dreaded the long trip home in the van, but hoped it wouldn't be quite so bad since they weren't going to be packed with all the stuff they had brought.

She still had the money her dad had given her, and she insisted that if they found any decent places to stay they would stop. Remembering how exhausted they had been when they arrived, they finally agreed. She also insisted that Alfredo take the rest of the money to buy materials for the church. He was thrilled, that money would go a long way toward building the church. Mary Lou knew her dad would be happy to know that his money was going to further God's Kingdom.

The closer they got to home, the more excited Mary Lou became. *It's strange,* she thought, *I haven't been homesick at all. I guess I was too busy. No time to think, which was just as well.*

16

CHAPTER

Alfredo stopped the van in front of Aunt Norma's house. "I'll call you.'" Barbara called to her as she jumped out of the van, grabbing her suitcase.

Mary Lou stood in front of the house for a while before picking up her suitcase and going to the door. Norma opened the door with Alice peeking over her shoulder. Since they weren't expecting her, they were shocked to see her. They were especially shocked at her appearance. She had on a long skirt which was wrinkled and not too clean after the long ride. Her hair was pulled back and hung in a long braid down her back. There was a little more gray in her hair and her face was nut brown from the sun. After kissing and hugging her, Alice peered at her. "You look like a squaw," she said bluntly.

"Mother! You never saw a squaw." Norma shook her head.

"Well, I seen pictures," Alice declared, "and that's what she looks like."

"You must be exhausted after coming all that way," said Norma. "Sit down and let me get you something to drink."

Mary Lou was glad to sink into a nice soft chair. "How's Dad?" she asked.

"Oh, he's fine," Norma replied. "He'll be tickled to see you. We had no idea you were coming."

"I didn't know I was leaving there until a few days before we left. I'll only be here a month," she added.

"You mean you're going back to that place?" Alice blurted out. "You look like they been workin' you to death!"

"Grandma, I'm fine! The Lord's work is being done there. We've seen a lot of people coming to Christ, I'm just glad to be a small part of it."

"How's Rosalie and John and the kids? Oh, and how's the church out there?" She wanted to hear about David, but she was afraid to ask directly. They might see through her inquiry. But of course they wouldn't. They had no idea how she felt.

Norma informed her that John and Rosalie were fine and that Andrea met someone and was planning to get married, perhaps at Christmas.

Alice broke in to tell her that David's in the hospital. "He's not doin' too good."

Mary Lou was shocked. Her heart began to pound, and for a moment everything became a blur. As soon as she could compose herself she asked, "What happened to him?"

"Well, from what we heard, he had a heart attack. They had to take him out from here, took him to Denver on a plane. When was that? Norma? Three weeks ago?"

Norma nodded. "I think so."

"Well, anyway, they brought him back and he's still in the hospital. Your dad was pretty upset," she added. "He looks on that boy like a son."

As soon as Mary Lou could speak normally she asked, "Aunt Norma, could you take me to the hospital? I want to see David."

"Shouldn't you clean up and rest first? You have to be dead tired."

"I don't think it's visitin' hours anyway," Alice broke in.

"I want to go now!" Mary Lou said firmly.

Norma and Alice glanced at one another with raised eyebrows and quizzical expressions.

"Of course," Norma said, "I'll take you now."

Mary Lou didn't say a word on the way to the hospital. When they got there, she turned to Norma. "Do you know what room he's in?"

"Well, he was in room 2 when your grandmother and I went to visit him. He didn't look very well," she added.

"Thank you, Auntie," she said as she got out of the car.

"Do you want me to come pick you up?"

"No, I can walk, I'm used to it."

Since it wasn't visiting hours, she knew that she would have to sneak past the nurse on duty. She was praying that she would be able to slip in without anyone seeing her. She steeled herself for what she might find if David was as bad as they claimed.

And so she was surprised to find him upright in bed reading a book.

"David," she whispered as she reached his bedside.

At first, he didn't recognize her, but then a delighted smile broke over his face. "Mary Lou!" he cried. "What are you doing here? I thought you were in Mexico!"

"I'm here on furlough," she said. "It's just for a month."

"Oh, is that all?" He seemed disappointed. "Anyhow, I want to hear all about what you've been doing there. Pull up a chair and tell me all about it."

"Well, I would, but I'm not supposed to be here. If they catch me, they'll throw me out."

"I won't let them," he promised.

"First, I want to know what happened to you."

He shrugged. "There's not much to tell, I collapsed. Fortunately, one of the guys working in the yard was there and rushed me to the hospital, and from there I was sent by plane to Denver." He paused. "I guess it would have been better if I'd gotten treatment sooner, but then, who knows? I guess I'm just fortunate that I wasn't alone at the parsonage. Any other day I would have been. Anyway, I have a pacemaker and maybe, just maybe, I'll be able to go back to work. I hope so," he said wearily. "That's my prayer anyway. Please, Mary Lou, tell me about what you've been doing. Tell me everything."

"Hmm, what I've been doing. Actually it's a little boring. I've never worked so hard in my life! I imagined myself saving the natives, but most of my time was spent cooking, cleaning, cutting wood, hauling water. There's never enough of anything. The last six months have been fun though." She proceeded to tell him about her class, teaching English to young people, telling them about Jesus.

David interrupted her, "I love you, Mary Lou," he said calmly as if he had been saying it for a long time.

"Well, I love you too," she said as if to a brother or a friend and proceeded with her conversation.

David reached over and took her hand shaking it a little, "No, Mary Lou," he said, looking deep into her eyes. "I mean I love you like a man loves a woman."

Mary Lou was stunned. The look in his eyes would be etched in her mind forever as if time had stood still at that moment. She couldn't believe what she had just heard. She could not have imagined this moment, not in her wildest dreams. In spite of herself, she began to cry, tears welling up in her eyes, coursing down her cheeks. She tried to brush them away with her hands.

David was immediately contrite. "I'm sorry, Mary Lou, I didn't mean to upset you, I don't know why I said that. I certainly hadn't intended to. It's true though, although I didn't realize what my feelings were until you left for Mexico. You just looked so beautiful when you talked about the work you've been doing." His voice drifted off.

Mary Lou dared not look at him. What could she say? Finally, she spoke. "It's okay, I've been in love with you a lot longer than that."

"Really?" He was amazed. "You certainly never gave any indication of it. Most of the time I wondered if you even liked me."

"Well, you were a man of God and I was a fallen woman."

"I never thought of you like that," he said soberly.

"You kicked me out as your patient," she reminded him, smiling.

"Yeah, I remember. I thought you were a spoiled brat. I can't believe the difference the Lord has made in your life. It's amazing!"

For a while they sat there, silent, amazed at what had just happened, each of them thinking, *Where do we go from here?*

About that time one of the nurses opened the door bringing a tray with David's medicine. When she saw Mary Lou she glared at her. "What are you doin' here? This is not visitin' hours. I don't know how you got past the desk." She turned to David, "Pastor Schwenk," she chided, "you're never gonna get well with people runnin' in and out all the time."

Mary Lou jumped up to leave. “I’m sorry,” she said. “I’ll see you tomorrow, David?”

“Until tomorrow.” He looked longingly after her.

That night, Mary Lou could not sleep. There were so many thoughts running around in her head. *There’s no way I can leave David now,* she thought. But what about Mexico? She had promised to return. Perhaps they could find someone else. After all, she hadn’t been part of the plan in the first place. She finally decided that David needed her more than she was needed in Mexico and that she was going to feel guilty no matter what.

She rose early the next morning, took a bath, and washed her hair. She dug out her second outfit, although clean, it was terribly wrinkled. As she surveyed herself in the mirror, she smiled. David had said she was beautiful. He must have something wrong with his eyes as well as his heart. But then, she had always seen him as beautiful as well.

She hugged herself with delight. *He really loves me. It was so wonderful, so amazing. How was it possible?*

She was singing softly to herself in the kitchen when her aunt and grandmother got up to make breakfast.

“Why are you so happy this mornin’?” asked Alice. “Did you see David? How was he?”

She had to stop herself from saying, “He was wonderful!” “He didn’t seem too bad,” she said. “I’m gonna see him again today.”

Alice and Norma looked at each other in surprise.

“I thought we were going to drive out and see your dad today,” said Norma.

“Could we go tomorrow if you don’t mind, Auntie? I really need to talk to David. I didn’t see him for very long before they chased me out of his room.”

“Well, I should think so,” sniffed Alice, “since you went sneakin’ in there when it wasn’t visitin” hours.”

“Okay,” said Norma, “but I know your dad will be anxious to see you. We’d like to hear something about what you were doing in Mexico ourselves, wouldn’t we, Mother?”

Alice nodded.

"What can I do to help you, Auntie?" asked Mary Lou. "I can't go to the hospital until this afternoon. I need to do something to pass the time away."

"You know, Mary Lou," said Norma, "I need to clean the bathroom upstairs and one of the rooms was vacated so I have to clean that."

So Mary Lou spent the morning helping her aunt clean, all the while rehearsing what she wanted to say to David.

Finally, it was time to visit David. She walked to the hospital, a spring in her step. She felt like running. She never imagined she could be so happy!

She checked in at the desk and found that David already had company. She was asked to wait until they left. "Pastor is a sick man," said the sister. "So many people are coming and going. We have to make sure he takes it easy. I'll make sure they leave in time for you to visit."

"Thank you," she said as she sank into a chair by the door. Actually, she was a little disappointed. She had been so anxious and now she had to wait and who knew how long.

At last the couple opened the door to leave. Thankfully, Mary Lou didn't recognize them. She was not up to making small talk.

She could tell that David was happy to see her. He reached for her hand and raised it to his lips to kiss her palm. "My word," he said when he looked at her calloused and broken skin, "what have you been doing, pouring cement?"

"I told you I was working hard." She laughed.

"David," she said urgently, "I don't have much time and I need to talk to you. David, I want to be with you." Before he could answer, she hurried on, "The only way I can be here with you is if we get married. I could stay here in the room with you, and when you leave I could take care of you." She paused, wondering if this was coming out the way she rehearsed it. In fact, she was amazed that she was even saying these things. If only she had more time.

He was looking at her with an amused expression. "Shouldn't I be the one proposing?" He smiled.

"What? Oh sure, I guess, but this is hardly, well, you know… normal, the situation, I mean." She felt flustered not knowing what else to say.

David let go of her hand and turned looking at the ceiling.

"I don't know, Mary Lou. Doc doesn't give me much hope of living a normal life. I think when he comes in here, he's surprised that I'm still here. If we get married, you might soon be a widow."

"I don't care what I am!" cried Mary Lou. "I just want to be with you! I don't want to just see you on visiting hours! We can live just one day at a time. We don't have to worry about the future. I want *now* for us. In fact, my time to visit you is almost over and I can't see you tomorrow either since my aunt and grandma are anxious to take me out to the ranch." She felt so angry, not at him, but at their circumstances.

He reached for her hand again. "You're right, Mary Lou, we do need to be together. I can't bear to think of not seeing you tomorrow either."

They sat quietly for a while. Finally, David spoke. "You can tell your family we're getting married when you see them. I never thought I'd get married lying in a bed. Actually," he mused, "I never thought much about getting married at all. I always imagined myself like a priest, married to God and the church. What about you, wouldn't you like all the trimmings of a nice wedding?"

"I had all that years ago," she said, "and no one was happy about it."

"What happened?" he asked. "You never told me about it. Actually, you never told me much about anything, if you remember."

"I remember," she said. "He found out he liked guys better than girls. He left me for a man that could promote his career."

David was genuinely shocked. "Mary Lou, I am so sorry. That must have been horrible for you!"

Mary Lou thought how naive David was. He had no idea that self-centered people bounce back pretty quickly.

"Well, that was a long time ago. I know I have to leave before they throw me out. Is it all right if I ask Alfredo to marry us?"

"That's fine if that's what you want." He kissed her hand again. "Good night, my darling. I love you." He looked at her lovingly.

Mary Lou didn't say anything. She realized she was not used to words like that or looks like that. All of her relationships had been based on each person trying to get their own needs met, the physical or the material. Even though she desperately loved David, she knew that it would be hard for her to totally let go. Before, there had always been a part of her that could never totally belong to another person, that part of her that was afraid of being hurt.

As she was leaving, she saw Dr. Mac coming down the hall.

He was surprised to see her. "Mary Lou, I haven't seen you in years!" he exclaimed. "I guess you must be healthy, or you have another doctor."

Mary Lou, observing him, decided he must be at least eighty and still practicing medicine!

"I am healthy, I guess. It's a good thing since I can't afford a doctor."

"What are you doing here?" he asked. "I hope none of your family is sick?"

"No, I'm here visiting David." She hesitated. "Dr. Mac, David and I are getting married."

He shook his head in disbelief. "What do you mean, you're getting married? Do you realize how sick he is?"

"I know how sick he is, but he's alive and I want to be with him!' When he leaves here, I want to take care of him." She was adamant.

"Well, he may never leave here. I guess you realize he can never be a husband to you in the usual sense." Being old-fashioned, he didn't say David couldn't perform sexually because of his heart, but Mary Lou understood what he meant.

"I don't care about that," said Mary Lou. "I have loved him for a long time and I want to be with him. I don't just want to see him on visiting hours. If he dies, I want to be there with him."

Dr. Mac shook his head in disapproval. As he looked at Mary Lou, he wondered why David would want to marry her. She looked as if she had slept in her clothes for a week, her hair was straggly, and she looked as if she had been in the sun too long. The last time he had seen her she had been in the hospital, a failed suicide.

"Well, Mary Lou," he said, finally, "I guess you and David are old enough to know what you're doing. Give my regards to your dad," he said, as he hurried off.

As Mary Lou watched him go, she thought, *I don't suppose anyone is going to give our marriage their blessing. It will just seem too improbable.*

As she rode with her aunt and grandma to the ranch the following morning, she wondered how the family was going to take this latest piece of news. Other than Rosalie, no one had any inkling of how she felt about David. This should be good news for a change, but she was not sure it would be.

When they arrived the whole family had gathered on the front porch in order to enjoy the cool of the morning.

She was so happy to see them, especially Andrea who was home on school break. It seemed unbelievable that she would soon graduate and then become a married woman. Again, she had this pang of regret that she had missed so much.

The boys too looked as if they had grown a foot just in the time she had been gone. Her dad looked the same, only a little grayer. As usual, Jake was there and he was aging fast. She wondered how the two of them were managing all the work that had to be done on a ranch this size. Of course, he had John and his boys who probably helped a lot.

After all the hugs and hellos, everyone settled back on the porch to ask about Mexico. They wanted to know what it was like, how she lived, and what she had been doing. She gladly and enthusiastically told about her job and her work with the young people. They couldn't believe that she actually washed on a wash board, killed and cooked chickens. They were amazed at how tanned she was and how healthy she looked.

Even John looked at her with admiration.

Finally, her dad asked her, "Are you plannin' on goin' back?"

This was the opening she had been waiting for. "I was," she said, "but something came up and I've changed my mind."

They waited for her to explain. "I went to see David in the hospital."

"Oh yes," her Dad said sadly, "this has hit all of us bad. He has meant so much to us as a preacher. But also as a friend. How did he seem? Any better?"

"Dad," she broke in, "David and I are getting married."

She knew they would be shocked, and that was putting it mildly.

Nothing was said until finally her dad said, "How did this come about?"

Mary Lou took a deep breath. "Dad, I have been in love with David for a long time." She glanced at Rosalie who was smiling. "And I found out when I visited him he feels the same way about me."

"I understand that he might never get well." Aaron felt bewildered.

"I know that," Mary Lou said firmly. "I spoke to Dr. Mac. But I want to be with him while he's living. And," she continued, "if he gets well enough to leave the hospital, I want to take care of him. He really doesn't have anyone else."

"And David agreed to all this? Was this his idea?" Aaron was skeptical.

"No, it was mine, but he wants to be with me too. He's just worried about me being a widow."

There was a long silence. She looked around at all her dear ones. "I hope we have your blessing."

Finally, Aaron spoke. "If you need my blessing, you have it. David's the finest person I know. He couldn't help thinking though that they made an odd pair. David was so solid and Mary Lou was, well, flighty was the only word he could think of.

Rosalie and Andrea, the romantics, were so thrilled they could hardly contain themselves. John and the boys sat impassive. Norma said nothing.

Alice broke the silence. "I hope you're not planning on getting married in that outfit." She eyed Mary Lou's attire with distaste. "Your hair needs fixin' too," she added.

Everyone, including Mary Lou, laughed, breaking the tension. Aaron and Alice were privately relieved that Mary Lou wasn't going back to Mexico.

Meanwhile, David, as he lay in his hospital bed, was having second thoughts about his decision to marry. He had no second thoughts about his feelings for Mary Lou. He knew he loved her deeply. She delighted him with her overt honesty. Just thinking about her caused him to smile. He knew she was serious about her faith and that was important to him.

However, the doctors had been very honest with him. His heart attack had left his heart in bad shape.

If he had another one, he would not survive. That wasn't all though. He never went through a day without pain due to his war injuries. In fact, that might have brought on his heart attack. He had visible scars on his face and his nearly useless hand. What people didn't see were all the scars on his body where the doctors had dug out shrapnel and sewed him up. He had lost his spleen.

Then there were the invisible scars which sometimes caused him to scream out in the night as he relived the horror of the war and the dying he had ministered to—bodies so torn up they were nearly unrecognizable as human.

Could he subject Mary Lou to this, perhaps watching him die before her eyes? But what could he say to her? She seemed so happy and he had felt so happy too. What would he say to her? How would he advise someone else with this predicament? He knew he would tell them to pray and ask God's guidance. Right now, that didn't seem to work for him.

The next day, Mary Lou arrived promptly at hospital visiting hours. She was so anxious to see David, to tell him that she had received her family's blessing on their marriage.

She could tell from the way his eyes lit up that he was happy to see her, but for some reason he seemed distant.

"Are you feeling okay?" she asked.

He nodded his head. "Mary Lou, I think we ought to discuss what we talked about, I mean, about our getting married."

Mary Lou's heart sank. "Are you having second thoughts?"

"I just don't know if you realize what you're getting into…I'm a broken man, not just my heart. I'm in pain most of the time. The doctors at the VA patched me up the best they could, but—" He paused, not looking at her.

Suddenly, Mary Lou broke in, "You promised to marry me!" She cried. "I should sue you for breach of promise," she said half-jokingly, half-seriously.

In spite of himself, David burst out laughing. "You know, you're brazen."

"I don't know what you mean by that," she said. "I just know what's best for me and I think it's what's best for you too. I told my family about us and they're tickled to death." She wasn't sure this was entirely true. "I think they're wondering what you could possibly see in me."

"My grandma is worried that I might show up at the wedding improperly dressed." Mary Lou laughed. She had picked up her clothes at her dad's house and she was dressed in her usual jeans and shirt.

"I think you're beautiful no matter how you're dressed," said David.

"I guess you have bad eyes too," said Mary Lou.

Since David had been in the hospital he had been letting his beard grow. Mary Lou noticed that he looked distinguished with his dark hair and beard. Her heart yearned to hold him close to her, to be able to snuggle in his arms. However, she determined to not say anything more about marriage. She would settle for what they had. It would be enough.

David could see how disappointed she was even though she did her best to hide it.

It was soon time for her to leave and David realized he didn't want her to leave. It occurred to him if they weren't married, she'd always be leaving. Maybe one day for good.

"Will you be here tomorrow?" he asked longingly.

"I will," she said, smiling at him.

"I was just thinking, Mary Lou," he said, "if we did get married and I got out of here, what would we live on? All I have is a small pension from the army. As they say, we can't live on love."

"Well, what were you planning on living on when you got out?"

"Doc says I can go to the nursing home which my insurance will cover."

"We could rent a room from my aunt or live with my dad. He would love that. Of course that is too far away from doctors and hospitals."

David didn't answer.

"Hmm, well, if we're going to be together, the proper thing is to be married."

"But," she continued, "I'm thinking you need more time to think about it. You shouldn't do anything you're not sure of. If you go to a nursing home, I can visit you there. I'm not leaving you," she promised, smiling.

They sat for a long time, holding hands without saying anything.

Mary Lou thought to herself, *If this is all I can have, I'm willing to settle for it. I am content.*

After a while, David spoke, "Mary Lou, you set the date and make the arrangements. I want to marry you, to become one with you, I want you for my wife."

Mary Lou s eyes welled with tears as did David's.

"I am so happy," she managed to say.

"I'm happy too," he said. "In fact, right now I have these feelings that I can't even express. I've never felt this way."

She realized that they had never even kissed. She wondered if she should make the first move. However, it would seem awkward with him propped up in bed and she sitting in chair. Since she wanted it to be special, she would wait until they were married and she could lie down beside him and they would kiss and it would be magical.

I have to stop thinking like a teenager, she thought, smiling to herself.

Since Mary Lou was in charge of the arrangements, she decided that she could get everything ready in two weeks before David (if there were no change in his condition) would have to be discharged to the nursing home. There was the license. Also, the hospital agreed that they could use the patio for the wedding, which meant the wedding would have to be very small, just very close family. She felt badly when she thought of all their friends whom they loved and who loved them would be left out.

Then there was Alfredo, Barbara, and Kate. She felt a pang of guilt when she thought of telling them, which, of course, had to be done right away. She prayed that Alfredo would be willing to marry them.

As she approached the house where they were staying, she rehearsed in her mind what she had to say.

They were so happy to see her, which made her feel even more guilty.

They were surprised when she told them about David, since she had never mentioned him.

She explained how she had loved him for a long time, never dreaming that he might ever love her too. As much as she loved Mexico and as much as she had wanted to go back, she wanted to marry the man she loved and take care of him for as much time as he had left, which according to the doctor wasn't much.

"I want you at my wedding," she said, "and, Alfredo, I'm asking you, if you would, please, would you marry us?"

Alfredo, with his big romantic Latin heart, readily agreed. "I would be honored, my friend," he said with a big smile.

Barbara, however, had begun to cry. She tried frantically to wipe away her tears, but it was useless. She was almost sobbing.

Alfredo rose, patted his wife's shoulder, and left the room.

Mary Lou was a little shocked. "Barbara, what's wrong? Why are you crying?"

"Well, for one thing," Barbara choked out, "I'm happy for you, but the idea that we're losing you is very hard for me." She rose and wet a towel to wipe her face.

She looked into Mary Lou's eyes. "You're like a sister to me. Far closer than my own sisters."

"Oh, Barbara, I love you too. You're the sister I never had!"

After Barbara had managed to calm down, she smiled at Mary Lou. "I don't know if I ever told you," she confided, "my family was not too happy when I married Alfredo."

"Because he's Mexican?"

"Well, yeah, not that they'd ever say so."

"But Alfredo's a man of God."

"I know." She sighed. "That's part of the problem. My family believes that religion has its place, but it's not something you discuss, and of course, Alfredo never discusses anything else, which makes my family very uncomfortable and it makes me uncomfortable when we're around them."

She paused, wiping her eyes again. "When I feel uncomfortable, I feel guilty, like I'm denying my Lord. And so we don't go see them much. Actually, they don't invite us much," she said ruefully. Barbara smiled through her tears, "I'm going to miss you so much, little sister."

"I'm certainly going to miss you too. Barbara, I want you to know, I've really prayed about this, it's not one of my usual fly by night decisions."

Barbara nodded. "I know that God has blessed you with this happiness. You're beaming all over, you know? You are radiant!"

"I know, I can hardly contain myself. I want to tell everyone I meet!"

Soon, Mary Lou rose to leave. "I'll see you at my wedding, if not before." They hugged one another, and Barbara watched as she walked down the driveway.

She is so full of joy, she thought, *but if he's as sick as she says, sorrow will soon follow.* Again, tears welled up in her eyes. *We must hang onto the moments,* she thought, *they may be all we have.*

Still, she could hardly bear the thought of going back to Mexico without Mary Lou, who had made herself almost indispensable. *Well, the Lord will provide*, she assured herself.

17
CHAPTER

The day of the wedding dawned bright and clear, much to Mary Lou's delight. The day before her old nemeses the wind had blown all day. But, she thought, she would be happy to marry David even in a hailstorm.

Her grandma had bought her an aqua lace dress with shoes to match. She had had some of her hair cut off with the rest hanging down in soft curls. As she observed herself in the mirror, she saw a woman past forty and fortunately who, due to her family genes, didn't look much over thirty. She needed no makeup as her skin was naturally tan. There were a few streaks of gray in her dark hair. Hesitating, she picked up a red lipstick, running it over her lips. Except for a little powder, none of the women in her family wore makeup. Barbara too, in her holiness denomination, wore no makeup. She decided not to wipe it off. She felt it made her eyes sparkle.

When she got to the hospital she found David sitting up in a wheelchair. His sister had brought his clothes and he was wearing a pair of Levis with a white western style shirt, all of which seemed too large for him. Mary Lou could not help thinking how handsome he looked. He still had his beard since she had told him how much she liked it. The dark beard did make him look even paler, however.

His eyes widened when he saw Mary Lou. He had never seen her dressed like that with her hair curled and even lipstick.

He reached for her hand. "Look at you!" he exclaimed. "You're a vision." He looked at her adoringly.

He couldn't help thinking of himself, a cripple who couldn't even stand for his own wedding! This couldn't be fair to Mary Lou.

"What are you doing up?" She demanded to know. "Did the doctor say you could get up?"

"I am not getting married lying down," he retorted, "no matter what he says. Come on, wheel me outside. Your family and mine are already here waiting. I want to introduce you to my sister and her husband."

I hope they like me, thought Mary Lou. *What are they going to think about David marrying someone they've never even met?*

The family was all there except for Jake, which was not surprising since, except for church, he never went anywhere where he might have to socialize.

Even Aaron was surprised at how beautiful Mary Lou looked. He could see that part of it was how excited and happy she was. She was absolutely glowing, and it showed in her face and her eyes. He worried about David though. He was pale and much thinner than he had been before. How long would it be, he wondered, before his little girl became a widow? Well, best to put all that out of his mind and just enjoy the day.

He could see that his daughter-in-law had brought a huge cake and enough food to feed an army. She had talked the hospital into letting her set up tables to hold the food and drinks even though there was not much room for it. Somehow, she had scrounged up enough chairs so that people could sit down during the wedding. Thanks to her, there were bouquets of flowers, some from her garden and some from the florist.

Mary Lou was overwhelmed. She was amazed at how Rosalie could always find a way to make everything, no matter how simple, look special.

As soon as she had the chance, she asked Rosalie if she and Andrea would stand up with her during the vows. Of course, they had wanted very much to be asked and they were thrilled. She couldn't help thinking that this was turning into more than she had planned. She noticed her brother with his camera, so there would be wedding pictures.

David introduced Mary Lou to his sister and her husband; their daughter was unable to attend. His sister was polite but not overly friendly. Mary Lou was too excited to worry too much about it.

About that time, Alfredo, Barbara, and Kate showed up. Alfredo was dressed handsomely in a black suit with a gray shirt and tie.

"I've never seen Alfredo in a suit," Mary Lou remarked to Barbara. "He looks wonderful!"

"He bought it especially for your wedding." Barbara smiled.

"He did?"

"Yes, he did. Of course, I hope I can get him to wear it more often."

"This is turning into a dream wedding," said Mary Lou. "So much more than I had planned, thanks to family and friends."

David's brother-in-law stood up beside David during the vows.

Alfredo took his task seriously. This was a solemn occasion, and he had no intention of rushing through it. He talked about Mary Lou and her miraculous conversion and how she had gone to Mexico and put her whole soul into ministering to the people there. Mary Lou thought he may have exaggerated a little. He spoke about how David, a man of God, who was struck down but not out, how he, in deciding to get married, was planning on making the most of every day that God allowed him.

He said, "None of us here have any idea how many tomorrows we have on this earth before our heavenly Father calls us home."

Mary Lou was beginning to think she might faint before they got to the part where they said "I do." Her hand was trembling uncontrollably when she held it out for David to put the gold band which had belonged to his mother on her finger.

He looked up and smiled at her and squeezed her hand. She felt her heart would break with love for him.

Alfredo asked Mary Lou to kneel, and he anointed her and David with holy oil, blessing their union. Mary Lou stood and then bent down to kiss David as he lifted his face to hers. *I'm still waiting for my real kiss,* she thought.

Everyone clapped and then moved in to shake their hands and wish them happiness. Mary Lou asked David if he were all right or if he needed to go back and lie down.

"Not until I get some of Rosalie's fried chicken, and of course, some cake. I'm sure it's out of this world." He grinned.

Mary Lou laughed. She hoped he wasn't expecting her to cook like Rosalie.

Aaron pulled Mary Lou aside. "Mary Lou," he began, "I talked to the church board and we agreed that if David should get well enough, or out of danger, you could come and live in the parsonage whether he's able to preach or not. We owe him a lot. Of course, if we find a full-time preacher, you'd have to move. Doesn't look like there's much danger in that. So far, no one's willin' to stay out there."

Her eyes filled with tears. "That would be so wonderful, Daddy! Right now, we just have to take it one day at a time."

"I just wish we weren't so far from doctors." Aaron sighed. "You could come live at the ranch. There's so much room there."

"Daddy, I'll keep all that in mind. I just thank you so much for everything. My cup is just running over right now. Every day is such a blessing."

She went to find David who was eating and talking to Alfredo. She was worrying that he might be overdoing it. But he seemed so happy and so alive. *I guess it's his body,* she thought. *Surely he'll know when to leave. I must not turn into a nag.*

It was out of her hands, however, when one of the nurses came to tell David it was time for his medication. "You really should rest," she said. "You've been up a long time, all this excitement…my word!

After everyone came to tell him goodbye, Mary Lou said, "I'll be there in a minute."

He nodded.

Aaron was busy loading up the tables and chairs which he had brought from the church, while the women helped Rosalie load up the leftovers.

Mary Lou wanted to thank everyone personally for making this day the happiest day of her life. However, she could hardly wait to be alone with David. He was still in his wheelchair when she came in the room, but he had changed into pajamas.

"I thought you would be in bed," she said.

"No, I was waiting for you."

"I have to go and change clothes. Aunt Norma is waiting for me."

He grinned at her. "Couldn't you just wear what you have on for a few days?"

She laughed. "Why, Pastor, I had no idea you ever noticed lady's attire."

"I certainly noticed today," he admitted. "I had no idea you could look like that, like an angel."

"Not quite," she said. "Anyway, I can't wait to get back in my jeans."

"I love the way you look in your jeans too." He smiled. "I hope you're coming right back."

"Don't worry, I'm never leaving you again. You'll see so much of me, you'll probably get tired of me."

"That will never happen."

That evening, the hospital agreed to put a large easy chair in David's room so that Mary Lou could stay with her husband. They claimed they did not have a rollaway bed available.

It was fine with them. They laughed and talked about the wedding until all was quiet. Then David pulled back the covers and Mary Lou slipped in beside him and they held each other, murmuring words of love and kissing passionately. Soon, David realized that Mary Lou had fallen asleep. He woke her and she slipped out of bed and went to her chair, pulling the coverlet up to her neck, falling fast asleep again.

David, however, could not sleep. He had never been that close with a woman and it had been wonderful. He knew in his heart he wanted more. Did he regret that he had put himself in this position? After all, if he had never gotten carried away and spoken of his feelings to Mary Lou. But no, he loved her more than he had ever imagined. He looked over at her. Even though he could not really see her in the darkness, he could tell that she was sleeping peacefully.

The next morning, Mary Lou left and went to her aunt's house for a shower and clean clothes. When she returned, David was again in his wheelchair.

"I'm getting out of here," he announced.

"You mean they're discharging you already. I thought that was next week."

"No, they're not. Mary Lou. I want you to get me a walker. I'm sure they have one, or maybe we can buy one."

"Are you sure?" she questioned, a little alarmed at his tone.

"Mary Lou," he said firmly, "when I was in the VA they got me out of bed when I felt if I took a step I would die! They got everyone up whether they had legs or not. I just feel people here, bless them, are behind the times."

Mary Lou hurried to the nurses' station to find a walker. They were very reluctant to give her one.

"The doctor has not ordered any such thing. The pastor is supposed to have complete bed rest," the sister said disapprovingly.

Mary Lou was firm. "He wants to walk, otherwise he says he's leaving," she lied.

They gave her the walker, which she took to David. When he gripped the handle with his good hand while she steadied the other and tried to stand, she felt she had made a horrible mistake. He just couldn't stand. But he tried again and again; his face turned red and he started to sweat.

Mary Lou was horrified, she had to turn her head. *Oh God, please, please, God, help. This is awful* she cried silently. At last he was able to stand, but only for a few minutes, after which he plopped back in the chair.

"I guess that's enough for now," he said, after which she breathed a sigh of relief.

Her relief was short-lived, however, when he said, "Maybe I'll try again this afternoon."

Even though she was now his wife, she knew she was not his keeper and she never would be. She could never ask him to think about her, how much she loved him, and didn't want to lose him.

And of course he did try again in the afternoon when they were alone in the room and it was the same nerve-wracking ordeal as before.

When the nurses notified Dr. Mack that David was out of bed and trying to walk, at first he was angry. But after talking to David, he realized the whole situation was out of his hands.

David told him that he had no intention of lying in a bed the rest of his life. He knew what shape his heart was in. He knew that it could give out any time. But he intended to live while he was living.

Dr. Mack nodded. "Do you want me to discharge you to the nursing home now?" he asked. "I think you'd have more chance of getting some therapy over there."

"Thank you, Doctor, I'd like that," said David. "I can't thank you enough for all you've done for me," he added.

"Well, I haven't done much," he said ruefully. "I sure didn't think you should get married in the shape you're in, and I damn sure didn't want you up trying to walk so soon, but you did it anyway. I wish you all the luck in the world."

David smiled. "I don't believe in luck, I believe in providence."

"Whatever," said the doctor. "I'll be checking on you while you're over there."

The next morning David left the hospital with Mary Lou following in his car which had been brought to town by some kind friends. When she walked into the nursing home she saw a sun room, which seemed pleasant enough. This was followed by a dining room, which led to a hallway with rooms on either side. Some rooms had more than one person in them and others were private.

Mary Lou was relieved to see that David had a private room. She wondered about it. Did his pension pay for it or did they give it to him because of his long service to their patients?

Unfortunately, they could no longer be together at night. Her aunt had kindly offered to let her sleep in one of her spare rooms.

Meanwhile, David, with the encouragement and help of the staff, was continuing to spend as much time on the walker as he possibly could. And, to Mary Lou's surprise, he was making progress.

He made a list of books he wanted from the parsonage, and he asked if she could drive out and get them for him.

She was thrilled at the thought of spending the day away from the nursing home.

David, however, seemed to thrive in that setting. He visited the patients on his walking tours, no matter what state of mind they happened to be in. Mary Lou couldn't see the point in visiting someone who sat there with a blank stare on their face. He, however, felt everyone needed a human touch no matter how far gone their faculties.

Some of the people were fairly sound in mind, if not in body, and they were so glad to see him. Usually, during the week someone came in to do a Bible study. Or if no one came, David would do the study. The same thing on Sunday morning, if church people didn't show up, he gave the Word and Mary Lou led the music.

Mary Lou was so elated when a friend of David gave them a small television. She hadn't watched any television since leaving California. Much to her disappointment, David announced that he didn't want it on since he had to study.

Why does he have to study? she wondered. "Why didn't you tell him you didn't want it?" she asked.

"I couldn't hurt his feelings," he admitted.

While David was thriving in their new setting, Mary Lou began to feel neglected. She decided to talk to Alice about the things that were bothering her. If she had expected sympathy, she came to the wrong place.

"You know, Mary Lou," Alice said, "you married a preacher and he's always going to belong to others. That's his calling."

"I guess so, I just hoped we'd have more time alone together. I do kinda wonder why he married me." She sighed.

"Maybe he fell in love with that little gal who took off for Mexico to build a church and save the Indians, and now he's found out he's married a shrew who wants his complete attention?" she asked with a raised eyebrow.

Mary Lou grinned at her. "Well thanks, Grandma. I guess you have given me something to think about."

"Maybe you better find something to keep you busy," offered Alice, as Mary Lou left for her drive to the parsonage to pick up David's books.

As she pulled up to the parsonage she noticed that someone had spent time keeping up the place.

When she went into David's room with her list, she was shocked. There were books everywhere, not just books on theology but history books, science books, even volumes of poetry. There were old magazines and newspapers with articles circled.

It took a while to find the books he wanted. After she put them in the car, she decided to sit on the porch in David's chair for a while and enjoy the sun. There was a slight breeze blowing through her hair.

It came to her that the people she saw every day in the nursing home would never again be able to enjoy the sunshine and the breeze the way she was. She resolved to change her attitude. Perhaps she could visit some of the people herself and try to make their day a little brighter. She knew that some of them never received any visitors at all.

She thought long and hard about what Alice had said. She realized that once again, she had based her happiness on someone else's thinking, doing, or saying. She had put another person in the place where God had to be and she was losing herself. Of course, the nursing home was a mission field just as important as Mexico or any other place.

Finding a place to put all the books into David's small room was a challenge. David was so happy to see his books. "These are like old friends to me," he said.

"I feel so dumb compared to you," she said with her usual candor.

"You are not dumb!" he retorted. "Well, maybe a little undereducated," he admitted.

"I'll tell you what," he said in order to redeem himself, "why don't I give you a couple of books to read, ones that I can guarantee you will enjoy reading?"

Mary Lou agreed even though she doubted whether she would enjoy reading them. She had never been much of a reader.

"Another thing," he suggested, "you said you were learning Spanish. Maybe you could go to the library and get a Spanish study book and we could work on it together. I took two years of Spanish in high school." He looked at her hopefully.

"Well, I don't know. What's the point if we have no one to talk to?"

"Mary Lou, the point is that we can enjoy doing something together?" he said calmly.

To her surprise, she did enjoy reading the books he recommended. She also discovered it was fun studying Spanish with David. He pointed out how quickly she learned.

He also insisted that she get out and go to her old church on Sundays. It was nice to worship there even though it was not quite the same without Alfredo and Barbara who had since left for Mexico.

18
CHAPTER

David had been in the nursing home for six months when he announced that he felt well enough to go back to Windy Hill if they would have him. He sent Mary Lou to talk to her dad. He knew that so far they had not found anyone to take his place.

Again, Mary Lou was petrified with fear. "That's twenty miles from the doctor, what if something happens?"

"Mary Lou, come here," David demanded. "Look at me!" Mary Lou knelt and looked him in the eye.

He cupped her face in his hand. "If and when I have an attack, I will die on the spot. It will not matter if I'm here or out there. Do you understand? I hope you're not alone when it happens, but you are a strong person and I'm confident you can handle whatever happens."

Mary Lou was not so sure. "Well, couldn't you wait till my dad comes in again and you talk to him? He said we could live out there."

"I know, but I don't want to just live out there...I want to go to work!" He was adamant.

"I have to talk to the bishop," he said, "but I want to know what your dad says first. He'll speak more frankly to you, I'm guessing."

"Okay, I'll go out in the morning."

Since there was no way to get hold of her dad, she just hoped he'd be around. Otherwise, she might be making the trip for nothing. Fortunately, he was out near the barn cleaning out cow troughs when he saw her drive up.

He was delighted to see her and came to meet her as she got out of the car. She ran to him and hugged him tight.

"Is there anything wrong? Is David all right?" He was surprised at her demeanor, she seemed worried or something.

"Oh, he's fine," she said. "In fact, that's why I'm here. He wants me to talk to you about his coming back to work."

"You mean he wants to preach?" Again, he was surprised. "What does the doctor say?"

"Well," she began, "David doesn't pay much attention to what the doctor says. Maybe it's a good thing. He's got himself out of bed and getting around pretty good on a walker."

"Well, you know I told you before, you could live in the parsonage temporarily."

"Dad, he doesn't want that. He wants his job back!"

"What do you think, Mary Lou?"

"I want whatever he wants," she said simply.

"Hmm, it would be a good thing for the church. Some of the people who drove quite a ways to hear him preach are droppin' out. Anyhow, I need to talk to the rest of the people on the board. As far as I'm concerned though, I can't wait to get him back. As soon as I hear from everybody, I'll come and let you know," he promised.

Mary Lou felt that if he felt that way, it was probably as good as done. She, however, had mixed feelings. It had seemed so safe in the nursing home.

She was right about her dad, they were soon packing their meager belongings and heading for Windy Hill. When they got there, only two people were there to greet them, her dad and another board member. As soon as she had parked the car and helped David out with his walker, they were anxious to show the couple some of the things they had done to help David, which hadn't been done before. There was a ramp with a railing leading up to the porch. They had also installed a shower so that he wouldn't have to get in the tub. There were other handicap improvements both at the church and in the new addition.

"This was all Rosalie's idea," admitted her dad. "She read about it in a magazine."

David was overwhelmed with gratitude. He remembered how, when he had first arrived after the war, how the love shown to him by these people had healed his body as well as his soul.

"We're giving you a week to get settled in," said Aaron. "There's plenty to eat in the refrigerator. I reckon you need a honeymoon." He smiled.

After they left, Mary Lou and David checked the refrigerator to see what goodies there were to eat.

The whole place was immaculate, even David's room had been somewhat organized with clean linens and newly washed curtains.

As the darkness fell, they both became slightly nervous. They had never actually slept together. Finally, they went into their room and sat on the bed.

David was the first to speak. "Mary Lou, I want you to see me."

She wasn't sure what he meant.

He began to remove his clothing. "I want you to see my scars."

Mary Lou was stunned. His body looked like a roadmap with some recent scars from his heart attack, red as on fire as well as old ones, which were slightly faded but still very visible.

"What are you feeling?" he asked.

"Well, I guess I'm a little shocked," she admitted. "I knew you had all these operations. It hurts me to think how much you've suffered. But if you think I'm turned off by them, your scars, I mean, I'm not."

"Mary Lou," he said urgently, "undress, I want to see your body."

She hesitated. "I thought the doctor said—"

"I don't care what the doctor said. I want to make you my wife."

Mary Lou suddenly felt shyness overtaking her. She felt as if she were blushing, red hot. *What is wrong with me?* she wondered. It was as if this were the first time she had ever been with a man. Finally, she lay beside him and they looked at one another; he with his visible scars and she with her invisible ones.

"You are beautiful," he whispered hoarsely.

They gave into their desire and consummated their marriage.

Mary Lou had no idea that David could be so romantic. He said such beautiful things to her. He called her his beloved, his darling, his sweetheart, as well as terms of endearment in Spanish, which he insisted they continue learning. It was as if he had saved all of his love just for her, which of course he had. She knew that he had avoided all romantic entanglements until now.

Of course, his first love was for his God. He wanted his first sermon since coming back to be perfect, and he worked very hard on it.

They still had time to enjoy one another. It was starting to get cold, so they would bundle up in blankets, sit outside watching the sun come up over the prairie. They just enjoyed watching the birds. David loved nature; he saw so much more in it than most people. Mary Lou too had regained her love of the prairie. She even loved the sound of thunder and lightning, even though she had a healthy fear of it.

It was decided that for now, David would only preach on Sundays. Someone else would do visiting, funerals, and weddings until he regained more of his strength.

Even though he was confident in his ability to preach, Mary Lou was a nervous wreck. "What if he falls down, he's still unsteady on his feet. Oh my," she worried.

When Sunday came, she walked with him to the church and stayed with him until he sat in his chair on the dais.

I feel like a mother at her son's first recital or something, she thought. *I am so frightened for him.*

Of course, all her family were there including her aunt and grandmother who had driven out for the occasion.

Rosalie led the music and the prayers, and Mary Lou found herself lost in the worship. A feeling of peace came over her. *What did I ever do to deserve the blessing I've received?* she wondered. *It's so amazing, considering the life I've led that I've suddenly received heaven.*

19
CHAPTER

David will be all right, and so will I. If the time I've had with him is all I'm going to have, it will be enough, she reassured herself.

David raised himself onto his walker and made his way to the podium. "Let us pray," he said. "Lord, your spirit is welcome in this place. Whatever we do and say here today, let it be to your glory. Let it be a sweet sound in your ears, a pleasant aroma rising to you. Once again, the Lord has raised me from among the living dead that I might preach his word."

He paused, as people shouted hallelujahs and praises to the Lord.

"Since I was a very young boy," he continued, "I've felt the call to serve the Lord as a preacher of his Word, to bring the good news to his people. There have been times, such as when I lay in the VA hospital with little hope of getting well or recently when again I was not given much hope of leading any life except as an invalid that I wondered if I had really heard the call or if I had imagined it. Today, as I'm able to stand here before you good people, I know for certain that the call was real."

Again, the people responded with shouts of praise and thanksgiving.

He went on to thank each and every one for their love and prayers without which he was sure he would not have survived. He reminded them of their own unique call by God.

"He always gives everyone plenty to think about," observed Mary Lou, "even me. There's probably plenty of ways I could be of service around here."

At first, Mary Lou and David were left pretty much alone to enjoy their life together. They read and studied their Spanish. David started playing the old piano in the parsonage, and he urged her to sing along.

"We'd make a good saloon duo." She laughed.

"Did you enjoy singing in a saloon?" He was curious.

"Well, not really…I looked at it as furthering my career as a great singer. What a laugh that was," she observed drily.

"I think you could have had a great career as a singer," he said. "You have a great voice. I guess the whole thing was mismanaged, too bad." He shook his head.

"That's an understatement," she said. "Besides, I no longer have any regrets. God had to bring me to the place I am now, and I can't think of any place I'd rather be. I can't put into words how happy I am."

Soon, David began to do other things other than preach. People started coming to him for counsel and prayer. He started to do a few funerals and weddings since the people couldn't imagine having anyone else.

The church began to grow and there were receptions and pot-lucks and vacation Bible school, all of which they were expected to attend.

Mary Lou began to worry. *Even I'm tired,* she thought, *how can David keep up this pace?*

And he couldn't. Suddenly she noticed that he was taking long naps, and it was hard for him to get up in the mornings. They no longer made love, but the affection between them grew deeper and the words of love more profound.

David's preaching grew more evangelistic, if that was the word. The congregation now consisted of more young people than in the past.

One Sunday it seemed to Mary Lou that the worship was charged, almost electric, with the power of the Holy Spirit. David asked for testimonies and prayers from the congregation, which went on for a long time before he finally gave the sermon. Even though they were running late, he gave an altar call, which he seldom did.

To her surprise, her two nephews, now young men, rose and walked to the altar and gave their lives to Christ!

Rosalie almost fainted with joy, even John had tears in his eyes. Mary Lou was crying openly. "Thank you, Jesus!" She breathed. She knew that Rosalie and John had been concerned as they saw them start to become a little rebellious, taking on some of the actions of their peers.

"I have the assurance of seeing all my family in heaven. What a blessing!"

On their next visit to Dr. Mac, Mary Lou had a chance to speak to him privately, as David was paying the bill. She informed him of the long naps, the falling asleep at odd times. How he was losing interest in the things he loved to do.

Dr. Mac looked at her, sadness in his eyes. "He's wearing down, Mary Lou," he said.

"Is there anything I can do?" she asked.

"I'm afraid not, even if he cuts down on his activities it won't make much difference. The pump is wearing out."

Mary Lou bit her lip to keep from crying.

"Mary Lou, he's happy! You know, I really regret advising him not to marry. You've been very good for him. He told me he wanted to live while he was living. That's probably good advice for all my patients."

"Will you be all right, Mary Lou?" he asked, remembering her suicide attempt.

"Oh, I will be," she answered. "Not at first, of course, but I'm not the same person I was then," knowing what he was thinking of.

Mary Lou was quiet on the ride home thinking about what the doctor had said. Anyway, there was no one to converse with as David had fallen asleep. He didn't wake up until they arrived home.

This is going to be a lonely road to go down, she thought. *If only David would talk to me about what he must be feeling.*

Soon, it was winter and everyone began to look forward to Christmas and Andrea's wedding. Of course, she expected Uncle David to officiate. Mary Lou prayed that he would be up to it.

Finally, she worked up to talking to David about his health. There was no easy way to say it. "David, you're failing, aren't you?"

"Yes, I know I am," he said simply.

They looked at one another, not knowing what else to say.

Finally, Mary Lou broke the silence. "Are you ready?" she asked.

He nodded. "I've been ready for a long time. You know," he said, "during the war I watched a lot of men die. I tried to comfort them the best I knew how. I realized the Bible doesn't really give us much information. Well, you know, Jesus said, 'In my Father's house are many mansions, I go to prepare a place for you. Still, you can't help wondering what you'll be doing there for eternity. I'm not saying I don't believe it," he said hurriedly. "I do. I just have a lot of questions without answers."

He paused. "I guess, as they say, when I was born into this world, I didn't know what I was getting into. Maybe it's the same thing." He smiled at her. "I'm sure it'll be good."

Mary Lou took his hand. "Please don't shut me out," she begged.

"I'll try not, my darling," he promised, "but unfortunately, dying is something you have to do alone."

20

CHAPTER

The day of the wedding was a bright crisp winter day. A foot of beautiful silvery snow lay over everything. Aaron came to help Mary Lou and David make the few steps to the fellowship hall.

He was more dressed up than Mary Lou had ever seen him. He even wore a white western shirt with what she assumed was a new black suit and a new hat.

"Daddy," she exclaimed, "I've never seen you so dressed up!"

"Well, now you know what to bury me in." He chuckled.

David had never worn his surplice and stole, but he did so this day. "I never felt comfortable in it. I wanted to dress in something the people in the country were used to. I never wanted to set myself apart," he explained to Mary Lou.

The sight inside the fellowship hall took Mary Lou's breath away. There were red carnations, silver bells, red and silver bows everywhere.

This is Rosalie's day, she thought. *She has spent plenty and she deserves it.*

All the congregation had been invited, as well as Rosalie's family, what was left of them, who came from out of state. The groom's family consisting of his parents as well as a brother and sister were seated on the front row. The place was filled completely.

David seemed to be fine as he went to sit in the front to wait for the bride and groom. Mary Lou was praying, "Father, help him get through today."

Someone started playing the wedding march as the groom came in with one of his brothers and his friends. Mary Lou didn't know much about him. David had counseled the young couple, but he'd not said much about him other than he was besotted with Andrea.

And well he should be, she thought. *I wonder if he knows how lucky he is.* He was twenty-four, but to her he looked like a skinny adolescent kid. David had also said the boy—his name was Byron—came from a prominent family somewhere in Nebraska. *Omaha,* he thought.

Well, I guess that shows Rosalie's power of persuasion if they're willing to travel over here in the middle of the winter in the middle of the sticks to attend their son's wedding. Mary Lou chuckled to herself. *He must have persuaded them that she was worth it. And worth it, she is,* she thought as she turned to see Andrea coming down the aisle between the folding chairs.

She knew that Andrea and Rosalie had spent hours making her dress. It was modest and gorgeous, made all the more gorgeous by the young woman who wore it with her radiant complexion and long dark red hair cascading down her back and framing her face. Her mother had allowed her a tiny hint of pink on her lips, which brought out the dark blue of her eyes. Mary Lou gasped when she saw her. She could hear some of the people near her catch their breath at the sight.

John couldn't keep his feelings to himself as he usually did, as he escorted his lovely daughter.

The look on his face is priceless, thought Mary Lou.

David got to his feet with the aid of his walker, but he put it aside as he prepared to perform the ceremony.

Why is he doing that? wondered Mary Lou. *He can't stand alone for that long.*

But he did. He had written a poem of love for Andrea and her husband to go with the usual ceremony.

Mary Lou was so surprised and proud. She had no idea he could write poetry like that.

Afterward, they feasted on Rosalie's superb cooking. She had really outdone herself, baking a huge three-tiered cake. Other ladies from the church had brought food as was the custom, so there was plenty to go around. She noticed that no one had asked her to bring anything, which was just as well since she wasn't much of a cook.

It was a proud day in the life of the Gerhardt family. Everyone, including David, and especially David, thoroughly enjoyed themselves. There was no liquor, of course, and no dancing, but there was total enjoyment in the conversation and laughter. People were loath to leave. Even the bride and groom seemed in no hurry to be off to themselves.

However, for some, especially the family as well as some of the congregation who had known Andrea since a baby, beneath the gaiety and excitement, lingered a tinge of sadness. Andrea and her new husband would be leaving for Omaha where he had secured a good position in an accounting firm.

Mary Lou perhaps felt it more than anyone. Her beautiful niece, who had always loved and admired her so much, even though it was unwarranted, was leaving. Even though it was not that far, as far as she was concerned, it might as well be in another country.

"Surely, since she's so close to her mother, we'll be seeing a lot of her," she comforted herself with that thought.

The day after the wedding was Sunday and David was having a hard time getting up. Thankfully, someone else was giving the sermon. Since David had officiated at the wedding, he had asked to have someone take his place.

Unbeknownst to Mary Lou, David had had a long talk with Aaron. He'd asked Aaron to stay after the Wednesday night Bible study as he needed to talk to him. Aaron had a sinking feeling that it was not going to be good. A man had to be blind not to see that David was failing.

David looked at Aaron with affection. *I wish I could tell him how much I love him,* he thought, but Aaron would not know how to handle this display of affection coming from him.

"Old friend," he said, taking Aaron's hand, "I'm about ready to check out. I guess you already knew that?"

Aaron nodded, doing his best to keep his emotions in check.

"It was important to me to marry Andrea, and I'd like to preach next Sunday. I'd like to announce my leaving and say goodbye to my friends. If that's all right with you?" he added.

Aaron nodded again, he knew he should say something, but what? This boy was like a son to him, not only a son, but so much more, his spiritual mentor.

David hurried on, “If it’s all right with you, I’d like for us to stay in the parsonage until you find someone.”

Finally, Aaron was able to speak. “Of course, that’s fine, but shouldn’t you be in the hospital? What will Mary Lou do, if God forbid, something happens to you way out here?”

“Aaron, I know you’re worried about your daughter, but you needn’t be. She has the car and a phone. She’s a strong person, she’s not in the dark about what’s happening, we’ve talked about it.”

Aaron shook his head. “I don’t know what to say.”

“You don’t have to say anything, as you know, I’m in good hands. And so are you,” he added, smiling.

Aaron got up to leave. He was anxious to go. He needed to be alone before he fell apart in front of David.

The following week was a tough one for Mary Lou. She had asked David not to shut her out and she knew he didn’t want to, but he was in that place where the very ill and the very old go; partly in this world and partly in the next. The place where the things in this world no longer matter much. However, he was working on his final sermon, his farewell sermon.

She looked forward to the nights when she could hold him close, but even then, she always woke up, checking to see if he still had breath. She dared not think about what she would do if he no longer had breath or what her life would be like without him. She dared not fall into that black hole, not yet, she must hang on for David’s sake.

Sunday finally came, even though she wished it never would. She didn’t want to listen to the final sermon. She didn’t want to hear anything final.

Snow was still on the ground, but it was another day of bright sunshine. As she and David made their way to the church, he stopped and breathed deeply. “I love this winter air,” he said, “I love the way the sunshine glistens on the snow. I have always loved this place. When I first came here, I knew I was home. It was winter then too.”

He seemed to perk up as they walked into the church. There was hardly anyone there as it was still early. Rosalie and John and the boys were there. Rosalie was arranging the music on the piano. Her boys were singing a duet with their guitars this morning. They rushed over to help David navigate the stairs to the dais.

Mary Lou moved to the back of the church in order to greet people when they arrived. She had made this her unofficial job. She was surprised to see her aunt and grandma. They didn't say anything to Mary Lou, but Aaron had gone to town and apprized them of his talk with David and the final sermon. When they saw David, they went up to say hello.

They each hugged him and told they were looking forward to the sermon. He decided they knew the situation as neither of them had ever hugged him before. It was with heavy hearts that they took their seats. Both their minds went to Mary Lou. "How would she take this, losing David?" They dared not think about it.

Mary Lou took a seat in the front row. She tried to pray, "Hold on to me, Lord. I don't know if I can take this. Help David. This is important to him. I want to pray 'Your will be done,' but, I can't, I want my husband!"

She couldn't concentrate on the music, the announcements, everything that goes into having church. And then it was time for David to make his way to the podium, which he did. Mary Lou could have sworn that he had an aura about him as he said, "Good morning," and smiled.

And then it happened, suddenly he had a strange look on his face and then he crumpled to the ground! Mary Lou grabbed the back of the pew, sure that she was going to faint. John was the first to reach him, almost flying up the stairs. Aaron and some other men scrambled upon the dais.

John checked for a pulse and then looked up at his dad and shook his head.

In the meantime, Mary Lou stood frozen; her grandmother had her arms about her waist as if to keep her from falling.

It was decided that even though David was dead, he must be taken to the hospital. A doctor would have to examine him in order to make out the death certificate.

John brought Aaron's car around. "Dad," he said, "I'll drive and you go with me. We'll put David in the back seat."

Mary Lou broke loose from her grandmother. "I'm going too!" she cried. "I'm going with David!"

"Wouldn't it be better if you came with Norma in her car?" Aaron stammered.

"No, no, no, I will hold David!"

There was no use arguing with her. She was adamant. She climbed in the back seat and gathered David in her arms, holding him close.

Aaron would have described the twenty miles to town as the longest ride of his life. He looked at John, whose face was grim as he drove faster than usual. He only looked at Mary Lou once and then quickly looked away.

She was making what he could only describe as a mewling sound, such as animals do in their grief. She was running her fingers over her beloved's face, trying to memorize, trying to hold on. But as soon as they reached the hospital and they came to get him, she let go, to her dad's relief. He halfway expected that she would not want them to take him.

She did not ask to see him again.

Dr. Mac came to the hospital as soon as he could, stopping to tell the family how sorry he was. He noticed that Mary Lou seemed to be in a stupor. She was not crying. Just staring into space.

"Mary Lou, would you like for me to give you something for sleep?" he asked.

She shook her head no.

Aaron asked her if she wanted to stay in town. "I'll be up tomorrow to help you with arrangements."

"No, I want to go home!"

"Home?"

"Yes, to the parsonage."

"Well, maybe someone can stay with you?"

"Dad, I want to be alone! No one can help me with this. Right now that is where I can find David." Aaron looked perplexed.

"Dad, I'm not going to do anything drastic! I would never sully my husband's memory in that way."

In the end, they left her at the parsonage to be alone with her memories. Aaron asked if he could pick her up the next morning to go into town to start making arrangements.

"I'll be ready," she promised.

It was getting late in the afternoon, the time when she and David would have their tea and sit on the porch, no matter the weather. And so Mary Lou changed clothes, threw on a jacket, made tea, and went to sit on the porch. She tried to observe everything the way he had. Soon the trees will be leafing out and the air will smell of spring. Whatever she was trying to do, it wasn't working.

She was trying her best to hold on to his spirit, but it was no good. "Where is he?' she cried aloud. "What is he doing? Oh god, it hurts so bad!" *I'm actually in physical pain,* she thought, surprised. *Maybe I'm having a heart attack!*

She sat at David's desk. He always did so much writing, maybe if she read some of his writing it would bring him closer. There were notes for sermons, his prayers for others, for himself, and then she found it, an envelope with her name on it. Hands trembling, she opened it.

"Mary Lou," he began, "I'm trying to write a poem especially for you. I haven't much luck, then I remembered another poet long ago who wrote the words that I feel."

As she began reading the words, she recognized the ancient verses from the Bible, paraphrased.

"You have captured my heart, My treasure, my bride. You hold it hostage with one glance of your eyes. With a single jewel of your necklace. Your love delights me. My treasure, my bride."

It was not signed. Was there supposed to be more? Well, it didn't matter. It was enough. She read it over and over.

She decided to go to bed even though she was sure she would never sleep again. She found the shirt David had worn the day before and put it on. She got into bed on David's side, using his pillow, clutching her poem. She felt if she could just cry, really sob, it might release the ache in her chest. She did manage to sleep however fitfully.

Aaron, however, could not sleep. Not only was he suffering from the shock and grief at David's sudden, dramatic death, but he was worried sick about Mary Lou. He should have insisted that she not be alone.

He breathed a huge sigh of relief when he drove up to the parsonage and saw her sitting on the front porch.

"How are ya, girl?" he asked as she climbed into the car.

"Not too good," she answered shortly.

They were quiet most of the way when Mary Lou broke the silence.

"Dad, what do you think I'll have to do to get David a military funeral?"

"Well, I'm sure Gary at the mortuary will know. I'm sure he's entitled to one."

"I think I'll have someone read his final sermon at the church and have him buried there. Maybe I'd better check with his sister," she said as an afterthought. "But he loved it so much there. I'm sure he would want to be buried there."

Aaron was shocked and relieved at how calmly she was making decisions. He had worried for nothing.

After they shook hands with Aaron's old friend, the mortician. Mary Lou calmly opened a box she had brought with her. In it were David's vestments.

"I would like to have him buried in these," she said. "His first love was being a preacher."

"Of course," said Gary, "is there anything else? We should have him ready for viewing by this evening around six o'clock. Have you decided on a day and time for the funeral?"

Mary Lou explained her wishes concerning the military funeral, his burial place, and so it was decided to hold it three days hence.

Mary Lou almost lost her calm when picking out the casket. "Oh, Lord, please help me. I don't want to think of him in one of those horrible boxes!"

Aaron could see that she was in trouble and he took her arm. "Mary Lou," he said. "Just pick something. It has to be done!"

He resolved that he would pay for everything no matter the cost. David had been his son by marriage, but he had been so much more than that.

Mary Lou agreed to stay in town so that she would be at the mortuary each evening for the viewing. She didn't want to, but there would be people coming and she should be there to greet them. David had meant so much to so many people.

To her surprise, she began to feel a presence with her, consoling her, guiding her. The Lord had promised that he would be her strength, and he was!

Also, she took comfort in the love poured out to her by the people who had known and loved David, people she had not known even existed. Some of the people he had visited in the hospital or even the jail came to pay their respects, telling her how much David had meant to them in their deepest need. Friends came from her former church, the girls she had worked with, her former boss. Flowers poured in until there was hardly any space for them.

Sometimes she sat alone with David's body. He looked so peaceful with his hands folded across his chest—the same hands that had caressed her and held her. "My darling," she cooed, "now you have a new body. No more scars, no more pain. Now you can walk and even run!"

Rosalie and John and their family came. Andrea would be there for the funeral. Rosalie made notes of who had sent the flower arrangements. Thank-you notes would have to be sent. Gifts of food were already arriving at the homes of the family. These too would have to be acknowledged. If Mary Lou wasn't up to it, she would be available to help.

Finally, the day of the funeral arrived. Mary Lou had spent the night at the parsonage. The women of the church had cleaned it until it shone. She knew this would be the last time she would be staying in this little home where she and David had lived and loved. The one place which, for her, true happiness had reigned.

She had packed her things and some special things of David's. His books she was donating to the church. They planned to make a place for a library.

She planned on living with her dad until she was mentally able to look for a job and a place to live. She knew she could stay there forever, but she preferred to be on her own.

The funeral was being held in the fellowship hall since they had decided there was no way the small church could hold everyone. And so it was, as Mary Lou walked over, the prairie around the church was beginning to fill up with cars and pickups as the small parking lot was full.

Someone, it wasn't Rosalie, was playing the piano as she walked in and took her place at the front with the family. The place was filled with flowers. David's open casket was placed in front. Everything would be done in order. The bishop was in attendance, and he would be saying a few words.

Mary Lou had chosen her brother to read David's last sermon. Usually, David used notes, but this one he had written out in its entirety since it was his farewell to the people he loved, the last, and the most important one of his life.

Some of David's favorite hymns were sung. Mary Lou didn't recognize the soloists, but it was beautiful. Probably they were friends of Rosalie's from somewhere.

People hung on to David's last words. He reminded them that he had come there after the war, broken in body, mind, and spirit, and they had loved him back to wholeness. The greatest privilege of his life had been to serve them as their pastor. He reminded them of sad times they had weathered together, of amusing things they had enjoyed. He mentioned most of them by name—the ones who had surrendered their lives to God at the altar, the ones he had been privileged to baptize into the kingdom.

One of the unexpected joys he had received was finding the love of his life, his wife. Mary Lou bit her lip. This was not the time to break down. Her dad reached for her hand, squeezing it.

He saved the Bible verse he had chosen for last. It was from the book of Habakkuk 3:17–18, and it was appropriate for country people who made their living from the land. It brought tears to the eyes of many as John read.

"Although the fig tree shall not blossom, neither shall fruit be in the vines, the labor of the olive shall fail, and the fields shall yield no meat; the flock shall be cut off from the fold, and there shall be no herd in the stalls: Yet I will rejoice in the Lord, I will joy in the God of my salvation. The Lord God is my strength, and he will make my feet like hinds feet and he will make me to walk upon mine high places."

Then the bishop spoke. He reminded the congregation of the time he had come to them wondering if they would accept someone with a handicap and how thrilled they were to accept David. He said he knew he couldn't take credit as much as he would like to, "But when I look out over all these faces today, I know that God had a plan for you and for David that I certainly couldn't see at the time."

There was more music and prayers and then the pallbearers carried David's body to the small graveyard. Taps were played and Mary Lou received a flag and then more prayers and then it was all over except the receiving line in which people came to shake hands or hug and offer their condolences.

After most people had left, Aaron gathered up Mary Lou and Alice and they left for the ranch. He felt as if he could hardly wait to get there.

"Mary Lou, everything was real nice," said Aaron. "You did good."

"Thank you," said Mary Lou.

That was the end of any conversation from then on.

Aaron wished he could think of something else to say in order to comfort her, but he knew he couldn't.

Alice knew it was useless. Mary Lou would have to grieve in her own way. All she could do was pray for her.

As soon as they stopped the car Mary Lou got out and went to her room. Her heart still ached, or something in her chest ached, maybe there was no heart there anymore.

How does someone prepare for something like this? she wondered. *I should have been expecting it, but somehow I wasn't. I just wonder how I'm going to get on with living.*

She tried to pray, but she couldn't. God felt nonexistent. *What would David say? God is always present whether we feel his presence or not.*

"Lord, I know you're here with me, I know you feel my heartache. I choose to believe that," she prayed.

David always said, "Faith is a choice, it is not a feeling. God will supply the feelings when you need them."

She wondered if she had depended too much on David and his faith, and now he was gone and it was just her and God.

She found herself wishing that she could just go to sleep and never wake up. She had no desire to eat and refused whatever Alice brought up for her to eat.

Finally, Alice got herself together and decided to confront Mary Lou.

She sat on the bed and put her hand on Mary Lou's head brushing back her hair.

"People say they know how you feel and they don't. But I do know how you feel. I do know that you never get over it, but in time the pain becomes bearable until it finally becomes a memory. I would suggest that you try to keep busy. As soon as you feel like it, I could use some help and so could Rosalie. In fact, your dad could probably use you. This is a busy time on this place, calving and branding and selling. Even with John and the boys, your dad has had to put on extra help 'sides Jake. You being good with a horse, I'm sure he could use you."

Mary Lou groaned and buried her head in her pillow.

Alice patted her shoulder. "Think about it," she said as she left.

In a few days Mary Lou did think about what Alice had said.

Maybe I will ask Dad if he needs help, she thought. *Maybe if I get out on my horse it'll help me to feel better,* though she doubted it. Although she couldn't think of anything he could possibly need her for. She had always made it a point to avoid anything on the ranch that looked like work. Being a girl, she had always gotten away with it.

Finally, she approached Aaron about being some help with the cattle. Aaron had been apprised by Alice about her conversation with Mary Lou even though he didn't necessarily agree with the idea. He finally thought of something even though he never expected her to ask him. When she finally did ask, he was ready.

"Dad, Grandma thinks it would do me some good to keep busy, do you have something I could do to help?"

"What about helping your grandma?"

"I can't stand to be cooped up inside right now. I'm not even sure I want to do anything to tell you the truth, but I would like to try doing something."

"Well, we have some new heifers calving, some are having problems, and we're not sure we got to all of them. Maybe you could ride over to the cedars and poke around in the canyons in case we missed some."

"Oh, mercy," Mary Lou said doubtfully. "What do I do if I find one?"

"Well, you could take a rope and try to pull the calf out, or you could come and get me or Jake."

The following morning as the first light of day came streaming through the window, Mary Lou began to regret that she had ever volunteered to help. After lying in bed for so long, she felt too weak to move. However, she managed to get dressed and go down the stairs to the bathroom, wash her face, and comb her hair.

When she came out, Alice was sitting by the window reading her Bible. "There's some breakfast for you. I packed you a lunch too. Your dad said your horse is saddled and waitin' for you."

Mary Lou ignored the breakfast, grabbed the lunch, and headed out the door. She felt a little resentment toward the whole family for thinking that she was ready for this.

Once she mounted her horse and started out, she began to feel somewhat better. She breathed in the fresh morning air as she looked toward the purple hills. *I have a feeling I've been sent on a wild goose chase just to get me out of the house,* she thought.

It was noon by the time she reached the canyons, and she decided to dismount and eat her lunch. She was surprised to find that she was actually hungry. No sooner had she found a rock to sit on, she heard a noise. She walked to the edge of the hill and looked down, and there at the bottom of the hill she saw what she had come to find. A young heifer was in labor and struggling.

Her first instinct was to get back on her horse and head for the house as soon as possible to find help. Even she, though as inexperienced as she was, could see that that would be too late. The closer she got as she led her horse down the hill, she could see that the mother had come to the end of her endurance and that the calf was most likely dead as it hung, partially in and out of the birth canal.

She tried not to panic as she remembered what her dad had told her to do. She had never in a million years expected that she would actually have to do something. "What if she tries to attack me?" That seemed unlikely though, considering the shape she was in.

Resolutely, she retrieved her rope and headed toward the calf. The mother tried to run, but it was too much for her. Mary Lou did her best to tie the rope as snugly as she possibly could to the calf's legs. Her plan was to tie the other end of the rope to the saddle horn and back up her horse. This plan was fraught with danger though. What if the horse got nervous and bolted? What if he refused to back up? Hopefully, the cow would move forward.

Mary Lou suddenly knew what to do. "Oh Father," she prayed, "I need your help as you can see what a mess I'm in. I leave this situation entirely in your hands." Suddenly, she felt calm and resolute.

The horse did back up, and the baby calf came out and fell on the ground. The cow let out a bellow and fell to her knees. However, she was fortunately able to get to her feet.

Mary Lou ran to the calf to see if there was any life left in him which there didn't seem to be. She remembered that when she was a child her job had been to take care of the orphan calves whose mothers had died for some reason or the other. She had taught them how to drink milk from a bucket.

She went to her canteen, poured some water into her hand, and stuck her hand in the calf's mouth trying to stimulate it to suck. Almost miraculously, she felt a feeble sucking on her fingers!

Eventually, she was able to raise the calf to its feet, which caused the mother to come running.

"Thank you, Father." She breathed.

The only thing she could do now was ride home, and hopefully someone would know what to do. She knew that the animals were too tired and weak for her to drive them home. Someone would have to come with the pickup truck to bring them home.

She had been gone much longer than anyone expected, and as usual her dad began to worry even as he tried his best not to. He breathed a sigh of relief when he saw her come riding up.

"Oh, Daddy," she cried as soon as she saw him, "you'll never guess what happened!"

He was surprised as she hurriedly recounted her adventure. He was also amazed that this was his daughter whom he always considered weak and fragile. He knew she would be all right. She had the strength of the Gerhardt's and, of course, her faith.

Mary Lou never stayed in bed after that. Somehow her experience with the cow and the birth gave her a feeling that with God's help she could do things she had never imagined possible, Of course, she told herself that it was no big thing. Other people did these things all the time. However, she knew, that for her it was a big thing.

In the coming weeks Mary Lou helped out with the work in any way she could. She especially liked working with the cattle.

At first, she couldn't bring herself to attend church. The idea of going there and not seeing David seemed like more than she could bear. She kept reminding herself that she was stronger than she thought and that she must do what she had to do and what David would certainly want her to do.

The first time was hard, but she forced herself to look at the parsonage where she and David had been so happy, to look at the graveyard where his body lay. She had designed his gravestone and had her Dad order it, but had never looked at it. She sat in her usual seat and looked at the pulpit where a new man was preaching. She felt his preaching didn't hold a candle to David's, but she listened and she felt the presence of God with her. This was where she belonged, in his house.

One morning Mary Lou went out to the mail box to pick up the mail and found a long letter from Barbara. They had written right after David died to tell her how sorry they were, but she had not heard from them since.

Barbara said that they had finished the school and were still, after all this time, trying to finish the church. The work was expanding, and Alfredo was starting a class to prepare about twelve converts who had professed a desire to go into the ministry. It seemed they never had a minute to spare.

After two pages of reporting all the things they were doing, Barbara got right to the point.

"Mary Lou," she wrote, "I know you had planned on returning here before you married David. I'm wondering if you might give it some thought now. We need help desperately. Now, if this is something you'd want to do, or if I'm speaking to you too soon after your terrible loss, just forget I asked you. I love you and I miss you. I just hope we'll be able to come for a visit soon."

Mary Lou collapsed on the porch swing, letter in hand. For a moment she was stunned. She had never given Mexico a thought since David's death. However, she did remember that when she left she had fully intended to go back. She remembered the feeling of comfort that what she was doing was important. Jesus said, "The harvest is plentiful, but the workers are few." She had felt that she was one of those workers and that what she was doing was God's will for her.

What about my dad? she wondered. They didn't carry on any long conversations, but they enjoyed each other's company. *Anyway, he's strong, and besides, if he gets sick I can always come home.*

She remembered how proud David had been of her when she told him about the work she was doing. "I'm sure he'd want me to go."

She decided not to say anything about the letter just yet. She needed to pray about it first.

Several evenings later after supper when she and her dad were relaxing on the porch, she brought up Barbara's letter. "Dad, she's asking me to come there and help with the work."

This time Aaron didn't hesitate. "If you want to go, I think you should go. This is a lonely life for a young woman, I know."

"Daddy, it isn't that…I'm not lonely. I'm content here. I just feel that this is something God had put in front of me, and I shouldn't say no. Even though I never would have left David to go back, part of me did have some guilt since I did promise I'd return."

"Well," he said, "I've always supported missionaries, and when they came to the church to tell about their work, I always felt like that was something I would like to do."

"Really, Daddy? You wanted to be a missionary?"

"Well, I guess not bad enough," he said ruefully. "I felt I had a responsibility to carry on where my dad left off."

"I guess that's the difference," said Mary Lou. "I have no responsibilities. I'll tell you one thing though, if you ever need me just send for me and I'll be here."

The following day, Mary Lou asked to borrow the car. To the question in her dad's eyes, she told him, "I want to go and say goodbye to David."

She had not made a habit of visiting his grave. It was not that it was too painful for her. It was just that she had no feeling of him being there. She had no idea why she was going now. Maybe she needed the ritual or whatever it might be.

She stood there admiring the stone which had his name as well as his rank and the war in which he served. What do people do when they visit graves? she wondered. Do they talk to the person who is no longer there, or pray?

She turned and looked at the church where she had found her Savior, indeed her very life, and the parsonage where she had lived with David, where God had allowed her a little taste of heaven.

Suddenly, she was overcome with gratitude to her Lord. "This is holy ground." She breathed, and she knelt and tried to find the words to praise him. Since there were no words adequate to what she was feeling, she began to sing, softly at first, and then she let her voice ring out across the prairie.

At last she was ready to leave. She walked to the car, turning to take a last look.

Mary Lou had no intention of having a send-off at church, and so the family was called to say goodbye the day before she left. Her aunt and grandma came from town. John and Rosalie came with their boys and food. This time they all knew this was a good thing for her, and so they visited and laughed and enjoyed the day and one another.

When they left they were sad. Even brother John had tears in his eyes as he hugged her goodbye. He had developed a new respect for his little sister. He had seen how she had held herself during a dreadful time in her life. He saw how she had worked hard all spring when they had needed her.

The next morning, Aaron drove her into town to catch the train. Norma and Alice came to see her off. They had brought a huge lunch for her to eat on her journey.

Aaron brought cash for her, admonishing her not to lose it. She thanked him profusely.

"Mary Lou, this is money you earned," he said.

At last, she boarded the train, and as it moved down the tracks, she looked out the window, waving until she could see them no more.

She was reminded that she had not ridden a train since she had left California. *That seems so long ago,* she thought. *A lifetime has happened since then.*

She remembered the despair she felt then, the longing to end it all, the deadness in her soul. She realized now that it had not been just the ending of her relationship with Larry, but also the life-long dream of being a big star, of coming back to her hometown having made the big-time, the little country girl having become "somebody."

That was a mess of pottage, she thought derisively. *I didn't realize that when I came home, through the magic of God's wonderful grace, I would be somebody, someone I never could have imagined I could be! I have no idea what God has in store for me, but I know I have come to a place of absolute trust and expectation.*

She sank down in her seat, closing her eyes, hoping to sleep. It was going to be a long ride. First, the train and then a bus and then Alfredo, Barbara, and Kate would pick her up. She could hardly wait to see them again!

ABOUT THE AUTHOR

Emma Sauer lives in San Pedro, California, with her husband, Frank. She was raised on a farm in Colorado and moved to California in her early twenties. For several years during the fifties, she lived and worked in Hollywood where she met many young girls, like the one in the story, who came looking for stardom and fame only to have their hopes crushed. Today, she is the matriarch of a large family. She's involved in her church as well as other ministries. For several years she and her husband have served as volunteer chaplains at the Los Angeles County Jail.

CPSIA information can be obtained
at www.ICGtesting.com
Printed in the USA
LVHW111149151120
671745LV00029B/278